ECHOES
FROM
A MISSING

CSN
Creative

CHRISTINA SUZANN NELSON

Cover design: Hannah Linder Designs

Chapter 1

KENZIE

April 30, 2024

Kenzie Danes arrived at the home where she had grown up, a house that held secrets within its compact frame. It also held warmth, determination, and made her part of something important.

Secrets and sanctuary, packaged together within walls of wood and plaster.

The top step cried out with the announcement of her arrival. Gram always said that the creaky plank was the only security system she needed.

"Hello." Kenzie pushed open the door and dropped her bag at the base of the coat tree.

"We're back here." Gram's voice held the remnant of a giggle, which usually meant she and Aunt Ginny were up to something.

Sure enough, Kenzie found the two women huddled around a cell phone at the kitchen table.

Light seemed to multiply in this room, bouncing off the lemon-yellow walls and gliding across the Formica counters. Kenzie pulled out the third and final chair and sat beside the women. "What have you all got going today?"

"We've been distracted by the Facebook again." Aunt Ginny's eyebrows bounced up and down as if what they'd seen bordered on scandalous.

Gram rolled her eyes. "It's just Facebook. You make us sound so old."

"I'm going to assume you were watching cat videos." Kenzie hugged Gram and gave Aunt Ginny a kiss on her fluffy white hair.

"Assume all you want, young lady." Gram's seat whined against the linoleum floor as she stood. "We aren't dead yet."

In reality, the videos were probably no worse than what one would find in a PG-13 movie, but Gram and Aunt Ginny—especially Aunt Ginny—had a way of turning everything into a giggle-fest.

Gram removed a plate covered in plastic wrap from the refrigerator. "There's tuna salad or egg salad. Pick quickly before Ginny chooses for you."

On cue, Aunt Ginny rubbed her broad belly. "I am mighty hungry today."

Kenzie drummed her fingers on the table and then chose tuna, hoping it would be the least offensive scent when she returned to her work as the county court reporter.

A buzz sounded from the rear of the house.

"That's the dryer. I need to run back and hang up my Sunday dress before wrinkles set in." Wrinkles were the bane of Gram's being. If they existed in Heaven, she'd likely turn away at the gate.

"Hey." Aunt Ginny fished in her deep pockets. She pulled out an envelope and handed it to Kenzie. "Stuff that away before she comes back."

"What is it?"

"The reason your grandmother needs to finally accept that her husband is dead." She leaned closer, her voice a loud whisper. "The bank is going to take the house. She put everything into keeping the hardware store going, and it's going to steal all that remain. She needs the life insurance money to get her out of this, but she refuses to go through the process of having him declared dead."

Gram stepped back into the room. "I don't think that dryer is working the best. The clothes were still quite damp." She took a seat. "What were you two chatting about while I was gone?"

Aunt Ginny snagged an egg salad sandwich. "I was just about to let Kenzie in on our little project. I think she'll be interested."

"Nonsense." Gram waved her fingers in the air as if shooing the subject away.

"What's the project?"

After a few swipes of the phone, Ginny slid it over to Kenzie. "We're trying to share our wisdom with the next generation. You know, for when we're dead or whatnot."

"Whatnot?" Kenzie let her sandwich rest on the plate.

"She means if we lose it up here." Gram tapped the side of her head.

Kenzie rubbed her fingers over the loose skin on her grandmother's hand. "I don't see that happening to either of you."

"You can't be sure." Gram topped Kenzie's hand with her free one. "They moved Margot Hansen into the memory care wing over at Hawk's Haven. We won't see that woman again until we meet in Heaven."

"You can still visit her. I'll go with you." Memories of Hawk's Haven visits were not positive for Kenzie. There was a smell in that building, something between urine and industrial-strength cleaner. Places like that provided ample reasons for a person not to want an overly long life.

"There's nothing scarier for women our age than being surrounded by dementia." Gram's sigh held an assemblage of fears Kenzie collected in her soul.

"I'm so sorry."

Gram took a long drink of water. "There's no reason for that. Getting old is a privilege—and like any privilege—it comes at a cost."

"I've never thought of it that way." Yet another reminder for Kenzie of how she was wasting the life given to her.

"Well, that will do." Gram pulled her hand free. "No more sad talk for us party girls."

"Okay. Well, I'd be willing to lend a hand." Kenzie started the video on Aunt Ginny's phone.

"Denny's coming over to help us out this afternoon." Aunt Ginny waggled her eyebrows at Gram. "He knows some stuff about editing. The YouTube guy says that's very important."

On the screen, Gram appeared—her wrinkled face puckered in concentration. From somewhere off-screen, Aunt Ginny talked about her first date with the man who would become Kenzie's Great Uncle Barry. "Your camera is facing the wrong direction."

Gram wiped a crumb from her lip. "When I turn it around, I can't see if Ginny has her big head in the shot."

"Are you both filming your stories?" Kenzie's entire life held a myriad of questions she wasn't supposed to ask.

Aunt Ginny tapped a finger on a small burgundy photo album.

"What's that?" Kenzie didn't recognize the book.

"It's from a time when I was young and in love. Sometimes, an old woman needs to look back on those moments and remember what it's like to swoon and be swooned over."

"I'm not sure I've ever felt that way." The edges of panic gripped her heart. Kenzie might never understand what it was like to have that kind of love.

"Hold out for it. I've never regretted my time with your Grandpa Bristol, no matter what happened." A steely edge shaped her words as they always did when memories from before Kenzie's mother came up. Clara Danes was a woman who had mystery in her past—secrets that might have very well gone to the grave with her body if she and Ginny hadn't decided on this project.

Until now, Kenzie hadn't questioned her grandmother's reasons for her private memories. With the album and Aunt Ginny's dogged determination, she realized there may be a chance to understand Gram's life as a young woman. "Would you tell me about meeting Grandpa? Did you love him from the beginning?"

Gram's gaze lifted to the ceiling, and she drew in a lungful of air.

"It's time, my friend." Aunt Ginny slid the album into the middle of the table.

"We met early in high school, not long after my family moved to Oregon. I thought Bristol was ... awkward, and I suppose he was. What young man of fourteen or fifteen isn't?" Gram pushed her plate and half-eaten sandwich away. "But he had eyes for me from the start. If it weren't for Ginny, I may never have given him another thought, but she assured me that Bristol was a man of honor." Her eyes searched Kenzie as if she were weighing her granddaughter's ability to be trusted. "That's why it was so difficult after he disappeared. People in a small town can be harsh with their gossip, and Oscar's Creek wasn't any different back then or now."

Kenzie's phone sang with the alarm she had set to ensure her timely return to the courtroom.

"You'd better get going. I don't want Judge Daniels coming after me when his best court reporter is late for work."

"I have a couple more minutes." It took only seconds for Kenzie to realize how she'd spent years of her life aching for the depth of transparency she now stood on the precipice of, yet couldn't quite bridge, thanks to the realities of life and responsibilities.

"Nothing doing. You go on now." Gram grunted as she pushed herself to stand. "We have the rest of my life for storytelling."

If it were that easy, why had this subject only now opened up? Growing up, Kenzie's mother had made it clear that Gram wasn't to be asked about Grandpa. He and Vietnam were next-level taboos in their family. She was sixteen before she realized her grandfather hadn't disappeared in Vietnam but on his way to the draft office. That information came from a social studies teacher who failed Kenzie's family tree assignment because of what he called "outright fabrications." Mr. Howard knew more about their family history than she did.

There wasn't much time to get into it back then. Mom's diagnosis of late-stage breast cancer came soon after that assignment. She was gone within the year, and Kenzie had lived with Gram for the rest of her time in high school. She had been so stunned with grief, she didn't have the mental space to question why Uncle Denny was the only man in their lives.

"Come on, now." Gram ushered Kenzie toward the front door. "There's nothing worse than being late."

In the living room, the television played a muted game show. "Thanks for lunch." Kenzie kissed Gram on the cheek.

"You look like there's something heavy on your mind. What is it?"

Kenzie scraped her thumb against a finger, pulling away loose skin. "It's nothing much. I've been considering something."

"What is it? We have no secrets."

That might be one of those agree-to-disagree things. If there were no secrets, Kenzie wouldn't be considering her next step. "You've probably heard about all the new things they can do with DNA these days."

"Oh, yes. I saw a program on the television about a man who discovered relations to British Royalty. Of course, it didn't change a thing in his life, but it was interesting."

"Right. Well, I've been thinking about taking one of those tests. I'm curious, and it would be nice to know if we had any health issues to be concerned about."

Gram reached over and squeezed Kenzie's shoulder. "The doctor tested your mom when she was first diagnosed. Her breast cancer wasn't genetic."

"True, but there are so many things they can determine now. I want to be prepared." She couldn't put every deep feeling into words. She'd started wondering about genetics when she thought marriage might be in her future. Even now, with her relationship with Christopher fully flushed down the toilet, her questions remained.

Gram nodded. "I understand."

"Anyway, I'm so glad you and Aunt Ginny are willing to film your stories."

Gram blinked away tears. "There is a season for everything." She took a deep breath. "A time to rend and a time to sew."

Sirens ripped through the air.

"What on earth?" Ginny's voice trailed in from the kitchen. "That's the kind of thing that could give an old lady a heart attack."

Whatever was happening wasn't in this neighborhood. Kenzie's skin prickled. Someday, Aunt Ginny or Gram might need an ambulance. Those thoughts were always on the edge of her mind, taunting her with the idea of more loss to suffer through.

"Well, I sure hope they get where they're going in time." Gram was always thinking of others. Right now, she was probably praying for whoever needed assistance, even as they stood there.

"I'll come by this weekend." Kenzie nearly ran right into Uncle Denny as she stepped out of the front door.

"Hey there, kiddo. You been to see our girl?" He hiked his jeans up to meet his rounded belly covered by his typical uniform, a plaid button-up over a plain T-shirt.

Kenzie nodded. "Have a nice visit." There had been an awkwardness whenever she saw Uncle Denny with Gram ever since Aunt Ginny let it slip that Denny was in love with her grandmother, the wife of his cousin.

Outside, tiny purple crocus poked through damp bark mulch, a bird sang, and the sun shone on her face. The earth was coming alive along with her curiosity.

She drove away and through one of the most beautiful neighborhoods in Oscar's Creek. As she reached the stop sign where the road went up the hill to the largest houses or down toward town, the screams of more sirens split the air. From behind her, an ambulance raced up, lights flashing. Whatever had happened had brought out the full force of Oscar's Creek's first responders.

Kenzie squeezed to the side of the road and watched as the emergency vehicle climbed toward the near-mansions.

She bit at her lip. Curiosity was a plague she'd fought her whole life.

Signaling to the left, she looked around as if she might get caught then turned up the hill.

At the corner of Cedar and Forrest, she found the road blocked off. The ambulance was silent now, the paramedics no longer in a rush. A young police officer emerged from the wooden double doors of a grand two-story home. His face was a pale and solemn mask, one Kenzie had seen on first responders in the courtroom.

Kenzie startled when an officer tapped on her window. She rolled it down.

"This street is closed. You'll need to turn around."

She nodded, put her car in reverse, and headed toward the courthouse, but not before catching the name on the mailbox. Stockdale.

Whatever had happened would be big news. Solomon Stockdale was from wealth and had acquired plenty of his own. The Stockdale name was splattered around town as a testament to his riches. Personally, she'd never been interested in knowing the man who'd left the rumor mill buzzing with stories of excess and entitlement.

Chapter 2

CLARA

December 1, 1969

I was a wife, an American, and a Christian. But that day may well have marked the beginning of the end of it all—if the good Lord saw fit to send my Bristol away to that nasty jungle on the other side of the world. My husband had been born on April 29, 1948. That was what mattered.

"Bristol, are you coming?" I hollered down the hall from the living room, where his parents had joined us to watch the draft numbers drawn—numbers that would determine the order young men of my generation would be called to serve in Vietnam. The tone of my voice was higher than usual and lacked the singsong quality I tried so hard to use in front of my in-laws. There was nothing left of me besides the nerves trembling under the surface and the love I had for the man who was taking forever to comb his hair.

We had only been married a few months, and that night I was already hosting an evening that was bound to be heavy.

I had only just begun to feel like a proper wife—not a girl playing house with a man who was still a boy. Bristol would turn twenty-two in April—if he lived to see his next birthday.

The doorbell had chimed, and I straightened my back as if it were me preparing for military service. I walked to the entryway to greet Bristol's aunt and uncle, Marnie and Albert. Bristol's sister—my dearest friend, Ginny—had been there the entire afternoon helping me set up for dinner.

"Oh, my." Aunt Marnie tapped her fingertips on her cheeks. She looked past me, and I realized Bristol had joined us. "You've done well for yourself with Clara. She's turned this house into a perfect home."

I looked around, taking in our tiny two-bedroom from her perspective. It was homey, though we lived on the budget of newlyweds.

His arm encircled my waist, pulling me to his side. "I'm a blessed man."

I snuggled in for a sweet moment. If I could have preserved that feeling of his body next to mine, I might have been able to face any challenge. He stepped away, ushering our guests into the living room, leaving me cold where his warmth had been.

"Howdy, Dad." Bristol reached his arm toward his father, though they had seen each other only an hour earlier at the family store, Danes' Hardware.

Hubert looked at Bristol's outstretched palm for a beat too long before seeming to remember the social construct and shaking his hand. My father-in-law was a tall, lanky man—a trait Bristol had inherited, though he had a thicker build. Hubert had never been one to overuse words, but lately, he had gone from quiet to closed off, and it made me feel uncomfortable in his presence.

Placing a hand on his shoulder, Bristol nudged his father toward the living room, offering him the recliner my husband usually took for himself.

The vinyl squawked as he fidgeted until he found a comfortable position, his gaze locked on the wall as if it were a television set.

A slap on Bristol's back jolted him forward.

"Good to see you, Bristol. Thanks for getting this rag-tag group together." Uncle Albert was the opposite of my father-in-law in every way. He was a stocky man who stood an inch or two above Hubert's shoulder. And he was a talker. Albert made his living as a salesman at his furniture store in downtown Oscar's Creek. From what he said—and he said it often—he did quite well there, too.

Bristol's cousins, Floyd and Dennis—Denny for short—worked for Uncle Albert. They had been born for the job in more ways than one. Though they weren't identical twins, they could pass for each other without hesitation. Both boys were short and stout, muscled like linebackers, and as smart as the furniture they moved.

That day, the boys seemed up to something—even more so than usual. They stood in the corner whispering and nudging each other.

I left them behind and returned to the kitchen, where Ginny pulled a casserole from the oven. She set it on the stove and tugged the oven mitts from her hands. "Had enough of the Danes side of the family yet?" With one finger, she pressed a stray blonde wave into submission.

"They're not so bad." I picked up a pile of plates and set them at the end of the table. We would be eating buffet style, as our little house couldn't fit the entire group in the dining area. A brown-and-yellow checkered cloth—one of our wedding gifts—draped the table, with a bouquet of dried flowers in the center. I thought it looked somewhat cozy and calming, though my heart felt like I was preparing a funeral reception.

Leaning around the corner, I motioned to Bristol, letting him know we were ready.

"Okay, folks," Bristol's voice boomed. I had always loved the deep tone that carried his words. "The girls have our dinner ready. Let's say grace and dig in."

We gathered in a lopsided circle, nine people coming together while avoiding the furniture obstacles. Bristol led us in a brief prayer, and I whispered an extra request for God to keep my little family safe.

As always, Bristol's mother, Patricia, fixed his dad's plate and delivered it to him before returning to the tail-end of the line to dish her own dinner.

My forehead tensed as I watched the ritual. Though Bristol had assured me a hundred times that he didn't want to be served, I couldn't help wondering if Aunt Marnie and Patricia thought I was a disappointment as a wife.

Bristol took my hand and pulled me in front of him. "You've been working since breakfast. Get a plate of this amazing food and sit with me."

"But Bristol..." He didn't understand how much I had to prove.

He tapped his finger on my chin. "Nothing doing. Everything's set out. We can clean up after we eat."

"But that's when the program starts." My voice was a fraction above a whisper.

"Then we'll do it after that."

My gaze darted around, pausing briefly on his aunt and mother.

"Don't worry about them. It's you and me against the world, remember?" His fingers intertwined with mine, and his smooth lips curved into a sassy smile.

"I remember."

As we ate, scattered around the living and dining rooms, the mood grew weak and limp, like paper confetti after a night of rain. No one wanted to mention why we'd gathered, but time ticked on, and we couldn't avoid the topic forever. As the man of the house, Bristol stood and made the move, switching on the television and adjusting the rabbit-ear antenna until we had the best image possible.

Gray figures moved around the screen—a jumble of people near the stage—while the familiar face of correspondent Roger Mudd leaned over the back of a chair, informing us of the process we were about to witness.

Aunt Marnie snapped her fingers. "Floyd, Dennis, come over here and sit by me." There was a shake in her voice.

A look flashed between the cousins. They had a way of communicating without words. While I couldn't understand what their looks conveyed, a new level of dread settled onto my shoulders.

Floyd and Denny sat on the rust-colored shag carpet at their mother's feet like they must have as young boys. Bristol's mother had chosen the farthest spot on the couch, her hand bridging the gap between her seat and the recliner, where she gripped her husband's arm.

Bristol tugged me onto his lap near the other end of the sofa.

On the television, Congressman Pirnie was introduced and stepped up to a large glass bowl to retrieve the first of the 366 blue plastic capsules, one for each day of the year—including February 29. As he pulled the sides apart, I felt the surrounding tension grow.

"September 14th," he announced.

The date was placed on the wall next to the number one. I couldn't think of a soul with that birthday, and I thanked God for that fact. They would be the first called up for service in 1970.

One by one, men from the Selective Service Youth Advisory stepped forward, taking turns drawing five or six dates. A few had issues with the system and refused to take part, silently stepping aside.

A boy with curly hair and freckles so dark they showed up on the screen pulled the ball containing February 23—the day Floyd and Denny had been born.

Aunt Marnie cried out, covering her mouth with the handkerchief she had been working between her fingers.

Patricia popped up and went to her sister-in-law, kneeling at her side. Even as she soothed the other woman, her gaze remained glued to the screen.

Number after number, date after date. I wanted to be brave for my husband and support him if he was meant to serve our country, but I wasn't sure I was made of the right stuff for that kind of sacrifice. At least, I wanted to want to, but there were so many other factors. I wasn't even sure how I felt about the war.

And then there was the family business. Bristol's father wouldn't be able to handle it on his own forever. He needed his son now more than ever. Bristol had worked beside him ever since he could count out a bag of nails.

My hand tightened on Bristol's arm.

He glanced at the screen.

April 29 was placed on the board next to number 191.

Uncle Albert put a beefy hand on my shoulder. "Don't you worry. This whole Vietnam thing'll be over long before they get to 191."

Aunt Marnie cocked her head to see her husband, her eyes rimmed red. "What about fifty-seven? Do you think the boys are safe?"

Seconds ticked by before Floyd elbowed his brother. The two of them hopped to their feet.

"I don't suppose that number matters much." He nodded at his twin. "Denny and me, we went down and enlisted this afternoon."

Denny puffed out his chest and gave his brother a nudge. "You're looking at a couple of army men."

I looked toward Aunt Marnie just in time to see her faint and slide off the chair.

Chapter 3

KENZIE

The town wasn't large, but it was the county seat, so most judicial cases came through Judge Daniels's courtroom. They handled everything from family disputes to major crimes, though those were rare. The only cases they didn't hear were traffic. Those belonged to Judge Sophia Lancaster, the youngest woman to be elected to the bench in the county's history. She was also Kenzie's best friend.

The court took a recess while the defendant went to retrieve the corgi, whose permanent custody was in question. The plaintiff, a man who looked as if he'd stepped off the football field, had requested a deputy supervise as he feared his ex-wife would realize the case was not going well for her side and dog-nap his "precious little guy."

Kenzie rolled her shoulders, then took advantage of the break and texted Sophia.

> *Hey, I had a weird visit with Gram today. Are we still on for dinner?*

A text buzzed in right after hers. She must have caught Sophia during a court recess.

> *I'm pushing these cases through as fast as possible. I had three citations for people driving too slow today!*

Kenzie caught the laugh before it escaped her mouth and drew unwanted attention. Court reporting was supposed to be a nearly invisible position. She liked it that way. Being noticed meant being vulnerable, and being vulnerable was a surefire journey toward heartache.

> *Let's meet in the lobby.*

The woman and the dog walked into the courtroom. The tan-and-white corgi on impossibly short legs chose that moment to relieve himself on the historic woodwork lining the walls. Any temptation Kenzie had had to get a dog dissipated long before the judge rendered a decision.

Judge Daniels awarded joint custody, giving the ex-wife weekends and every other holiday, while medical decisions were to be agreed upon mutually. This couple would likely be back before the end of the year—one of them having broken the agreement.

The courtroom cleared, and Kenzie finished her paperwork. Second thoughts about dinner filled her. The introvert in her was screaming for alone time, but she'd committed.

Sophia was already in the lobby when Kenzie arrived. Somehow, her friend looked as fresh and put together at the end of the day as she did at the beginning.

Sophia had a look that made men stop and stare. During the day, she wore her hair up in a bun, but as soon as court let out, she allowed her dark tresses to hang free over her shoulders, somehow drawing even more attention to her dramatically dark eyes.

Kenzie shot a glance at Sophia's red spiked heels, then at her worn flats with holes sprouting at the toes. Kenzie could put in a bit more effort, but why bother? Nobody ever looked at her.

"I would kill for sushi. What do you think?" Sophia tucked a loose strand of hair behind her ear.

They approached the entrance where Deputy Travis remained at his post. Kenzie nudged Sophia's arm. "I think you shouldn't talk about murder until we're out of the courthouse."

Deputy Travis closed his eyes as he shook his head. "I didn't hear a thing." Travis, like every other man in the building, seemed to have a little crush on Sophia. Little did any of them know there wasn't a chance. Soph had been happily committed for nearly nine months, but Kenzie was the only person in town who knew about the long-distance romance.

They said goodbye to Travis as they stepped into the waning sunlight.

The Japanese restaurant they favored was only a few blocks from the courthouse. "Declan found a job in town. He's hoping to find a place and be moved by June." Sophia sighed.

Nasty thoughts ticked away in Kenzie's brain. It was not that Declan wasn't a nice man. He was about as close to perfect as Sophia herself. That selfish nature Kenzie tried so hard to beat down kept taunting her. Sophia was Kenzie's last single friend, and it would likely not be long before she and Declan married. Then they'd start a family. And Kenzie would be that friend Soph used to do things with from time to time before life took off.

"Kenz?" Sophia slowed her pace. "Are you okay?"

Kenzie's stomach soured. *Well, yes, I'm great, if you consider being a selfish cow a good thing.* Ugh. She could hear Sophia reminding her about positive self-talk. "I'm fine. That's big news."

"I told him that Wednesday nights are reserved for you, forever and always." Sophia reached her arm around Kenzie and pulled her into a side hug as they approached the restaurant.

Kenzie tipped her head onto her friend's shoulder. "You're too good for me."

"I feel the same about you." She swung the door open, and they wove their way to the back, where they took their favorite seats near the sushi chefs.

The great thing about sushi was the brief wait for food after a long day of work. The server took their orders and served them two Diet Cokes within minutes of them sitting down. "Okay. I've been jonesing for details all day. What happened at your grandma's place?"

Kenzie unwrapped her straw and plunked it into her drink. "It's nothing big. Not anything like your news about Declan."

Sophia threw her head back. "Quit minimizing your life. I want to hear what happened."

"Okay, okay." Kenzie started to preface the story again, but caught herself before the words managed to escape. "She started talking about my grandpa. I mean, it's not like she's never mentioned him before, but he was kind of a taboo topic in our home. Gram and Aunt Ginny are working on a project. They're recording their stories for posterity. Gram even had an album out—one I've never seen before. I think the reminiscing has been good for her. It wasn't so much what she said about Grandpa but the way she looked when she talked about him. She kind of sparkled, if that's not too cheesy to say."

"She still loves him." Sophia took a long drink. "That's quite beautiful." She shrugged. "I mean, isn't that what we're all looking for? A love that lasts a lifetime?"

"But she hasn't seen him since 1970. He could be dead or living it up in Canada with his second family. What if he found someone he liked better than Gram? Maybe he was too much of a coward to tell her. She spent her entire life waiting for him when she could have moved on."

"It's just so sad, like a classic movie where the man goes off to war never to return and the wife dies of a broken heart." Sophia blinked tears away.

"The Army claims he never went off to war. He never even showed up for his intake."

"Maybe they brought him in as a special operative." Her eyes went wide. "He could have been the 007 of Vietnam."

Kenzie nearly choked on her Diet Coke. "My friend, the judge with the mind of a fairytale writer."

Sophia held up a hand. "Not a writer. Never a writer, but a reader for sure."

"I did a DNA test, but I keep thinking, why open that box? It could be filled with long-lost cousins I wouldn't know what to do with." Kenzie smirked. "I've got all the family I need, thank you very much."

"You have three relatives."

Kenzie tapped her chopsticks on the rim of her plate. "Six, if you include Aunt Ginny's son and his family in Chicago."

"Which you see every five years or so? I don't count them." She shrugged.

The sushi arrived in a bowl shaped like an ornate wooden boat.

Sophia mixed wasabi and soy sauce in a tiny dish. "Declan can't stand sushi."

"Thanks, Soph. You're a good friend." Leaving Kenzie as the re-dundantly single one, never finding Prince Charming or even Mr. She-Could-Work-With-This. The topic had been front and center at last month's therapy appointment with her counselor, who had posed an interesting question. Did Kenzie even want a relationship? Her answer had been no. She wanted the "taken" title, the no-longer-the-third-wheel friend. Even with as little experience as she had, Kenzie knew she had no good reason to get serious with a man. "Thanks, Soph. You're a good friend."

"Because I'm such a good friend, I'm going to see what I can find out about your grandfather from a judicial standpoint."

Kenzie's eyes watered as she swallowed a chunk of wasabi. She sucked down a gulp of soda. "I doubt you'll find anything. My grandma is the kind of woman who made it through sixty years of driving without a single infraction. Grandpa may have been a draft dodger, but I would bet that's about all you'll get."

"There must be something." Sophia stuffed another piece of sushi in her mouth, then cringed.

"Too much wasabi?"

She nodded as her eyes watered.

"I can't pin it down, but there seemed to be an urgency for Gram and Aunt Ginny. It could be about their friend and her dementia, but I can't help wondering if it's deeper than that."

Sophia sniffed. "Your grandmother has spent a lot of time not know-ing. That has to be tough. People don't up and disappear."

"Aunt Ginny says she needs money for the house. Apparently, she took out another mortgage at some point to keep the hardware store going. Ginny wants her to have Grandpa declared dead."

"That's usually a tough process, but after this many years, it shouldn't be too difficult. An attorney could help her with that."

Kenzie wiped the corner of her mouth. "She doesn't want to do it. I think it's like giving up hope."

"Sometimes hope is worth more than anything else."

"Maybe so." Kenzie dropped her chopsticks onto the side of her plate. "There's this nagging feeling in the pit of my stomach. I think I owe this to Gram. She deserves the truth."

Chapter 4

CLARA

Christmas Day, 1969

My mother had wanted me to marry Walter Clark because he had what she called *potential*. When I told her the only potential I saw in Walter was his potential to hurt someone, she scoffed. Now, I braced myself as Bristol and I waited on her front porch, our arms heavy with presents and pies. Walter Clark might have been a medical student, but he was also a class-A jerk. The man who stood next to me was the kindest of men. We might never be wealthy, but I didn't care. With Bristol, I was safe and content.

The door swung open, and my mother stood as straight as a pole, her feet wedged into heels that had to be pinching every one of her toes. Her hair was styled in its typical auburn perfection, and she wore a lace-trimmed apron over her waist-cinching dress. "What are you waiting for? Come on in before we lose all the heat."

My mother worried about the temperature in her house more than most people worried about communism and bombs.

Once inside, Mom took the pies. Then Bristol and I arranged our gifts under the tree.

My brother, Bobby, sat on the floor, his shoulder leaning on that of his girlfriend, Star. Mom had spent the better part of the college break trying to uncover Star's "real" name with no success.

Dad pushed up from his recliner, an act he didn't care for, to turn up the volume on the television. On the screen, news from the front blared, stealing away the comfort of Christmas.

Bobby rolled his head back. "How can you watch this, Pop?"

"Because I'm a thinking American. I got my education like a real man, on the battlefield preserving your right to avoid the war while going to college on my dime." He flicked ashes off the end of his cigarette into the clay ashtray I'd made in school. "Bristol knows what I'm talking about. Don't you, boy?"

Mom strode into the living room waving a dish towel. "I won't have any of this war talk on Christmas." She snapped the television off. "We're here to enjoy time together regardless of differing opinions."

"Yes, dear." He took another pull from the cigarette. "I just don't see what Bobby's fighting so hard against. Nixon's already pulling out troops."

Mom's eyebrows raised, and she stared down at Dad.

A scream from outside broke the silence of the room.

At the window, Mom parted the drapes. She sank to her knees as the scene two doors down unraveled. Men in military dress uniforms stood at the Baldwins' home, where Mrs. Baldwin had her face now buried in her palms. "Oh, Chuck."

Dad murmured something I couldn't understand as he cupped her shoulder with his hand.

"Not Tim." Bobby's words echoed like a shot had been fired right here in Oscar's Creek, Oregon.

The room grew unsteady, and my breath seemed stuck in my chest. Childhood memories replayed in my mind—images of Bobby and Tim riding bikes and taking off to places they wouldn't let me follow. I'd had a secret crush on Tim in elementary school. At three years my senior, he'd seemed so grown up. I'd loved the way he run, his golden hair swaying in the wind, creating the picture of speed.

But Timothy Baldwin would never run again.

Bristol's hand took mine. Only in the warmth of his grip did I realize how cold my fingers had become.

"This is what I'm talking about." Bobby's voice seethed with anger. "Nixon is going to let every young man in this country die for a cause that has nothing to do with us."

"Oh, give me a break." Dad went back to his recliner. "Pay attention, boy. It's Nixon who's been pulling troops out of Vietnam. You heard what he said about the risks of pulling out completely."

"What I heard was a bunch of political nonsense."

Dad was up again. "Are you calling Nixon a liar?"

"What if I am?" Bobby stepped closer to Dad.

Bristol's hand ripped away from mine as he lunged between them. "Come on, now. It's Christmas. I think we're all a little busted up about Tim Baldwin. But we're family, and family sticks together."

Bobby took a step back. "You're right, man." A heavy breath heaved from his chest. He switched his stare to Bristol. "I don't want it to be you next. I have friends in Canada. You got to go before it's too late and some G.I. Joe comes knocking on Clara's door."

A coldness coursed through my body. In the last few weeks, I'd done everything within my power to keep thoughts of Bristol and the draft banished. I'd held on to the hope that the war would end, doing my part as the "great silent majority" and supporting our president's plan to bring our troops home through Vietnamization. After all, there were young wives in Vietnam too, and America had the power to lessen the bloodshed.

I sank onto the sofa, pulling a crocheted afghan over my lap. Why couldn't Nixon's policy work without taking my husband?

"Bristol is not about to run off like a coward." Dad pulled the top off a decanter, then poured himself a glass of whiskey.

"I don't think choosing to stay out of a war that's none of our business and keeping alive at the same time makes a person a coward. Those who refuse to kill innocents are the true heroes."

Star's head bobbed in agreement. The girl never seemed to say a thing. Even the scene we'd just witnessed on our childhood block didn't crack her peace. Star had never gotten under my skin before, but all of a sudden, I wanted to rip those ridiculous John Lennon granny glasses off her perfect nose and smash them under my foot.

I turned my body away from the scene, then found myself surrounded by Bristol's arms. His shirt grew damp with my tears. Growing up, I knew right from wrong. My parents weren't perfect, but they made sure we went to Sunday school and stayed out of trouble. Yet nothing had prepared me for Vietnam; right and wrong weren't clear anymore. Protesters told us the war was unjust, that we had no business over there, but our country's leaders touted our responsibility to kill the communist monster. I'd been taught to respect authority, our country, and those we voted into office, but they wanted to take my husband.

A vision of Abraham and Isaac nearing the place of sacrifice popped into my mind. Did Sarah understand what was happening out there in the wilderness? I think she would have understood my feelings, even if I couldn't wrap my brain around them.

The oven door slammed, followed by the clanking of pots and pans. "Chuck, I need some help in here."

Dad looked at me. "Go see what your mother needs."

In the kitchen, Mom moved like a dancer from one side dish to the other. She'd lined up Tupperware in a row with military precision.

"How can I help?"

She looked up, her features twisted as if trying to figure out why I was there.

"You called?"

"I called for your dad." She brushed her palms along her apron. "I'll need help carrying this stuff."

"I'm happy to set the food on the table."

She spun on me, piercing me with her glare. "This food is no longer for our table. It's for the Baldwins."

It took a moment before I could speak. "Mom, I'm sure they have a Christmas dinner already cooked."

"Young lady, this is what neighbors do." Her tone halted all further discussion.

I peered around the corner, catching Dad's eye.

He dropped his chin to his chest, smashed out his cigarette, then got up. "Peggy, what in the world are you doing?"

This time when she turned, her eyes were brimming with tears.

Dad scratched the back of his neck. "I'll get my coat."

Ten minutes later, Bristol and I stood with my parents on the Baldwins' front step. The icy air wove down the collar of my wool coat, and my stomach twisted into knots.

Mr. Baldwin opened the door and ushered us into the house without a word.

"I've brought dinner, Jerry. I'm so sorry for your loss." Mom went toward the back of the house where the kitchen and dining room mirrored the layout of my parents' house. We followed, each with our warm Tupperware containers. When Mom had set out each dish alongside the ones that had somehow already arrived, she turned back to Mr. Baldwin. "How's Fran?"

Mr. Baldwin dug the toe of his shoe into the shag carpet. "Not so good. She's taken to her bed."

"Well, I'll go see to her this instant." Mom was gone before anyone could argue.

With a shrug, Mr. Baldwin lowered himself into an armchair. The way he moved was like he'd aged fifty years since I'd last seen him. "Go on. Take a seat."

Bristol, Dad, and I sat side by side on the floral sofa with the pattern I'd once envied.

The sound that rose from Mr. Baldwin broke my heart in half. He buried his face in a throw pillow and openly wept.

Hot fear swept through me. I wanted to wrap my arms around my husband and not let anyone take him to Vietnam or anywhere else. How would I survive if I lost him?

Chapter 5

KENZIE

A woman without a mother knows the beauty of a grandmother better than anyone else.

Kenzie pulled off her work shoes and slipped her feet into sneakers before climbing from her car to get Gram. They had a standing dinner date every Thursday night. It wasn't like Kenzie would have a date with a man to get in the way. Ginny spent the evening playing Canasta, a game Gram refused to learn because she insisted it was for old people.

As Kenzie opened her door, a familiar voice startled her. "Don't get out. I'm here, I'm here." Gram scooted along the sidewalk with the smooth gait of a woman half her age. She threw her oversized purse into the backseat, then climbed in next to Kenzie. "I'm glad I caught you. There's no sense in you coming inside when we're not staying."

"I don't mind."

"That's not the point. I can get myself out of the house, and I don't need you coming in to assist me like I'm a hundred and twenty. If you go treating me like an old lady, I'll wind up being one." Gram cupped her hands in her lap, her gaze straight ahead as if the discussion were closed and it was time to move on.

Kenzie's stomach growled as she drove toward the Noodle Nest. "I've had noodles on my mind all day."

"Noodles? At your age, you should have a man on your mind. But noodles are an excellent alternative. I've been meaning to ask you, how's Sophia and that hunky guy she's seeing?"

"He's moving to town." Kenzie cringed as she picked up on the jealous edge in her tone.

Gram clapped her hands. "That's wonderful news. She's been alone for a long time."

Hunger gave way to a wave of guilt. Gram was right. Ten years had passed since Sophia's then-fiancé took his own life, leaving her broken and wondering. With the way time moved on, Kenzie had nearly forgotten about Thomas, but Sophia wouldn't have, even if she hardly ever mentioned him anymore.

There'd been many tough days when Kenzie brought meals and the two of them sat in silence. Then Sophia began to breathe again. She took that grief and made it ambition. She graduated from law school and passed the bar exam on the first try, going right to work for the district attorney's office, then public defense, and now she was a sitting judge.

Kenzie's life had lacked trauma, but it also lacked achievements.

"What's so heavy on your mind?" Gram adjusted her seatbelt.

"Not much. Work, I guess."

The Noodle Nest was only a few blocks from Gram's house—close enough for Kenzie to walk but a long distance for Gram. After parking, Kenzie retrieved Gram's purse. The straps stretched with weight. There must be a brick inside.

Inside, the scent of garlic and tangy sauces flavored the air. They took their normal table along the front window. Kenzie dropped the purse near Gram's feet, where it landed with a thud. "What are you toting around in there?"

Gram's eyebrows lifted. "Wouldn't you like to know."

"Um. Yes. That's why I asked." The banter between them was one of Kenzie's favorite parts of their relationship. It soothed away her worries and set the world back into proper rotation. "Are you going to tell me?"

"Let's order first. I'm literally dying to have food with fat and salt." She unfolded her napkin. "Ginny is back to *healthy* cooking."

"I'm sure you're not *literally* dying from lack of fat and salt."

"You don't know. I'm convinced people pass on just to get away from the bland menu old folks eat. Ginny is trying to kill me. She keeps tossing out anything worth eating."

The server appeared at the table. "Ladies, it's always a pleasure to see you both. What can I get you today? A couple of Diet Cokes to get started?"

"You get us." Gram patted her menu. "I'd like that chicken ramen, a little light on the spice but not mild."

"Same for me, but don't go light. I want to sweat." Kenzie wiped a finger over her dry forehead.

"You've got it. I'll get this going." She twirled on her toes and left.

Gram leaned forward in a conspiratorial manner. "Before we talk about anything else, I have to ask, do you know anything about what happened to Brooklyn Stockdale?"

The courthouse had been buzzing with speculation, though they weren't even supposed to talk about cases. "Nothing that hasn't been on the news. I drove by when the first responders were at the house. Until I heard it was Mrs. Stockdale, I'd assumed the husband was the one who was dead, with everything they say about his shady business dealings. It sounds like it was definitely murder. What have you heard?"

She leaned back and crossed her arms. "That she may have been fixing to leave that good-looking husband of hers."

No doubt about it, Kenzie shouldn't be talking about this. "What makes you think that?"

"Ginny and I were at the old folks' gym, and Billy Jo Emerson said she heard it at that fancy country club she belongs to."

"Either way, I understand he wasn't even in town when his wife was killed, so we can't go condemning him for her death without cause."

"I suppose you're right." Gram took a breath, her gaze on her clasped hands. "I've been thinking a lot since Ginny's insistence that we tell our old stories. There are things I'd planned to let die with me, but watching people slip away has made me wonder if I'm being fair to you."

Kenzie bit her bottom lip, wanting to argue but knowing a word from her could stop the flow of memories.

From her giant purse, Gram pulled out a photo album. "It's a long story, and I'm out of practice telling it." With shaking hands, she opened the cover, the plastic cracking from lack of use and age. "This is the first picture of me and your grandfather together." She pushed the book toward Kenzie.

Two teenagers smiled toward the camera. The colors had faded into hues of browns and yellows, washing the images in a haze. Gram was a beautiful young woman. Chestnut brown waves brushed her shoulders, and a spray of freckles dotted her smooth face.

Bristol's hair was so light it appeared white and without the slightest wave. He had parted it to the side, neatly combed.

Kenzie reached a hand to her own head, feeling the smooth silk of her straight hair, something neither her mother nor her grandmother had.

The way Kenzie's grandfather looked at his wife, even through the fading of time, sparkled with love. Seeing them like that, so young—younger than Kenzie now—brought tears to her eyes. The loss Gram must have endured when he disappeared had never been so front and center in Kenzie's world.

Photo after photo, Gram took her on a journey through the building of their relationship. "It never occurred to me that I could lose Bristol. He was steady. Even after the draft lottery, I refused to imagine him not coming home to me because it was too much." Gram rubbed her palms together, the friction filling the silence while she stared out the window.

"So, you didn't have any idea he was leaving?"

Her chin rose. "A lot happened in 1970. Bristol was under a great deal of pressure." Darkness clouded her eyes. "Everyone says he took off. Maybe he did. Maybe there was more going on than I wanted to believe. But I know Bristol. He wouldn't have left me if he had any other choice."

A shiver prickled Kenzie's skin at her use of the present tense. Could he still be out there? Did Gram know more than she was sharing?

"I waited by the window for months after President Carter granted amnesty to draft dodgers." Her gaze bore into Kenzie's. "If Bristol was out there, he would have come home to me then."

Kenzie startled as the server clicked two bowls onto the table. Warm scents of garlic and soy sauce pushed away the tension that had grown between them.

Gram swirled noodles around her fork. "It was a long time ago." She took her first bite and, once again, pulled up the drawbridge on the topic.

Chapter 6

CLARA

January 1970

It was a strange year, even as we lived through it. People were either consumed by the happenings in Vietnam, or they ignored the conflict altogether. The nation was inundated with images straight from the front—images we weren't ready to take in, images we had to either fight for, fight against, or banish to the corners of our minds, making them no more than scenes from a movie.

I switched off the television, wishing I could still let the reports from Vietnam feel far away. No challenge to my safe and happy life. A blue capsule and a dead neighbor had taken away that luxury. In a matter of months, it could be me standing on our tiny front porch while men in uniforms laid out the news of Bristol's death. Did Nixon understand what he was doing to the wives and mothers of this nation?

"Babe?" Bristol placed a hand on my waist. "What's happening?"

Anxiety attacked at the bone level, but I couldn't let Bristol know. He faced a worse evil in a place without the familiar to keep him grounded and connected to hope. "I must have gotten lost in my thoughts. I can't decide if I will make pork chops or spaghetti for tomorrow's dinner."

The long breath that whistled from my husband's tight lips told me he wasn't immune to worry.

"And what is it that has your mind busy?" I shifted the focus.

His arm wrapped around me, pulling my body tight to his. "I'm worried about the cousins. They're young and hot-headed. They're the kind of kids who don't make it home." As if realizing he'd given too much of his thoughts away, Bristol's hold tightened. "I shouldn't be going on like that. I've been listening to my Aunt Marnie too much. The boys will be fine. It's Vietnam that better watch out."

His chuckle was a low vibration in my ear, a hollow placation to the reality we lived in.

I stood tall and kissed his cheek before stepping away. "There's work to be done. I told your mother I'd be at the furniture store by 12:30 to help set up."

Bristol tapped his watch. "You'd better get going then." He pulled the keys to our car from his pocket and handed them to me. "I'll be down there as soon as I finish up at the shop." A coldness clothed his features.

Bristol's joy at working in the family hardware business was waning with his father's deterioration.

I struggled for something comforting to say, but every phrase I could think of would sound trite under the weight of my husband's circumstances. A wife was supposed to support her husband. There'd been lessons in high school about that subject, but none of them tackled how to help your husband when he was watching his father fade away and had the threat of war sitting on his shoulders.

"Your lunch is on the counter in the kitchen." I ran a palm over his smooth cheek. "I wish I could stay and sit with you while you eat."

"Nonsense. Go on now. Mom will be a frantic mess without you. I'm sure Aunt Marnie is useless at this point." Bristol led me toward the door. "I'll see you soon." He grinned, and the dimples on each cheek drew tight like perfect tucks in a cushion.

***

The furniture store seemed like a strange place to hold a farewell party, but Marnie insisted they needed all the room they could get, and the church was having the carpets replaced. She spoke as if this was to be the don't-miss event of the season. I spent most of the afternoon hearing arguments between my husband's aunt and uncle about keeping the inventory from being stained or snagged by guests.

The furniture store was closed for the day, allowing the family time to set up and prepare. Each time a potential customer peered through the window, a growl vibrated from Uncle Albert's chest.

If Marnie noticed, she gave no indication.

Bristol's mother walked in from the back room. Her nose wrinkled as she turned her head away from the bundt cake topped with sliced oranges she carried to the table.

"What is that?" I leaned close and sniffed. Citrus mixed with something pungent I couldn't identify.

"It's a Harvey Wallbanger cake. Mrs. Houchin sent it over. The recipe came from her sister in New York City, and it's all the rage. She seemed particularly proud of that fact." Patricia set it on the food table, pushing the cake behind a plate of bacon-wrapped smokies and a bowl of fluffy Cherry Cloud—my favorite Jello dessert.

"It's nice of everyone to bring food." Marnie pulled a lace-trimmed hankie from her shirt sleeve and dabbed her eyes. "I just pray this is the last time they'll be bringing meals for the sake of my only children."

I caught the tail end of an eye roll from my mother-in-law, but I was somewhere between two battling emotions. Part of me was done hearing Marnie talk about her boys as if they were saints sent straight down from Heaven by the Creator himself. The other part couldn't get the images of Tim's family walking down the aisle at his funeral, dressed in black, out of my head. I wouldn't wish that fate on anyone.

"Where are those boys?" Marnie turned in a circle as if both stout figures could possibly be hidden behind her own ample frame. "I told them to be here before guests arrived." A look at her wristwatch only added a deeper furrow to her brow.

Patricia brushed at her apron, then reached back and untied the long strings. "I tried to get Hubert to close the store early today, but he would have nothing to do with that idea. He said he'd send Bristol over, then he'd close up not a minute before the allotted time."

"I'm sure Bristol will be happy to stay with him." The stories he'd shared about his father's slipping mind had me worried about leaving Hubert at the hardware store alone. He seemed fine in the morning, but by the time the sun had set, he was confused and edgy. Yet Patricia lived in a world of denial, pretending day after day that her husband wasn't becoming senile, and her son wasn't heading off to a jungle where men who didn't know a thing about him would seek to take his life.

The bell above the front door jingled as guests arrived. Aunt Marnie bustled forward, her hankie clamped between her thumb and index finger. At the same time, a sound from the back of the store drew my attention. Uncle Albert shoved his two boys toward his desk in the corner where he unwrapped red-and-white mints before cramming them into the mouths of his sons.

"There they are." Aunt Marnie touched the hankie to her dry cheek. "There are my grown men." She sighed as she waved the boys toward the group of women who had congregated around her.

Uncle Albert gave them a nudge, and the three moved toward the awaiting crowd where men shook hands and women leaned in for delicate kisses on powdered cheeks.

"Ginny." Patricia's voice was a hiss.

Her daughter looked up from one of the display sofas where she had been reading a book.

With a dip of her head, Bristol's mother made it clear what she wanted, and Ginny hopped up, joining us behind the long food tables.

Ginny leaned on my shoulder. "Want to count how many times someone says, 'Oh, Ginny, haven't you grown?'"

I stifled a giggle but almost lost it when Mrs. Bacho came by and stopped to eye the Harvey Wallbanger cake. "Ginny, dear, I almost didn't recognize you. Haven't you grown into a beautiful young lady?"

"Thank you, Mrs. Bacho." Ginny grinned as she offered her a napkin. "You are so kind."

When Mrs. Bacho was out of earshot, I let a giggle run free. "You will pack your bag right now and move to Hollywood. There isn't an actress out there who could top that performance."

A chill ran across my skin as my husband planted a kiss on the back of my neck. "Guess who."

"It sure better be Bristol Danes or you're in big trouble, mister." I turned, my gaze taking in his rumpled shirt with smudges on the sleeves, but it looked pristine along the chest where a work apron had protected the fabric.

He placed another warm kiss on my forehead. "I got here as soon as I could get Dad out of the store. It's getting bad. At one point, when I reminded him about the twins' party, he thought it was a birthday celebration."

With discreet movements, I twisted to see my father-in-law. He stood next to Patricia, his old, calloused hand wrapped in hers as if she had become a source of security. There were so many pieces to marriage I couldn't quite fathom. I laced my fingers through Bristol's. The warmth from his hand gave me hope that I still had a lifetime of memories to make with this man, despite whatever awaited in Vietnam.

Shouts, more like chants, rang out over the buzz of polite company. Bristol and I edged past guests to the display window. Gathering across the street with signs, flowers, and enough beads to string a full-size Douglas fir stood a group of folks protesting.

I anchored my fists to my sides. Bobby and Star were among the group, pumping fists and making a racket with the rest. While I wasn't one to agree with this war, I couldn't grasp the heartlessness it took to holler things like "baby killer" at young men who hadn't even left the country yet. Many waved signs bragging about their ability to help draftees flee. Wasn't there a law against this?

As the chanting grew louder, the sounds of conversation quieted. Some guests moved closer to see what was happening, while others congregated at the back of the store as if afraid the war would crash through the glass into their lives.

But it already had. Our picture-perfect town had fallen to the power of politics, hatred, and regret.

***

My feet ached by the time the last guest managed to get away from Aunt Marnie and out the door.

"Oh, Albert." Aunt Marnie dabbed at her eyes again with her dry hankie. "I wish they all didn't need to go so soon."

Uncle Albert patted her shoulder, but his eyes were anything but sympathetic to his wife's emotions. "Marnie, that's enough now. People have homes and families to get on with. The only thing you could have done to make this shindig last longer was to get out a bowl for everyone's keys."

Aunt Marnie gasped and stepped back from Albert, which put a huge smile on his face and made me have to hold back a laugh of my own.

"I'm just teasing." Uncle Albert ran a hand over the five hairs he still greased across his bald spot. "It was a nice send off, even if the boys have been MIA for most of the night."

"Well, boys will be boys." Aunt Marnie brushed herself off and turned toward me. "Clara, you are a godsend. I hope the twins find nice girls like you to settle down with. Lord knows they need all the help they can get in that area."

My cheeks cramped with the tension of my smile. I never knew what to say to comments like that one. If even half the stories Bristol told me about the boys had any truth, it would take more than a woman to rein them in.

Uncle Albert pulled out a cigarette. "Vietnam will take the wind out of their sails, I'll tell you that." He lifted his chin and turned toward the back of the store. "Isn't that right, Hubert?"

"What's that?" Hubert's voice had an unfamiliar edge to it.

Uncle Albert flicked a lighter, producing a flame. After a couple of starter puffs on the cigarette, he exhaled a stream of smoke. "Vietnam. I was telling Marnie here that the boys will learn a few things about being men over there. Of course, it's nothing like the Great War."

Hubert sniffed the air. "I left the burner on. There's a fire." He pulled his hand out of Patricia's and started swatting at his legs. "Get out of here. The whole place is going to burn."

"Bert, what's gotten into you?" Uncle Albert took hold of Hubert's arm.

Flinging himself free, Hubert turned in circles, clarity coming back into his eyes. "I got to go back to the store. That's all. I left the burner in the back room on."

The smallness of his voice cut my heart. Over Hubert's shoulder, I saw Bristol. Oh, how I wished he could have missed that scene.

"I've got it, Dad. I'll go back. You and Mom go on home."

"I can take care of my business, boy." Hubert's hands folded into fists.

A vein pulsed in Bristol's neck. "I know you can. But I left my billfold there. You're always getting on me for being so forgetful. Well, I went and did it again."

The bulge in Bristol's back pocket told a different story.

"Mom looks tired. Why don't you both get on home, and I'll take care of everything."

Aunt Marnie moved to step in, but Uncle Albert took hold of her arm.

Patricia yawned, her hand patting her lips. "That would be wonderful, don't you think?"

My husband gave me a knowing look, then guided his parents out the back of the store.

"What on earth was that all about?" Aunt Marnie swung her gaze from me to Uncle Albert.

Uncle Albert ground out his cigarette in an ashtray. "A man has the right to his own business, and whatever is going on with Hubert is his and his alone. That's my final word on the subject." He stepped out the front door and stood with the light from the streetlamp illuminating his stooped figure.

Before Aunt Marnie could go on, I scooped up the rest of the unused paper plates and hastened to the back.

Bristol stood at the door with a hand raised in farewell to his parents and sister.

I threaded my arm around his waist. "I'm so sorry."

Bristol kissed the top of my head. "Me too." He blew out a long breath. "I'm going to head over to the store. I want to be sure Dad didn't really leave something turned on. Do you mind driving home on your own?"

"We could go together. It's mighty chilly outside."

He brushed his thumb across my cheek. "Do you mind terribly if I go alone? I need the walk. It'll help me clear my head."

"I understand." Though what I really wanted to say was, please let me help you. The burden on his shoulders was a heavy one, and though he'd never let me, I longed to take some of the weight.

***

The clock ticked loudly in the silent house as I waited for Bristol to return. Outside, snow had fallen and tiny ice crystals formed at the edges of the windows. I pulled my housecoat tight around my body.

Our back door squawked as it opened, making my heart pound in my throat. Bristol usually came to the front door. A floorboard whined. My arms trembled in the air that had turned cold.

I flattened myself along the wall between the kitchen and living room, grabbing the ashtray we used for company. My pulse pounded in my ears, eliminating all other sounds.

A figure stepped around the corner, and I screamed as my arms were caught and pinned above me.

"What are you doing?" The familiar voice brought my fear into submission.

"Oh, my goodness. I'm sorry."

Bristol stood in front of me, barely visible with only the light from the moon coming through the windows. "I'm sorry I scared you. I thought you'd be in bed."

"Why did you come in the back?"

He brushed his arms. "There was slush on my shoes. I didn't want to traipse it through the living room. I'm freezing cold. Let me take a quick shower, then I'll be in for bed."

Before I asked any more questions, Bristol was down the hall. A minute later, the shower water started. Something wasn't right. There'd been a strange smell in the air, something familiar I couldn't place. It was like a perfume that had been mixed with something metallic and gone bad. My mother would remind me that a woman has no business questioning her husband, not that she took her own advice.

I padded down the hall to our room and climbed under the blankets. My husband was trustworthy, wasn't he?

Chapter 7

MATTY

February 1970

When I moved my pregnant wife to Oscar's Creek, I had safety in mind. I served my country proudly in the Korean War, though the horrors of war were something I longed to leave far behind.

My time with the military police left me qualified for not much else besides civilian police work. I'd tried a few other careers, but nothing stuck, and I'd felt like I was failing my family. Keeping the peace in a small town seemed like the best answer.

I did my research and checked the statistics. Oscar's Creek had few violent crimes, and there hadn't been a homicide reported since 1963. The one before that was in 1948. When I accepted the detective position with the tiny Oscar's Creek Police Department, I was playing the odds. Missing dogs and young people out past curfew were what I'd signed up to handle.

It was the beginning of my third week on the job when we got a call about a woman found unresponsive. They could have just said dead. The woman had died hours before someone dumped her body into the creek.

People in these parts talked about their creek as if it were a raging river bringing salvation to town, but in reality, even in winter, a man could wade through without getting his elbows wet. There'd been no chance for the body to wash away with snags reaching up from the depths to take hold of whatever passed by. The killer wanted nothing more than to keep their identity hidden.

As a detective still in training, I was tethered to a partner for the time being. Mike Morgan was stout and surly, the kind of man who reminded me of a bear after hibernation, hungry and ill-tempered. He took an immediate dislike to me when I refused his offer of a shot of whiskey at the end of our first shift, calling me just another pansy.

We came upon the scene minutes before the paramedics arrived. It only took a glance to see they weren't needed for their life-saving skills. Morgan called dispatch, letting them know we had a fatality and needed the medical examiner, while I approached the two teens who'd called it in from a pay phone.

"Good morning, boys." I motioned for them to follow me a few steps farther up the path. "What brings you out here so early in the morning?"

The older-looking one, a kid with carrot-red hair and freckles that reminded me of a teen Opie Taylor, dug a stick into the moist earth. "Scouting, sir. I'm a merit badge short, and Dillon said he'd help me before our meeting this afternoon. I've got to put together a display of local floral and fawnies."

My eyebrows raised. It was a good thing this kid had help with him. "I was a scout myself." I flipped my notepad over to a clean sheet and scribbled a memo to the scoutmaster. "Turn this in, and I'm sure you'll be in line for a badge." After getting the pertinent information and a statement about what they'd seen, I let the boys go home with stern instructions to tell their mothers what had happened, but not to tell anyone else.

Without a doubt, the entire town would know by dinnertime.

Memories stabbed at my mind as I joined Morgan beside the body. He didn't seem the least bit bothered by the lifeless woman before us. Such violence without the mandate of war. I couldn't make sense of why one human would snuff out the life of another.

The trail was silent aside from the gurgle of the water and squish of soil beneath our feet.

"It took me a minute," Morgan jerked his head toward the body, "but I recognized her. That there is the Campbell girl. Her daddy is one of the doctors in town. I told dispatch to send the other one to certify the death. We'll get an autopsy. That might give us a clue as to what happened here."

The cause of death wasn't a mystery. Angry purple marks encircled her throat, and burst capillaries dotted her eyes. We could call the means of death right now: murder.

Coming down the hill, a shortcut to the path we stood on, came two more officers. They did as we already had, searching the ground for any kind of evidence, but the rain from the night before had masked whatever may have been left in the way of footprints or drag marks. They secured the area with tape and barricades.

With others on the scene, I stepped away from the sight that would haunt my dreams for weeks, maybe years. A gravel country road was at the top of the hill. Our squad cars now blocked passage on the road.

The volunteer force swarmed around, setting up roadblocks and managing traffic with curious drivers.

A walkie-talkie squawked in the hand of a man near me. "Doctor Swift requests access."

The man looked at me, and I nodded.

A moment later, a brown sedan pulled to the edge of the gravel.

I'd met Dr. Swift before today. He was the doc who'd done my physical for the department. He was a pleasant man, probably in his mid- to late fifties, with dark eyes and hair that was sprinkled with gray, yet his skin was so pale I wondered how often he came outdoors.

I approached the doctor at his door, and we shook hands. "Thank you for coming."

"I was asked not to contact Dr. Campbell about this. Can you tell me why?"

The tight pinch of his expression told me he already had a feeling as to the circumstance. "We believe the deceased is Dr. Campbell's daughter."

He pressed two fingers against his forehead. "Betty. She was one of my first patients here in Oscar's Creek. A real spitfire from her first word." His gaze shifted to the treetops, towering firs that stretched toward a crystal blue winter sky.

This was the first time I felt the blessing of being new to town. Though the loss of this young woman broke my heart, it may have shattered if I'd actually known her.

Chapter 8

KENZIE

Kenzie woke with the room still dark, not even moonlight broke through the thick clouds that had blanketed the valley for weeks. She tapped her watch, and the time glowed brightly enough to illuminate the mess of blankets bunched across her body: 5:37 a.m. Too early to get up, too late to bother with sleep.

She sat up, looking deeply into the corners, wondering if the sound that woke her was real or part of a dream.

The spin of Hector's wheel squawked. As if sensing her wakefulness, the guinea pig went full force into the day. He'd be whistling for her attention soon. To Hector, Kenzie's fluttering eyes meant only one thing—breakfast veggies.

"Hush. It's not time yet." Kenzie pointed to the violet hue out the window.

She had formed a habit of storing her laptop under the bed when she was ready to sleep, which never seemed to frighten her then. It was in the mornings—when she reached under the drape of the bed skirt, her fingers searching for the cold metal—that a shiver of discomfort chilled her and her mind spun stories of hidden creatures waiting to nip at her fingers.

The screen lit up, making her blink her eyes as they adjusted to the light. She had spent the previous night searching for any signs of her grandfather, finding almost nothing.

Disappearing in 1970 equaled a life that didn't matter within the world of technology. Yet, the more she thought about the man absent from her own family story, the more she needed to find where her grandfather's ended, assuming he hadn't remained on this side of eternity, living his best life with an entirely different branch of the family tree.

What would she do if she discovered he was still alive and had chosen not to return to his wife and child? She wouldn't hesitate to break Gram's biggest rule.

She'd lie.

Not all truths were meant to be known. If she'd had the choice, Kenzie would have forgone the full story behind the breakup of her only long-term relationship. Christopher could have made up a story, like he was forced to move to some horrible big city for work. She would have stayed here—probably. They would have grown apart and eventually gone their own ways on good terms. Instead, visions of her former coworker—a woman Kenzie had introduced him to—wrapped in his arms the day they announced their engagement, continued to haunt her. He had proposed to this woman a full three weeks after he had dumped Kenzie.

Men were capable of all kinds of deception.

Renewed fury brought her fully awake.

If Bristol Danes, a man whose wife had loyally awaited his return for years with his name always a whisper in her prayers, turned out to be just another man taking advantage of the woman who loved him, then she was done with the gender forever. Maybe down the road she would want a child—a female child—but she could do that on her own too, like her mother and her grandmother did. Kenzie had turned out fine without some guy telling her what to do.

She grabbed her phone and punched out a text to Sophia.

> I'm going to do whatever it takes to find out where my grandfather went.

Before she could set the phone down and get out of bed, it pinged.

> Great. But why not wait until the sun comes up?

Kenzie slapped her palm against her forehead.

> Why isn't your phone on Do Not Disturb?

> It is. You're on my list of people who come through.

Kenzie's hand went to her chest, a motion that surely made her look like an overly dramatic actress from the 1920s. She may be single in perpetuity, but she had Sophia. A good friend was all she needed.

Her phone pinged again.

> There's someone I want you to meet. Are you free for lunch?

Betrayal of the worst kind. A fix up.

> No more men!

> He can't help that he's a man. It's not a setup. He's the investigator I told you about. Lunch?

> I can't wait.

If only sarcasm was effective in text.

> *Let's do this in my office. Privacy.*

Something about meeting with the investigator made Kenzie want to know everything she could about life in 1970. Probably another holdover from her relationship with Christopher. He had a way of making her feel inferior, as if she'd never quite understand the world as well as he did. *Well, Mr. PhD could just ...* Hector's voice sang out like a tone-deaf congregant from his cage, urging her to feed him and interrupting her less than kind thought.

Kenzie got up to start the coffee, then positioned her laptop on the card table she used as a dining room table. Gram would have a fit if she saw it, but Kenzie's apartment was up a flight of stairs so steep it was like mountain climbing to get to her place, so Gram had never been inside.

The history of draft dodging in the United States revealed a heated debate. Everyone seemed to hate someone. Those who served were angry at those who ran. Those who dodged the draft had bitterness about those who went to war. The discussion boards, fifty-five years after the events, still pulsed with emotion. In some ways, the things she read felt like another world, but in others, it was far too familiar.

The landscape of the 2020s was as divided as ever.

Two cups of coffee later, she had a decent understanding of the laws that had surrounded the draft, including the amnesty given to those who evaded the draft. It was only seven years after Bristol's disappearance that President Jimmy Carter granted the pardons.

Kenzie's mind conjured images of the man from Gram's photos making a new family in Canada with a wife and five little blond-haired children. They lived on a small farm with chickens and a couple of goats. Bristol was probably sitting on the old farmhouse porch at this very moment, bouncing a great-grandbaby on his knee while his illegitimate wife watched from the window. It was a stolen life.

The alarm on Kenzie's phone blared a zippy song, and she jumped, knocking her knee on the table and sending a half cup of coffee onto its side. Liquid swept across the surface. She snagged the laptop and her phone before they became collateral damage.

That was the time-to-leave-the-apartment alarm, and Kenzie was still in her pajamas, decorated with a splattering of java.

She threw a towel over the mess and went to change. It would have to wait.

On her way out, Kenzie heard a ping. She glanced at her phone screen. The results from her DNA test were available.

Chapter 9

MATTY

Oscar's Creek was the seat of a rural county. Dr. Swift acted as the medical examiner and with that came the responsibility of the autopsy; at least, that was the expectation in a typical Oscar's Creek questionable death.

"Why aren't we sending the body on to Salem?" I stood with Detective Morgan outside the room in the basement of Flynn's mortuary. From what I'd been told, there was a room just on the other side of this door that was used in events like the one we were in the middle of now. "They would be able to gather evidence we can't here."

Morgan scoffed. "Aren't you high and mighty? What makes you think you know what Dr. Swift and the resources and knowledge of Oscar's Creek is capable of? You've been here all of a minute."

"In a case like this, I think a transfer will be expected." The sandwich I'd had for lunch sat like a lump in my stomach. I could handle the sight of death better than dealing with pompous men who put their community and self-facing pride above a case, especially a murder.

Stepping into my personal space, Morgan wagged a finger near my nose. "You listen up. I'm your superior. This is my case, and it will be handled in the way I see fit. If you have any issue with that, you're welcome to scurry on out of here to some wuss-ified city department."

I shifted back, my legs bumping against a row of plastic seats bolted to the cement floor. The man was a jerk, but he had a point I couldn't argue with—this was his case, and I was new to the local force. It was my job to do as I was told.

The door swished open and with it came icy air and the scent of formaldehyde. "Gentlemen, come on in." Dr. Swift's white gown made me think of a mad scientist doing experiments in a basement lab. On his head, he wore a matching cap and an additional light. Another lamp shone over the table where Betty's body lay still; a sheet draped her from forehead to feet. "I wanted you to join me here so we could go over the injuries to the exterior of Ms. Campbell's body."

The doctor pulled the draping from her left leg. The knee had a series of abrasions. "This wound is very recent. I'd say it took place the night she was killed."

"That seems standard. Why would you want us to see a skinned knee?" Morgan crossed his arms over his chest.

"It's not the injury per se, but the absence of further external injury that caught my eye." He re-covered the leg. "Aside from a few bruises, all of which could easily have originated prior to the attack, Ms. Campbell only has one other injury." With both gloved hands, he pulled the sheet to just below her collarbone.

Betty's eyes were closed. Her hair, combed back from her face, laid like an orb around her head. Her skin was gray and appeared almost fake, as if she were a plastic replica of the woman she must have been before whatever violence took the life from her body.

Dr. Swift ran a hand over Betty's neck, which was splotched with deep purple marks. "You can see right here," he pointed to a series of bruises shaped like lines, "this is the imprint of a hand."

I rubbed my hand over my jawline. "Can you get an idea of how large the hands were?"

"I'm afraid not. As you can see, the bruising is extensive. I'd venture to guess the attacker was shaking her as he strangled her." Swift shook his head. "This is no way for a young woman like Betty to lose her life."

Was there any acceptable way for someone so young to go? I couldn't think of one.

"Come with me." Dr. Swift re-covered the body before walking over to a wall with a mounted light table. "And before you ask, there was no evidence of sexual trauma. You can put this down as plain murder." He flipped a switch and a series of x-rays lit up. "There's evidence of past breaks." He pointed to an arm bone. A lighter white line ran through the center of the ulna. "This is from a break I put a cast on a couple of years ago. There are a few others. Betty was a bit clumsy, but I don't see any new fractures aside from the hyoid bone, which is generally associated with strangulation." He flipped off the light board.

Morgan pulled out a pack of cigarettes and worked it with his hands. "Looks pretty cut and dried. Thanks, Doc." He moved toward the exit.

I didn't follow. Morgan wanted me to act like his dog, but there were still questions that needed answers. "Did you find evidence that she fought off her attacker?"

"One broken fingernail, but that could have happened at the same time she scraped her knee." Dr. Swift snapped rubber gloves from his hands. "I'm afraid there was quite a bit of alcohol in her system."

"Thank you for giving us a rundown."

Dr. Swift nodded. "I'll go ahead with the interior inspection, but I don't expect to find anything unusual."

Morgan remained quiet aside from the smacking of the cigarette pack against his palm until we entered the stairwell. "Boy, you need to learn your place."

For once, I made the wise choice and didn't respond.

Chapter 10

KENZIE

Kenzie arrived at her spot in the courtroom seven minutes late, giving her three whole minutes to prepare. And exactly as she'd experienced every other time she'd been late, the morning was a series of chaotic moments that amounted to far more than the seven absent minutes.

The judge pounded his gavel and declared lunch recess at precisely noon. "We will reconvene at one o'clock. Do not be late."

No doubt he intended those last words for Kenzie. The man seemed to know everything that went on in his courtroom, even when he wasn't present, which was certainly thanks to the friendly and gossipy court clerk, Billy.

Judge Daniels rose, not glancing at her as he exited. His lunch, the same French dip sandwich with fries and coleslaw that he'd eaten every day since Kenzie had worked there, would be waiting in his office.

Grabbing her purse from under the desk, Kenzie was suddenly aware of its light weight. Forgetting to make lunch was common for her, but this morning she'd thrown a few things together so she could eat while meeting with the investigator and Sophia. Unfortunately, her food remained on her kitchen counter.

She located a shoe that had somehow come off and slipped it back on her foot.

"Are you heading to the food trucks?" Billy smiled as if wanting an invitation.

"I've got plans with Sophia." She swung her purse over her shoulder and took off for the meeting.

Sophia and a man with hair cut so short he might as well shave it stood near the table at the far side of the office.

"Well, there she is." Sophia motioned to the tall stranger. "This is my friend, Kenzie. And Kenzie, this is Frank."

A sudden memory surfaced. She'd never forget a name like Frank when it was assigned to a man in his thirties. Sophia had attempted to set them up in the past, and Kenzie had refused. Frank couldn't have been the only detective Sophia could have contacted. He stood there all ex-military or something like that, as though Kenzie wouldn't be able to resist him once they were in the same room. Bold move. "Yes. The *investigator*."

Frank's eyebrows pressed together, forming three identical vertical creases above his nose. "That is my job. Nice to meet you." He held out a hand.

Kenzie took it and gave it the quickest shake possible. "Then I assume you have some information to share with me." She directed the challenge toward Sophia.

"Frank worked for the public defender's office when I worked there. He's a good guy." Sophia rolled her eyes as she set two brown bags on the table, sliding one to Kenzie.

Inside the sack, Kenzie found one of Sophia's nearly gourmet sandwiches, sliced apples, and a Diet Pepsi.

This is the level of hot mess she'd sunk to: her best friend was setting her up and preemptively supplying lunch because she knew Kenzie would forget her own.

Frank opened a file, which he pushed to the center of the table. "Sophia gave me a bit of information to get started with. I'm sure you know there isn't much available through the normal channels."

"Wow. You really went for it. How much do I owe you?" The chicken and avocado sandwich lost some of its original appeal.

He shook his head. "Consider this a favor for a friend."

Kenzie's gaze jumped to his.

"For Sophia." His clarification left an awkward pause in the room. "I mean, we could be friends too, but we met like five minutes ago."

Had Sophia thought they'd be a good match because he was as socially embarrassing as she was?

Sophia tapped her fingers on Frank's forearm. "Tell Kenzie what you found. It's really interesting and probably nothing, but Kenz, be prepared."

Frank slid a notebook out of his pocket. "I looked back at any crimes on the record in 1970, starting at the beginning of the year and moving forward until your grandfather's disappearance. I wanted to see if his case was a solitary event or if any other disappearances or crimes could be connected. What I found was Betty Campbell." He flipped through papers in the file until he came to a photograph, which he handed to Kenzie. "This is Betty's graduation picture. She was eighteen and working as a receptionist until she met the age requirements to begin training as a flight attendant."

"What happened to her?" Kenzie took the photograph. In it, a pale-faced girl with dark bouffant hair, curled out at the ends, stared at something above the camera. "Did she disappear too?"

"In a manner of speaking. Ms. Campbell was found dead on the morning of February 16, 1970. She had been strangled, then her body dumped in a secondary location near the river."

Blood pounded behind Kenzie's eardrums. "Do you think my grandfather was killed by the same people?" She placed her elbows on the table and rested her chin on her fisted hands.

"I didn't think so, but I took a look through the case file to be sure." He looked between Sophia and Kenzie. "This is outside of my official position as an investigator, so I'd appreciate it if you kept this information between the three of us."

Kenzie nodded.

"The file contained a list of people interviewed in conjunction with the crime. Bristol Danes was at the top of the list."

"Why? Did he witness something? Did he know her?" Alarms were sounding throughout Kenzie's body.

"There's honestly not a lot here, but it seems Mr. Danes was the primary suspect."

Kenzie shook her head. "That can't be. My grandmother would have told me." She recalled images of the two of them arm in arm, so much love between them. Was it possible the man who had looked perfect in black-and-white photos could have been masking a dark secret life, one that led him to run from more than the battlefront?

Of course it was. She should know better than anyone after all the deception she'd witnessed in the courtroom day after day.

"I hope I didn't overstep, but I checked in with my uncle. He's a retired police officer and started here in the early 1980s. He remembered one of the officers who investigated Ms. Campbell's case. His name was Matty Yawl. My uncle was able to get me a phone number. The guy is still alive, but he's old. I thought I'd give him a call and see if I could pick his brain."

"I want to be there." Kenzie wrapped up the remaining half of her sandwich. "Please. I'd like to come along and hear what Mr. Yawl has to say."

Sophia's chair squeaked as she pushed back from the table. "I don't see why she shouldn't." She nudged a baggie of red pepper slices closer to Kenzie. "It's not like this is an official case for you. You're talking to a man about a story from the past."

"All right." He scratched at the back of his neck. "I'll make a call and see about setting up a time. This guy is in his mid-eighties. I have no idea what kind of shape he's in or what he'll remember from well over fifty years ago, but we'll give it a try."

Kenzie leaned back in her seat and stared up at the ornate ceiling with painted beams and crown molding. She'd wondered if her grandfather could be the kind of man who'd run out on his devoted wife and start a new life somewhere else. That thought had made her feel guilty, yet she'd now learned the same man was a suspect in a crime only a true monster could commit.

The Danes women clearly were not good judges of character when it came to men.

Chapter 11

CLARA

I fell asleep before Bristol joined me in bed, and he was up before I woke in the morning. Another mark against my home economics skills. Wrapping myself in my powder pink terry-cloth robe, I slipped into my matching slippers and made my way to the kitchen.

Bristol sat on a stool, his hands surrounding a mug of coffee.

"I would have made that for you." I wiped coffee grounds from the counter into my hand and deposited them into the trash can.

He cleared his throat. "I'm perfectly capable of making a pot of coffee on my own." There was a snap in his voice that alerted my senses.

"I'm sure you are. In fact, I see that you did." My tone had grown frosty. "I'm sorry. How about breakfast? I'm starving." I wasn't, but it seemed like the thing to say, a bridge we could both walk across.

Before I could get an answer, a sharp knock sounded from the front door. Who would come calling at not even seven thirty in the morning?

Bristol held out a hand to stop me. "You're not dressed. I'll get it." Worry lines creased his forehead, and I realized this could be about his father.

Rocks sat in my stomach as I rushed down the hall. I pulled on a pair of trousers and a button-up shirt, ran the brush through my hair, and pinched my cheeks to add a tinge of pink to my pale face. Whatever news had come to our door this early in the morning, I wanted to be there, a cushion for my husband who'd endured far too much recently.

What I didn't expect to find were two police officers. One was tall and slender, not much older than us, and the other, a man with just enough girth to feel intimidating, was graying along his temples and mustache. I recognized him right away. Detective Morgan was the same age as my father. They were not friends. In fact, Morgan wasn't friendly with many people outside his sprawl of cousins. He came from one of the long-time families who viewed themselves as Oscar's Creek royalty.

"What's happened?" A wave of cold went through my body, a byproduct of countless nightmares where authorities arrived at my doorstep to inform me of my husband's death in combat.

The taller one moved toward me, cutting a divide between Bristol and me. "Ma'am, we're asking your husband a few questions. It's bitter cold out here today. Would you have any coffee available?"

"Of course." I rushed into the kitchen and found only enough left in the pot for one cup. Pouring that down the drain, I started over, moving as fast as I could manage. I brought down two cups from the cupboard and set them on a tray with sugar and a small pitcher of cream. Before the final burble from the percolator, I pulled the carafe and poured steaming liquid into each mug.

"Mrs. Danes?" The tall officer came around the corner. "I'm Detective Yawl. I was wondering if I could ask you a couple of questions." He pulled a small spiral notebook from his breast pocket and flung it open as if I'd already agreed.

"Of course." I picked up the tray. "Let's join the others in the living room."

"This will only take a moment." He tipped his head toward the counter.

I replaced the refreshments. "What can I help you with?"

"What time did your husband arrive home last night?" His pen waited millimeters above the paper.

"I'm not sure what you're asking. Bristol didn't come home until after the send-off for his cousins. They're off to Vietnam today. You know the boys, I'm sure, Floyd and Denny. They're a handful. I'm sure their mother will be relieved to have them away from home for a while." My mouth was running a race and making little sense in the process. Of course, Marnie wasn't glad the boys were going to war. What kind of mother would she be? "That's not what I meant. No one wants them to go. I mean, should anyone be going to Vietnam? Do we really belong there?"

"Ma'am?"

"I'm sorry, what was the question?"

"What time did Bristol return home last night?"

I picked at my cuticle, a habit that vexed my mother. "I'm not sure. It was before the snow started to fall."

It was 10:17. I'd looked at the clock the moment after seeing him in the kitchen. Something told me I shouldn't commit to a time.

"What time did you get home from the event?" Detective Yawl looked at me over the top of his notebook, one eyebrow scrunched.

I tapped my toe on the yellow linoleum. "It couldn't have been any later than eight thirty, maybe nine." Vague was my strategy, and I was committed to it.

"And why didn't your husband return home with you?"

I swallowed hard, then regretted the action, wondering if it gave me the look of someone hiding information. "Bristol was checking on the hardware store. You see, his father is having some memory problems, and he thought he may have left the burner on in the back. There's a little stove back there where they brew coffee and such. Bristol went back to be sure everything was safe. He's a good man. He takes care of things."

"And that took him ten minutes? Twenty?"

"There's really no telling how long it can take at the store. One task has a tendency to lead to another."

"Yes, I'm sure that's true. Would you say your husband was home before or after midnight?"

"Oh, before, for sure."

"What about ten? Was he home before ten?"

My throat shrank into a barely usable straw, keeping words from forming. I shrugged one shoulder.

"Are you saying you don't know?"

"It ..." My voice was a squeak. I cleared my throat. "Maybe. Why are you asking me all these questions? We didn't do anything wrong."

Detective Yawl finally picked up a cup of that coffee he'd insisted on and took a sip. "Mrs. Danes, do you know a girl by the name of Betty Campbell?"

"Sure. She was a few years behind me in school. What does Betty have to do with this?" My mind raced over the rumors I'd heard about Betty's recent behavior. Our little town wasn't a vital center for the hippies, but free love, and all that went along with it, was taking hold here like anywhere else.

"Did you see Betty last night?"

I skimmed my memory, thinking through the people who'd attended Floyd and Denny's party. "I don't think so." Her parents were a bit pretentious, not the sort Marnie would invite.

"Betty Campbell was found dead this morning. She'd been brutally murdered."

Air forced itself from my lungs as if I'd been punched.

"I hope that helps you understand why these questions are so important."

My legs shook. "Could we go into the living room?" I motioned toward the coffee. "It's getting cold."

Detective Yawl leaned back, glancing around the room. "Yes, ma'am. I think that would be fine."

Without waiting for Detective Yawl, I snagged the tray and joined my husband on the sofa. With the drinks set on the coffee table, I figured the men could help themselves to what they needed. I slipped my hand around Bristol's arm, feeling his tension through the thin fabric of his shirt.

"Is that all, officers?" Bristol's gaze swung toward the door.

"So, you're saying Ms. Campbell was in fine health when you saw her last night? She hadn't been hurt in any way?"

"She'd been drinking. When I came across her, she had tripped on the sidewalk. I helped her to her home. That's all that happened."

"If I could take a look at the clothes you were wearing last night, that would help us to settle this matter." Detective Morgan's face was as icy as the snow outside. "Ma'am?" He looked to me. "Could you get those for us?"

Bristol held a hand up. "I'll get them. This whole thing is ridiculous." He slumped down the hall, returning a few minutes later with a shirt and trousers.

Detective Yawl held the shirt up to the window, inspecting the fabric. "You're sure this is the shirt you were wearing last night? It's certainly very clean."

"I only had it on for a few hours. I changed after work for the party."

That wasn't true. My stomach soured. At the party, I'd noticed the stains on his sleeves, the ones I planned to soak out today. The shirt was nearly identical, but the one I'd seen last night also had a snagged thread at the corner of the pocket. I remembered because I was sure either Patricia or my mother would mention how I needed to mend it. The one Detective Yawl held had perfect stitching.

Detective Morgan unfolded a bag he'd pulled from an inner pocket and held it open.

"Wait, a minute." Bristol stepped forward. "You can't take my clothes."

"Sir, you said yourself that you had nothing to hide. They will be returned to you when the investigation is complete."

"That could be months, years even. No. I do not consent to your taking my clothing. As you've already seen, there is no evidence here."

With a deep sigh, the detective held the bag out, not quite handing it to Bristol. "Your choice, but I can't help but think this doesn't shine a very nice light on you. Of course, I think it will help us get a warrant, and that might be to our benefit."

"And like I've already said, I have nothing to hide." Bristol held up a hand. "Keep it."

The two men exchanged looks. "We'll be in touch if we have more questions. I'd be expecting another visit." Detective Morgan led the way out with Detective Yawl following a few feet behind.

With the door shut between us and the police, I was finally able to release a full breath. "What in the world was that about?"

Bristol shrugged, moving toward the kitchen as he spoke. "I saw that girl last night. It wasn't a big thing. She'd been drinking, and I helped her home."

I chewed the inside of my cheek as I picked up the tray and followed him. "What do you mean? When did you see her?"

"On my walk home." He poured another cup of coffee, then added two scoops of sugar and a splash of cream. "She was sitting on the curb. I couldn't just leave her there. But you know what they say about Dr. Campbell. I was afraid I'd get my head blown off if he saw me with his daughter in the condition she was in. Don't worry about this. It's no big thing."

My palms pressed into the Formica, and I leaned closer. "It becomes a big deal when she turns up dead."

"She was alive the last time I saw her." He stood quickly, nearly knocking over the stool. "Let it go, Clara. It was a coincidence. I'm sure they'll find out what happened to her. She was plotzed. I wouldn't be surprised if she'd managed to wind up dead all on her own."

I sucked in a breath. "Bristol Danes. I can't believe you would say such a thing. A young lady is dead."

"Not much of a lady, the way I see things."

My mouth hung open as I watched him go. That was not the man I knew, the man I loved with all my heart. What had happened the night before to change my compassionate husband into the kind of man who dismissed another human life as if it held as much value as a penny nail?

As quickly as my thoughts betrayed him, Bristol turned back. "I'm sorry. That was uncalled for."

The tension in my shoulders loosened a degree. "Did something happen you're not telling me?"

His eyes met mine and stayed there for a beat too long. "No. I'm tired, and this situation has me on edge. Really, I'm sorry."

I nodded. "Of course." I wove my arms around his waist and snuggled my head into his chest. My mother always said, "When you find good fortune, don't go digging deeper." That was the first time in my life, I believe I understood what she meant.

Chapter 12

MATTY

My desk wasn't much bigger than a school kid's. It sat in the middle of an open room with the captain's office just over my right shoulder. I swiveled my chair, peering through the window of that room as Morgan presented *our* case without me.

On my desktop sat a tower of paperwork—the punishment for being the new guy on top of questioning Morgan. My *supervisor* had burrowed so far under my skin, I'd probably still feel him picking away at my nerves fifty years from now.

Connie Blackwell's desk, at least twice the size of my own, sat near the entrance. She was the real hub of the department. Connie typed away while barely pausing to answer the phone. "Thank you, Debbie. I appreciate the heads-up."

The door opened, and a man came in as Connie stepped from behind her desk. "May I help you?"

"Good morning, Connie. I was hoping to get a quote for the paper and an opportunity to meet the new detective." The man wore a trench coat that fell nearly to his ankles, not a surprise as he couldn't have been over five feet six. He removed a fedora and worked it in his hands. A dark mustache curled over his upper lip, blurring his expressions.

Connie crossed her arms. "You're welcome to meet Detective Yawl, but if I hear you hounding him for information you're not privy to, I'll remove you from this building." Her chin rose. "Am I making myself clear?"

"Perfectly." He dipped his head as if granting her authority.

"Detective Yawl." Connie ushered me over with a wave of her fingers.

I was a big believer in the freedom of the press, but I didn't care for talking to reporters. Standing, I took a moment to stretch my legs, then joined them. "I'm Detective Matteo Yawl." I held out my hand.

The reporter had a grip that didn't match his small frame. "John Fox. Lead reporter for the Oscar's Creek Tribune."

It was a struggle to hold back my thoughts on what "lead reporter" could possibly mean in a newsroom that couldn't require more than two people to run it. "How can I help you, Mr. Fox?"

"I wonder if I could treat you to lunch at the diner. It's important to meet the new people in town when you're in my position."

I darted a look at Connie, but she didn't offer me an excuse. A glance at my watch told me what my stomach was already saying. It was time to eat. "All right. But I'll pick up my tab."

"Have it your way." He placed the hat back onto his head, possibly self-conscious of the balding scalp he attempted to cover with a swirl of long hair and a handful of Top Brass.

I grabbed my coat and hat from the rack at the side of Connie's desk. "I'll be back in an hour. I have a couple errands to run after lunch."

She peered at me over the top of cat-eye glasses. "Don't let that man pressure you to say anything you don't want printed."

Fox held the door, and I walked through, wondering what I'd gotten myself into.

The diner was a swarm of activity—conversations mixed with the clinks of utensils on plates. We waited at the hostess station until a woman in a white dress and checkered apron saw us to a booth and dropped menus in front of us.

"The meatloaf is good here." Fox pushed his menu aside and turned his coffee cup up, sliding it to the outer edge of the table.

A moment later, a waitress placed water glasses on our table and filled Fox's coffee cup. "You two know what you'd like?"

Meatloaf sounded good, but something told me not to take suggestions from the man across from me. I ordered an open-faced hot turkey sandwich instead.

After she left, Fox pulled his cup close. "Detective Yawl, tell me a bit about yourself." He stirred an inordinate amount of sugar into his coffee, then topped it with cream. "What brings you to our little bit of paradise?"

"My wife and I like the location, and there was a job available. It's as simple as that."

"I'm betting you were counting on a place like this being safe, no major crime issues."

I nodded my head, fearing he was taking me somewhere I didn't want to go. "Well, yes, that was part of the thought process."

"And here you are, already investigating the murder of the town doctor's daughter." His spoon swirled around in his cup, the coffee now a light tan.

"You get right to the point."

"I find people don't care for a lot of filler in their news or in their conversation. What can you tell me about the investigation?"

My imagination went to Morgan answering this question. It wasn't a wonder why Fox picked me to fish for information. "We are at the beginning of our investigation."

Fox pulled a notebook and pencil from his shirt pocket.

"We've made the death notification to family already, so I can confirm that Betty Campbell's body was found early Saturday morning and that the death is considered suspicious."

"Any suspects?"

"Not at this time."

"Would you tell me if you had a suspect?"

I couldn't help but smile. "Probably not."

"Good to know." He scratched a few notes. "How was Miss Campbell murdered?"

I opened my mouth to answer, then really took in his words. "Mr. Fox, I believe I said her death was considered suspicious. I did not classify it as murder at this point."

"But you believe someone killed her."

"I believe the evidence will lead us to understand what happened to Miss Campbell. We need to take the time now to carefully evaluate this case and not jump to conclusions until we have the proof to back up those conclusions."

"And you believe Bristol Danes is in possession of this proof?" His mustache twitched with smug satisfaction.

"I'm not sure what you're referring to."

Our waitress appeared, set our plates in front of us, and refilled Fox's coffee cup.

His mouth twisted. "I hate it when they do that. It's nearly impossible to get the cream and sugar right again."

I cut a bite out of my sandwich. Gravy covered the meat and bread, creating a smell that made me think of my mother's cooking.

"Bristol was seen with the victim the night of her death. Wouldn't that make him a suspect?" Fox shoved a forkful of meatloaf into his mouth.

"It will make him a person of interest, but I wouldn't say a suspect."

Fox's eyes lit up, and I replayed my words in my head.

"Let me make myself very clear. Mr. Danes is not a suspect at this time. Please, do not print that he is." The turkey and gravy were suddenly heavy in my stomach. "I assume you'd like a story that is truthful rather than filled with speculations."

Who was I kidding? This guy had one thing in mind—selling papers.

I chowed down on my lunch, ready to get the heck out of there. With the last bite in my mouth, I wiped my face and motioned to the waitress for my check.

"One more thing before you go." A smug look lifted the right side of his mustache. "What do you think of Detective Morgan?"

Chapter 13

KENZIE

Saturdays were a mixed blessing. Kenzie didn't have to work, but that meant long mornings with only Hector to share her thoughts with. Her phone buzzed with a text.

> *Yawl can meet at noon. You in?*

It was Frank.

She typed a reply.

> Yes.

And noticed the time. He'd only given her a twenty-minute warning.

> *I'll pick you up.*

Before she could type in her address, another text came through.

> *I know where your place is. I'll meet you outside the building.*

Creepy.

Kenzie had barely made it to the sidewalk when a pickup pulled up to the curb, its diesel engine growling. Frank jumped out and waved over the top of the hood. This man wasn't easy to put in a box. She hadn't given much thought to the car he might drive, but didn't investigators prefer the kind of vehicle one would describe as nondescript? Frank's truck was anything but. Not only did it signal his arrival half a mile before he got there, but the paint was a metallic red that sparkled like crushed glass in the sun.

He came around the bed and opened her door.

There should be a ladder that dropped out of the thing so a person could climb in. Kenzie tossed her bag onto the seat then hoisted herself up using the running board. "Nice spy mobile."

Frank chuckled low in his chest, much like the sound of the engine. "I borrow my mom's Camry when I want to be sneaky."

No wonder he wasn't married. She'd stumbled across a mama's boy who still played cops and robbers with his life.

Inside, he snapped on his seatbelt and turned the radio volume down. "Mom likes to drive my truck, so it works out for both of us."

"So, you live with your mom?"

He cocked his head to the side. "No. Well, I live on the farm where my parents live, but in a totally separate place."

"Okay."

He pulled onto the road. "You make it sound like I live in the basement gaming all day while my mom does my laundry and keeps me fed."

She shrugged. "I didn't say anything."

"Girl, when you say 'okay,' it speaks about a book's worth of words."

Kenzie twisted her mouth to keep the smile from blooming. "Do you think this Detective Yawl will be able to help?"

"He wouldn't give me much on the phone. I got the feeling he was in some kind of hurry, but he said we could swing by. Hopefully, a face-to-face will get him talking."

Kenzie watched out the window as the scene changed from local businesses to neighborhoods with kids playing ball in the streets and the occasional cat standing guard from a wooden fence.

"There it is." Frank parked and cut the engine, leaving them in relative silence. He pointed to a one-story home at the end of the cul-de-sac. An assortment of children's toys decorated the front lawn.

"Isn't this guy in his eighties?"

"Maybe he lives with family."

The door flew open and a tall thin man with a head full of silver hair burst out. Two young boys and a little girl wearing bright pink cowgirl boots ran after him. The four of them disappeared around the house, reemerging a moment later on the other side where the man allowed himself to be caught and dragged to the ground.

"That cannot be the right Matty Yawl." Kenzie squinted at the wrestling match taking place in the short-cropped grass.

"Only one way to find out."

As they approached the house, the man took notice. "Okay, crew. Let's take a break. Go see if Grandma has those bubbles ready. I need a few minutes to chat with these folks."

The little girl gave them both critical stares. "Who are you?"

"Maisey." The man tapped her on the shoulder. "Head inside."

She did as she was told but not without a couple more glances over her shoulder.

"Excuse her. She's a future detective." He held his hand out to them. "Matty Yawl. You must be Frank and Kenzie."

They shook hands, and Matty ushered them to a table with four chairs.

Frank pulled a notebook from his shirt pocket. "Thanks for taking the time to meet with us."

"It's no problem. I'm retired, so time is my greatest commodity." He grinned. "Those three are my great-grandkids. They come over every week to keep us from getting old."

"They seem to be doing a fine job of that." Frank's eyes were wide, not disguising his amazement.

Kenzie nodded, her mouth suddenly dry.

"So, you'd like to know about the Betty Campbell case. It's not every day that we have a homicide around here, especially one we were never able to solve." He shook his head. "I was working with Mike Morgan back then. That man was a surly old coot even in his forties. He wanted to pin the crime on anyone he could, just to say the case was closed."

The seat squeaked with Kenzie's movement. "Do you mean you don't think Bristol Danes was involved?"

"Now, that's not at all what I said. We had good reason to keep Bristol in our sights, but the thing that stood out to me was how completely innocent the guy had been until that night. Usually, the folks we'd pick up on violent crimes were acquainted with the law in some capacity prior to committing acts of violence. Bristol Danes was, by all standards, a good guy."

Matty tapped his finger on the edge of the metal table, producing a hollow ring. "I wasn't convinced the guy had anything to do with Betty's case, just the wrong place at the wrong time until a few months later when he up and vanished."

Frank's pen hovered about the notepad. "Were you involved in that case too?"

"The way I remember it, there wasn't much there. Young men were skipping town on the regular during those years. I went to Vietnam in '65. It was a different war then. I returned home to no spitting or cussing, only a mama glad to have her kid home safe. The boys who went later, they fought two battles—one in Vietnam and the other in their own hometowns. I couldn't blame draftees for making the run for the border. What got me about Bristol Danes taking off was the situations he left behind. If I remember correctly, his wife was expecting, and his dad's health was failing. Best I could tell, he didn't say a word to his wife about his plan. She was heartbroken."

When Detective Yawl finally took a breath, he looked from Kenzie to Frank as if expecting an onslaught of questions.

The Vietnam era, aside from what happened to her grandfather, was a time Kenzie hadn't given much thought to. It sounded like a world designed by fiction, not something that took place less than sixty years earlier. Hippies, protests, drafts, and a war that didn't make sense.

Frank crossed his arms and leaned forward. "But the case is still open, so you didn't have enough evidence to pin it on Bristol Danes or anyone else?"

"We never even found the primary location. This case was cold from the first day. There was a piece of jewelry the victim always wore, a necklace with an oval-shaped blue stone. We never retrieved it. The newspaper ran a photo of the pendant. It was our hope that someone would find it and we would be closer to at least finding out where the original crimes occurred. To this day, there have been no sightings." He stood and stretched. "I visit all the pawn shops in the county each year. I take that photo and remind them that the piece is part of a murder investigation. I've even offered a reward. Nothing."

He looked at his watch. "I promised the kids we'd jog down to the park before lunch. I hope you got what you needed. I'd sure like to see this case solved before I kick the bucket."

From the looks of the man, Kenzie would beat him to the grave. She really had to start exercising. "Could we get a copy of that picture?"

"Of course. Let me run to my office." The screen door snapped as he went inside.

"What do you think?" Frank looked her way.

Kenzie shrugged. "I don't feel any closer to knowing if my grandfather was a murderer, a coward, or just a jerk."

"There's another possibility. He could have been a good guy who got mixed up in something he had no guilt in."

"Then why run?" It all came back to that. If he hadn't done anything wrong, if Bristol Danes was a victim of unfortunate circumstances, why run away from the wife who loved him and his unborn child? A decent man would have stayed and fought to prove his innocence. Unless it really was all about staying out of Vietnam.

The door opened, and Matty walked out, all three great-grandkids in tow. He handed a sheet of paper to Frank. "This is the flyer I give to the pawn shops. I hope it helps."

They stood. "Thank you for your time."

Matty nodded. "Let me know if something comes up that I can help with. I've said it already, but I'd sure like to see this thing closed."

"We will." Frank placed his hand on Kenzie's arm, guiding her toward the truck. "Thanks again."

"Yes, thank you." Kenzie turned back as the little girl climbed into Matty's arms, resting her head on his shoulder. An ache lodged in Kenzie's chest, the missing piece she hadn't realized was missing. Her whole life, she'd been without that relationship—no father or grandfather to lift her into his arms and make the world feel safe and secure. Had Bristol Danes known what he was doing to the next generations?

The drive back was quiet—Kenzie in a world of her own thoughts, wondering about who and what had come before her. All of a sudden, she felt an ache to open the app on her phone and look through the DNA results she'd been ignoring, but not in front of Frank. He was getting enough information about her family.

Frank cut the engine when he arrived at Kenzie's apartment building. Did he expect to come in?

"Thank you for arranging that meeting. It was ... insightful." She tugged on the door handle, and it popped open. "Don't feel like you need to keep working on this case. It's not like it's time-sensitive or anything. I can take it from here."

His head hung in an exaggerated manner. "Is it always so hard to help you out?"

Clips of arguments with Christopher flashed through her mind. One of his big complaints was feeling unneeded. Wasn't that a good thing? Didn't it give a partner the freedom to have a life without worrying about someone else?

She shrugged. "I'm pretty independent."

The mood shifted as he leaned toward the passenger side of the truck. "There's a difference between independence and hardened."

"Maybe so." She stepped back. "Thanks again. I need to get something from my car, so, well, I'll see you." Kenzie's gaze followed her feet as she turned away. At her car, she fiddled with the lock then opened the door, pretending to search for something.

When Frank finally pulled away, she let loose a long breath. What gave him the right to challenge her that way? They hardly knew each other. She slammed the door with more force than she meant to, causing the vehicle to shudder. That was when her eye caught a glimpse of something on the windshield. A piece of paper had been tucked under the wiper blade. Likely an advertisement.

She tugged it loose then unfolded the page.

Leave the past alone.

A jolt of fear rushed up her spine. She turned her head back and forth, feeling eyes watching her, but the narrow road was empty except for Mrs. Perkins walking her black-and-white cat near the corner of the block.

Kenzie shoved the paper into her pocket and headed toward her apartment, all the while talking her fears away. The note didn't have a name. It could have been meant for anyone. It was probably just a prank.

But in her heart, she understood it was meant for her.

Chapter 19

CLARA

For the first time in our marriage, our home was filled with an unease that held Bristol away from me. Something had happened. And he wasn't telling me what.

I went about the house, one task to the next, fulfilling the role my home economics teacher had told me would be the completion of my heart's desire, but mopping and cooking fell flat. In my estimation, Mrs. Harper had been wrong about quite a few things. A woman could be very happy at home, but she could also be happy in the workplace.

In the last few weeks, I'd begun taking care of the bookkeeping for the hardware store—a fact I didn't share with my mother-in-law who thought Bristol was the one making the calculations. As it turned out, I had a knack for numbers, and the job gave me a feeling of satisfaction that needlework couldn't contend with.

I pulled the ledger from the drawer of the desk and set it on the table with a freshly sharpened pencil, but then I remembered the load of laundry I'd failed to start that morning. I jotted a note on my scratch paper, then tucked the pencil into the bun I'd twisted my hair into.

The hamper held more than a day's worth of cleaning. I scooped up the clothing and tossed them into a plastic basket. As I picked it up, I noticed another shirt poking out from behind Bristol's dresser. I placed the laundry on the bed and reached for the runaway, stopping with my fingers grazing the collar. A rust-colored smudge sat next to the smallest line of bright red.

Bringing the fabric closer, I sniffed. Bristol's scent still clung to the fibers, but something earthy and metallic was there too. And that red. I scraped it with my fingernail. The waxiness said everything I didn't want to hear. It was lipstick.

At the window, I held the shirt up to the light. Smudges covered the front with two clear spots on the sleeve. It was blood.

I eased down onto the edge of the bed. What was going on? Bristol wasn't a liar. Yet, he'd told the police he'd only seen Betty for a few minutes, and he'd showed her to her door with no injuries or concerns. Then, where did the blood and lipstick come from?

"Knock, knock." Ginny's voice trailed down the hallway.

I hopped up, turning circles in my small room before shoving the shirt into the back of my nightstand drawer. "Back here."

"Hey, there." Ginny flopped onto my bed, her chin in her hands and her ankles crossed over her bent knees. She looked like a girl at a slumber party. "What do you have planned for today?"

"Laundry."

Ginny rolled onto her back. "I'm never getting married. You make it look like an absolute bore."

"I do not." I collapsed onto the mattress beside her.

"Then prove it. Come sledding with me."

I rolled toward her, propped on one elbow. "I can't do that."

Her eyes rolled. "And why not?"

I started to tell her, but then realized my entire excuse was a series of meaningless chores that could wait. Even the bookkeeping was up to date. "Fine. But only for a couple of hours."

She hopped to her knees on the mattress. "My brother is so lucky I'm here to make sure his bride doesn't turn dull."

I gave her a shove as I got up. "We'll see who the bore is on the hill."

***

We took the long way to the sledding hill, avoiding my parents' house and my mother's judgment. All the while, my mind would not let go of Bristol's blood-stained shirt.

The sledding hill was lined on each side with bundled people pulling sleds up the hill while laughter and squeals rang out from the center as blurs of flying youngsters zipped down the snow-covered slope.

By the time we reached the crest, my right foot was in agony thanks to a leak in my boot.

Ginny positioned our sled, the runners pointing toward the edge. "Do you want front or back?"

I stared down the run, my breath gone from the climb. "Back." I had doubts about Ginny's ability to steer us safely to the bottom. I wanted it to be my boots against the rod that shifted the runners left or right.

My feet were barely settled into place when Ginny started us forward with a push off the ground with her gloved hands. The flash of a camera startled me. The snow was packed from use, and our sled shot along the surface before I could see who held the camera. I clasped my hands around Ginny's middle. The fluff of her coat and scarf obscured my vision of the path in front of us.

At the final moment of the ride, one runner clunked over something hard, and we turned abruptly to the left, both of us tumbling full speed and rolling until we stopped in a pile, giggling and sore.

I stumbled twice as I made my way to our sled. Grabbing the rope, I trudged toward the side.

A group of girls stood in a tight circle, their words hushed. Narrowed eyes looked my way.

Instinct had me checking myself for any wardrobe malfunctions, but I found nothing. The closer I came, the quieter their words became.

Ginny jogged up to my side. "That was a hoot. Let's go again."

I turned to her, noticing more eyes aimed at me. "I think I've had enough." I reached down, rubbing my knee as if I'd hurt it. "I'm going to head home."

"Not yet." Ginny looked around. "What's going on?"

I shrugged. "No idea." But that wasn't true either. Word got around town fast when something tragic happened. Put this many people in one place, and the story soon grew from a small fact to a mountain of speculation. I thanked God the newspaper hadn't made a mention of Bristol yet. There would be no way back for us from allegations printed in black and white.

Ginny marched up to the group of girls. "What? You clearly have a problem. What is it?"

I tried to tug Ginny by the arm. I loved her, but Ginny had a way of barging into a situation like a bull through a tiny gate.

A girl with bright pink ribbons tied to the ends of braids and a stare covered by cat-eye sunglasses spoke up. "We just think it's awfully crass of you both to be out here having fun when Betty Campbell's mother is at home crying over the loss of her daughter."

"Betty Campbell?" Ginny crossed her arms. "What happened to Betty?"

The group exploded into explanations of the girl's body found near the river.

"That's horrible." Ginny held a hand over her heart. "But what does that have to do with us? You're out here. Why shouldn't we enjoy the snow like everyone else?"

The girl's eyebrows rose over the top of her sunglasses. "Why don't you ask your sister-in-law?" The girl turned, dismissing us.

"Come on, Ginny." I tugged her arm. This time she came.

When we were a couple blocks away, Ginny stopped. "What's going on?"

I nudged her forward. "I'll tell you, but please, let's keep moving." My foot was soaked and had turned to ice, and everywhere I looked, I imagined people staring at me from behind their curtains.

By the time we arrived back at the house, Ginny was fighting tears, and my eyes stung from the many I couldn't stop.

"There's no way Bristol was involved in this." Ginny hung her coat on the rack near the front door.

My foot prickled with the heat penetrating my frozen toes. I curled up on the sofa, pulling my legs up and stuffing my feet under a cushion. "You and I know that, but the town is looking for someone to blame, and Bristol was seen with her."

"Because he's a good guy."

"I never thought Vietnam could seem like an escape." As soon as the words were out of my mouth, I regretted them. These rumors would pass. My husband returning to me in a casket was a grief I didn't think I'd survive.

Chapter 15

KENZIE

A spring storm swirled around the trees outside Kenzie's bedroom window. She retrieved Hector and snuggled him into her side, then opened her laptop. Maybe it was a sign that she was no longer young—her thirties were a bit rougher than she'd imagined—but the DNA results were easier to read on the larger screen.

She skimmed through the results about far-off places, not surprised to see she had strong Danish roots. It all came down to a little of this and a little of that, not the kind of information that would change her life.

Further down, she found the section she'd anticipated since the day she'd sent in the kit. Did she have any close relatives other than the few she already knew?

She was surprised to see Gram's brother pop up. Though Kenzie had never met Bobby in person, she knew that he'd spent the majority of his life living in a commune somewhere in southern Florida. He had no children from what Gram understood. He didn't seem to be the kind of man who would send in his DNA, but then again, maybe he wasn't so sure about his childlessness.

There were a few very distant relatives—distant in the way that nearly everyone must be connected since the creation of Adam and Eve.

The final entry was for someone who preferred anonymity. No picture or truly identifying information was available other than three things: the relative was male, between the ages of sixty and eighty, and lived in Oregon.

Kenzie continued to stare at the blue circle where a photo could have been added. Why investigate your ancestry without sharing who you were?

Hector climbed onto Kenzie's shoulder, chirping his guinea pig sounds in her ear.

"I'm with you. This is weird." She opened another tab and searched for anyone in Oregon with the last name Danes. There were thousands, none of whom was actually from the same Danes family as Kenzie. Finding this one hidden relative would be impossible.

She stroked her hand over Hector's soft fur before reaching for her cell, swiping to the text thread with Frank. No, she owed him enough already. Another request would add to the pile of obligations she had no way to repay.

A crash sounded from the window beside her bed.

Hector dove under the pillow, and Kenzie nearly joined him.

With her heart thudding, she scooted off the mattress to investigate.

Outside, the street was dark aside from a dim security light from the building next door. Rain pelted the window, and the limbs from the tree alongside the building waved. No cars drove on the road below, and no one would be out for a stroll in this weather.

Her mother had been deathly afraid of storms, a fear Kenzie never understood the root of, but tonight, it had attached itself to her.

Chapter 16

CLARA

Word spread around town like wildfire. Bristol closed the store early, taking advantage of Saturday being his father's day off. By the time he stumbled into the living room, he looked ten years older than he had a day earlier.

I set myself to the task of making dinner out of the leftovers Aunt Marnie had sent home from the party. The phone rang. "Hello."

"Is this Mrs. Bristol Danes?" The voice on the other end of the line had a staccato beat.

"It is. How may I help you?"

"I'm calling from the Gazette. Do you have a statement about your husband's involvement in the murder of Betty Campbell?"

Cold flushed across my skin as my heart pounded, and a wash of dizziness swirled through my head.

"Ma'am?"

"How dare you!" I slammed the phone onto the hook, shaking the ringer.

"What was that about?"

I swallowed as I turned to see Bristol standing near the dinette. "Nothing."

"It sure didn't sound like nothing. Who was it?" His eyes begged for answers, while the weakness in his voice made me want to protect him from more hurt.

The phone rang again.

I picked up the receiver and then replaced it without answering. "It was the paper. They wanted a statement about Betty's case." What were we going to do?

"This is absolutely ridiculous." He paced the short length of the kitchen. "I helped the girl to her house. That's the end of the story. What would give the newspaper a reason to seek us out?"

"You know how rumors fly around here."

"I saw it with my own eyes at the store today. The only people who came in were gossips looking for information I do not have." He scratched his fingers into his scalp. "This will pass. The police will find out what happened to that girl and life will move on."

"Bristol, I found your shirt—the one you were really wearing the night you helped Betty Campbell home."

He looked up, a wash of sadness passing over his gaze. "And you think I had something to do with Betty's death?"

"Of course not, but I want to know why you didn't give it to the police like they asked."

"I'll tell you why." He looked down at his hands. "Because I was afraid they'd look at me the way you are now. It looks bad, but I promise you, I did nothing wrong."

I knelt down beside him, taking his hand in mine and holding it to my cheek. "I believe you."

He kissed the top of my head. "We just need to hang in there. This will blow over."

As much as I wanted to believe him, I'd grown up here. I understood all too well how long the gossip chain stretched. An elephant's memory was no match for that of a small town. When the telephone rang again, I picked it up, pushed down the hook, then set the receiver on the yellow Formica. The dial tone filled the room. Opening a drawer, I stretched the cord and closed the phone inside, muffling the sound. "Let's have a quiet dinner in the living room." I dished two plates while Bristol poured a couple glasses of milk.

We sat behind the TV trays we'd received as a wedding present and watched as David Brinkley reported on the latest news around the world, much of it involving the war in Vietnam and protests here in the States. Life had felt safe when Bristol and I made our vows, yet only a few months later, the world was crumbling around us.

"Clark Donalson got his letter."

I didn't need to ask what kind of letter my husband meant. It was always the same now. The letter was from the draft board, and Clark had been called up like so many other young men. "I'll give Dee a call tomorrow and see how she's doing." I dabbed at the edge of my lip with a napkin. "She's expecting, you know."

"I'd heard that. It puts things in perspective. At least we don't have a baby on the way." His gaze remained glued to the television as if everything we were discussing was no more than the happenings on an episode of *The Brady Bunch*.

As the news ended, the theme music for *Hogan's Heroes* played.

The girls I went to school with were quickly becoming victims of Vietnam. There should be a show depicting those left behind, but who would watch it? We were supposed to be brave, keep the home while our men went to war, all while protesters spit words like "baby killer" at returning soldiers. And of course, we were to smile the entire time.

"I want you to start teaching me how to run the hardware store."

Bristol's gaze darted toward me. "Why would I do that?"

"I'll need to help your parents while you're gone, and it would be helpful to maintain the income."

"You don't need to do that. I can't have you forced into working at a hardware store of all places." He stuck his fork into a chunk of meat that had to be ice cold by now. "The military will give me a wage, and we don't even know that I'll be drafted."

"But it's likely, and your father can't manage on his own. I'm sure your mom will want to help, but don't you think she has enough on her plate with caring for your dad? You saw how he was last night. It's getting bad, and the nights are the worst."

"I don't know how much longer we can keep letting him come to work. He yelled at a young guy the other day, chased him right out of the store because he was sure the kid was stealing."

"Was he?"

"Stealing? No. Not at all." Bristol walked across the room and snapped the television off. "I ran after him and apologized, but I doubt we'll get his business again."

"I think you've made my point. You need me at the store." I cocked my head to the side, mimicking my mother's no-nonsense stare. "You've said it yourself, I'm as smart as any man you've ever met. The world is changing. Women can do whatever they set their minds to. And I'm setting mine to keeping the hardware store running for us and for your folks."

Bristol scratched his head, then pulled me up from the couch. "I know you can handle it. I just wish you didn't need to."

"I know. But I'm not complaining about the work. I'm already managing the books, and I enjoy the challenge. There's no reason to think I won't love getting to spend more time with my husband."

His arms wrapped around me, bringing my ear to his chest, where I relaxed into the sound of his steady heartbeat. Bristol was a good man. No matter what anyone said, he couldn't have hurt Betty Campbell or any other woman.

"Why don't you come along Monday morning? You can see what it's like, and if you don't want to work there, all you have to do is say so. I can hire someone to manage the store if I get shipped out, and there's always Ginny."

I leaned back and stared up at his eyes. We both laughed. Ginny was my sister-in-law, my best friend, and an all-around great gal, but she'd never stick her hand into a bucket of nails.

My finger traced its way down Bristol's arm until our palms found each other. I kissed him gently, then led him away from the mess of dinner and toward our room. I didn't want to miss a minute with this man, but I couldn't help the sour feeling in my stomach—the one that told me our time was short.

Chapter 17

MATTY

The forest smelled of rotting leaves and mud. A cacophony of sounds made it hard to determine if progress was being made. The river rushed by only a few yards from the path, and feet pushed along the ground, moving debris in the search for any missed sign or clue.

Sam Wright was out there with his hounds, hoping they'd pick up the scent and turn this needle in a haystack into something more manageable.

With last night's rain, there wasn't a track to be found. I wondered if the dogs were even capable of finding evidence that might have been thoroughly diluted or washed into the soil.

As I searched, my mind kept betraying the task at hand and wandering to John Fox's last question. It had been more than a casual wondering about how I was getting on with a new coworker. Fox had meaning behind his words.

"Found something!" The shout came from a patrol officer who'd volunteered time after his regular shift. He waved a hand in the air while his other hand braced him on a thick tree trunk.

I jogged that way, but Morgan had been closer. "What is it?"

"Maybe nothing, but look at these initials." He pointed to the bark where "B.D. Loves B.C." had been carved with careful lettering.

Morgan lit the cigarette hanging from his lips, puffed three times, then blew out a stream of smoke. "Looks like Mr. Danes isn't so innocent." His words were intended for me, a reprimand for not agreeing with his initial assessment.

"I hardly think this will stand up in court as evidence of anything." I snapped my lips shut at the scowl that met my words.

"Smith," Morgan pointed at the young man. "Get someone over here to photograph our little love note." With a jerk of his head, Morgan ushered me away from the tree. "Is there any chance you're going to learn to keep those opinions of yours in your head?"

I held my lips tight together, but inside I let loose a gush of thoughts. Wasn't it my job to have opinions and thoughts? Wasn't I supposed to use my brain to decipher the evidence available to me? What exactly were the people of Oscar's Creek paying me to do? I couldn't follow Morgan's every command and keep quiet.

My grandmother always said to pick your battles with care. It was the war you aimed to win. I knew this wasn't a battle worth laying my career on, but I had every intention of following up with the Captain about Morgan.

I stepped back from him to take in the team searching the area for clues. The trunk of the tree had been the only thing we'd found all afternoon.

At the edge of the clearing, a man stood with arms stiff at his sides. I recognized him immediately as Dr. Campbell. Dealing with family members was the worst part of my job. I couldn't manage to keep my heart on a professional level. Their pain became mine.

One look at Morgan berating a volunteer, and I knew there wasn't another choice. I wiped my handkerchief over my damp forehead, then made my way toward the father of our victim.

"Dr. Campbell."

"Detective." His eyes remained on something off in the distance.

"Sir, you really shouldn't be here." I reached for his arm, but he shook my hand away.

"Do you have children, detective?"

"One on the way." I swallowed hard, thinking about my wife, so pregnant she had trouble getting up from the davenport. If I lost my job, we'd have to make another move.

"My daughter died here. I need to see the last place she took a breath." He pulled in a lungful of air. "Did you know I was there when she took her very first breath? My wife went into labor three weeks early, during an ice storm. We lost a tree. It just missed the back bumper of our Oldsmobile. Before I could do anything about getting her to a hospital, Betty forced her way into this world."

I searched for something to say, but everything seemed petty when talking to a man who must have been heartbroken.

"That's the way my daughter was, always pushing forward into the next thing." He stood in silence for another moment, then turned, walking slowly back to his car.

Chapter 18

KENZIE

Kenzie pushed away thoughts of the note and the mysterious relative as she passed behind her parked car at the curb in front of Gram and Aunt Ginny's.

She tugged at her braid. How did a person ask an elderly woman if it was possible the love of her life was a murderer?

She knocked on the door, but no one answered. Aunt Ginny would be at her bridge tournament, but Gram had planned to stay home. When no one answered, she turned the knob and stepped in.

Inside, the house smelled of scalding milk, a scent only familiar due to her own lack of cooking skills.

"Gram, it's me." She headed toward the kitchen. "I wanted to catch you before your hair appointment."

Gram's head laid slumped over her folded arms at the kitchen table.

Kenzie rushed over, dropping to her knees. "Gram?" She gripped her cold hand. "Gram. Please be all right." This was a time for praying if ever there'd been one. Kenzie's whirling mind took notice of how she reached for the familiar comfort she'd taken in the warmth of her grandmother's faith. "Please let her be okay."

A wet stream of incoherent words flowed from Gram's slack mouth.

"I'm here, Gram. I'm going to get help."

The slightest pressure came from Gram's fingers.

Kenzie stood and located the cell phone in her pocket. It took three tries to get her thumb on the screen correctly to unlock. A beeping sound resonated from the hall smoke detector, and an acrid odor burned her nose. She jumped up as she punched in 9-1-1, turning off the stove where Gram had been making Cream of Wheat and sliding the pot to the other side.

The phone shook at her ear as she hollered answers to the operator's questions. Within minutes, the sweet sounds of sirens approaching mixed with the still-blaring smoke detector.

Kenzie stepped back as the room grew busy with medical professionals. The EMTs exchanged information and administered treatments as Kenzie pressed herself farther and farther into the corner, watching her only direct family member, her anchor, fight through a medical crisis. She wasn't ready to be alone.

***

The hospital waiting area consisted of plastic and resin—materials that could be sanitized with ease but did little to comfort family members waiting for news about their loved ones.

The door whooshed open, and Uncle Denny lumbered in. His head swiveled on his neck like an owl looking for prey.

Kenzie waved and caught his attention.

"What happened?" The gravel in his voice was like another layer of guilt settling onto her soul.

"She was slumped over in the chair when I got there."

"For how long?" He wiped his palm across his bald scalp.

"It couldn't have been too long. She'd been cooking."

The redness in his cheeks softened. Denny grabbed her shoulders and yanked her toward him, surrounding Kenzie in a rough hug. "Don't you worry. This is going to be okay. She's the strongest woman I've ever known."

When he released her, Kenzie stepped back and took refuge in the scooped seat of an orange resin chair. The two of them sat in silence while the clock, an institutional black-and-white analog, ticked by the minutes.

"Denny?" Kenzie recognized the childishness in her voice and tried to correct it.

"Yep."

"What was my grandpa like?"

Denny scraped his hand through his shaggy beard. "Bristol was a good guy. He was my cousin."

"Yes, but what was he *really* like?"

"You've got to remember, I was only eighteen the last time I saw him. Me and my brother Floyd were heading off to the jungle. We were full of youth and thought we could do anything. Life hadn't taught us to keep our heads down yet. I'm not sure how accurate any of my memories will be."

"What about Betty Campbell? What do you—"

Denny was out of his chair faster than Kenzie would have thought possible. "What kind of game are you playing?"

"No game." She leaned back, swallowing. The way he loomed over her gave her the feeling of being a small child again. Kenzie shrugged one shoulder then the other, finally standing and stepping to the side of Denny. "Her name came up, and I wondered what you knew about her. That's all."

"Betty Campbell is not a name that just comes up." He crossed his arms over his round belly. "Your grandmother is in there fighting for her life. I can't imagine what she must have been through while I was in Nam, but I know it's not the kind of thing she needs brought up again."

"Are you the family of Clara Danes?" A woman with blonde ringlets pulled mostly into a braid and blue scrubs approached them.

"I am." Kenzie edged around Denny. "Kenzie Danes. I'm her granddaughter."

"I'm Dr. Ness. I've been evaluating your grandmother. She's had a stroke, and we're treating her for that now. Unfortunately, we don't know exactly when this happened. That makes it a bit more difficult to speculate on her prognosis. Depending on how long parts of the brain were without oxygen, she may have lasting effects. The good news is that she's stable now, and we're doing everything we can to give her the best possible outcome."

Kenzie's head swirled with scenarios; none of them included Gram walking out of there the way she'd been even a day before. "How long will she be here?"

"I'm sorry. It's too early to make that determination. I've sent her for one more scan, then they'll get her set up in a room. Someone will come get you soon and take you up there."

"Thank you." Kenzie's shoulders curved. Gram had a lot of pride. She could only pray the stroke didn't rip another beautiful layer of hope away from her grandmother's life.

As the doctor left, Kenzie dropped into the seat.

Chapter 19

CLARA

I readied myself for the walk to the hardware store about an hour after Bristol left home. He liked to be at the shop early, giving himself plenty of time to prepare for the day. I suspected the solitude before his father arrived was an added benefit. While I could have joined him, I ushered him out the door with the excuse that I needed time to get the house in order before I could leave.

Pouring myself another cup of coffee, I took time to sit at the kitchen counter and stare at the melting snow on the other side of our sliding glass door. Somewhere under the slush, the bulbs I'd planted last fall lay dormant, waiting for the warmth of spring to call them to life. When I'd tucked them into their earthen beds for the winter, I'd been so innocent of the twists and turns a life could take. It was me and Bristol—nothing would ever tear us apart.

Tears cast a blur in my vision as I remembered the simplicity of the life we'd shared only half a year ago. Now we had Betty Campbell's death, Bristol's father, and the closing in of the terrible war in Vietnam.

My mother and four years of home economics classes had done little to prepare me for this always changing world. No matter how great my cooking, it wasn't going to fool my husband or myself into forgetting our troubles.

I needed someone I could share my fears with, but there was no one. My mom would tell me to try harder, and I hadn't developed the kind of relationship with Bristol's mother that would allow such intimate conversation. Ginny was my very best friend, but she was also Bristol's sister, and she had to be suffering from her father's changes as much as Bristol was.

The cuckoo clock sang out.

I looked up to see the ridiculous bird spring from little wooden doors and cry out the time. I'd bash the thing and bury the whole contraption in the backyard if my mother hadn't warned me at least ten times that Aunt Shirley and Uncle Philip were known for their surprise visits. If they came by unexpectedly and the clock was not hung in a prominent place, the result would be catastrophic.

I wondered now if my mother really understood what that word meant. I'm not sure I'd known the depth of its meaning until recently. *Lord, please let this be as deep as it gets.*

My red coat hung on the coat tree by the front door, screaming at me to be on my way. Still, my feet were hesitant. The outside world seemed filled with dangers I'd never known before.

Slipping my arms into the sleeves, the cold of the fabric reminded me of the chill I'd experienced when finding police officers on my front porch. My mother would have been mortified by the sight, a spectacle for the neighbors. I'd never been more grateful to have her out of town visiting my grandparents.

Outside, the street looked very much like it had a week ago. Much of the snow was gone, leaving slush in the gutters but the sidewalks were clear. Snow never seemed to stay a long time in our part of Oregon.

Pulling my hood over my head, I moved along as if the wind were shoving me forward, yet there wasn't even a breeze and the sun shone like we'd shot into spring without warning.

I arrived at the hardware store in record time, my toes numb in my thin flats, but my body hot and my head pounding with the effort of keeping my gaze away from the houses I'd passed.

The bell jingled as I entered the shop. Behind the counter, Bristol's head popped up, a welcoming grin on his face that faded at the sight of me.

"Golly. That's not the reaction a woman wants from her husband." I unbuttoned my coat and folded it over my arm.

He came around the counter and gave me a peck on the cheek. "Sorry. I'm happy to see you. Business has been slow this morning." He held my upper arms in his palms, pulling me close, then kissed my forehead. "Mom called. Dad's not well. She's going to keep him at home."

I nodded, unsure what to say. Hubert's changes were a subject no one wanted to discuss, especially Bristol's mother. My heart hurt for her. The man she loved was slipping away right in front of her. Life could be so cruel.

The door jingled. I swung around to find a boy in the doorway, his crew-cut hair standing like spikes on his head.

"Can I help you, young man?" Bristol's voice didn't lift with the welcoming tone he usually had for customers.

The boy's eyes narrowed and his nostrils flared.

For a moment the three of us just stared at each other. Then the boy stepped back and let the door shut again.

"What in the world was that about?" My body trembled with a shiver.

"That was Betty Campbell's younger brother." Bristol returned to his post behind the counter. "He comes in occasionally to get this or that for Dr. Campbell. I guess he's heard the rumors."

I dropped my gaze to the rough-hewn floor planks. "They'll find whoever hurt Betty and life will go back to normal. You'll see." But even as I said the words, doubt devoured my hope. Why couldn't I bring myself to ask him where the blood had come from? Was there really a part of me that could believe my sweet husband was a murderer?

Bristol dragged a broom from the back of the shop and started to sweep the already clean floor. "One day at a time, I suppose."

It was a worthy goal, but my mind couldn't help thinking that each of those days brought us closer to Bristol's very likely summons to Vietnam.

The clock moved slower than molasses straight out of a freezer as minute by minute ticked by without a single customer and nearly as few words from my husband. When the phone rang, I jumped at the break in the silence. "Danes' Hardware, this is Clara. How may I help you?"

"Hey there, Clara. It's Ginny." Even through the phone line, I could tell she was near tears.

A long breath whistled from my chest. "Hey. Is everything okay?"

"No. I've done something. Mama is going to be livid."

I waved my hand in the air to get Bristol's attention. "What is it? I'm sure it's not as bad as you think." Most things weren't. Although the past few months were trying their darnedest to prove me wrong.

Bristol still hadn't noticed my waving, so I tossed a screwdriver toward his feet. That did the trick. He jumped as if I'd shot him. When he looked my way, I motioned him over.

"Ginny, just tell me what you did."

"Daddy was having a real hard morning. He was hollering and making a huge fuss. He ..."

"He what?"

Bristol leaned an ear closer to the receiver.

"He struck Mama. Knocked her to the ground. He's not in his right mind, I know that, but I was so scared. I called Dr. Swift."

A vein bulged at the side of Bristol's neck, and I was sure it wasn't his sister at the end of his rage.

"You did the right thing. Bristol and I will stand behind you."

Ginny hiccupped. "Easy for you to say. You all don't live here. Mama and Daddy refused to see the doctor. And now, he's on his way to the house."

I covered my mouth with my free hand. Dr. Swift and Bristol's father had been friends since their school days. Of course he'd make a house call as soon as he heard there was a concern.

Bristol tugged the phone from my hand. "Gin, we're on our way over. Hang tight." He dropped the receiver onto the cradle where a ring reverberated throughout the store. "This has gone way too far. I understand wanting to give Dad the respect he's earned, but all that goes out the window when a man hits a woman. In his right mind, my dad would have been the first person to say the same." He tugged our coats from the hooks along the back wall.

"What about the store?"

His gaze swept around the room. "We might as well go rather than pretend we're waiting for customers who'll never arrive." Bristol grabbed the sign that hung from the door, flipping it to closed.

All the nervous energy that had built up in my chest now bubbled at the back of my throat. My hands clenched, and my breath came in short puffs. This was not the life I'd planned, not the sweet romance of the newlywed life, taking care of my husband and home. Instead, everywhere I turned, people were not who I thought they were. Situations that should have been purely fictional had formed our daily reality.

"Are you coming?" Bristol stood before me wearing his winter coat, his gloves hanging from one hand.

All the possibilities, at least the worst of them flew at me as if flung by David's slingshot directly at my forehead. If customers stopped patronizing the store, how would we afford our rent? How would Bristol's parents? Would Hubert need specialized treatment? Would he need to be confined? What if Bristol was arrested? What if he wasn't and instead was shipped off to Vietnam? What if it was me standing before a casket draped in the American flag, one containing every dream I had for the future?

Chapter 20

KENZIE

Kenzie took the day off. Not an easy thing for a court reporter, but fortunately, there was a woman in records who was trained for the job. Berta had held the position prior to Kenzie being hired. Berta was also outspoken about how much she hated the courtroom.

Hospitals were bound to have visiting hours, but Kenzie didn't bother to check before arriving to see Gram. It would be harder to turn her away in person than over the phone.

Gram had never been one to be sick in any way. As far as Kenzie knew, she'd only spent time in the hospital when she gave birth to Kenzie's mother. There'd been no surgeries or severe illnesses. Gram barely ever had a cold.

The last time she'd paid a visit to the hospital, all filled with masks and hand sanitizer, was to see Uncle Denny after the doctor placed a stent to prevent another heart attack. Kenzie came from hard stock. Denny had returned to the furniture store two days later, as if having a metal tube inserted near his heart was nothing more than getting a tooth filled.

Without making eye contact with the nursing staff, Kenzie approached room 216. She stepped through the door, but her vision was obscured by a curtain. Kenzie halted when she heard Aunt Ginny's voice with an unfamiliar seriousness to it.

"Clara, enough already."

Gram huffed.

"I understand your desire to honor Bristol. I loved him too, you know. He was my big brother. But this little trip to the hospital should have made it clear to you—you're not going to be around forever."

"I don't doubt that."

"Well, are you okay with leaving Kenzie with nothing just because you're hardheaded?"

"I am not hardheaded."

"You absolutely are."

The conversation quieted, and Kenzie reached for the curtain. "Hello." She let her voice ring out to foster the illusion that she'd just gotten there.

Gram lay under a white blanket, a heart monitor beeping a steady rhythm at her side.

Near the window, Aunt Ginny lay back in a rust-orange recliner. "Clara, look at that, Kenz is here to see you."

Gram pushed a button, bringing the top of her bed up.

Kenzie held out a hand. "Hi, Gram. Don't sit up on account of me."

"Nonsense." Aunt Ginny pushed the footrest down with a great deal of effort, then rose to her feet. "She's not frail."

Gram's eyes blinked. "Oh, my goodness. Such a fuss." Her words were a bit slower than their usual cadence, but they didn't lack the internal strength Kenzie always associated with her grandmother. "Shouldn't you be at work?"

"I took the day off to spend with you." Kenzie eased onto the side of Gram's bed.

"What a bother I am. Berta must be fit to be tied." She reached a shaky hand to her mouth, dabbing at escaped saliva. "This is ridiculous. I'm slobbering all over myself like an old Great Dane."

Aunt Ginny chuckled. "That's fitting."

There was nothing wrong with Gram's ability to shoot her friend a dose of stink eye. "They're letting me out of this death trap today."

Kenzie swung her gaze to Aunt Ginny, who nodded.

"What are you looking at her for? I'm the one in the hospital, and I'm not here for lack of mental resources. The doc came in and said I'm doing well, and I can complete my recovery at home."

"Well, he did say all that, but she'd threatened to leave regardless of being discharged." Aunt Ginny rested her hand on the lump in the blanket that was Gram's foot. "The stroke seemed to increase her spunk."

"It was a TIA." Gram kicked at Aunt Ginny's hand.

Aunt Ginny crossed her arms. "Which is a mini-stroke."

A nurse came into the room, breaking up the conversation. She pushed a wheelchair into the bit of available space. "Good morning. Mrs. Danes, I hear you're being discharged. Dr. Ness wanted you to be seen by occupational therapy before she signs the papers. Would you mind coming for a ride with me?"

Gram dabbed again at her mouth. "I can walk."

"Hospital policy. All our guests ride."

Kenzie thought for a moment she was going to say "ride for free" but thought better of it.

Aunt Ginny and Kenzie moved out of the way, and the nurse helped Gram into the chair. "We'll be back in about half an hour. You're welcome to stay here or you could get some breakfast in the cafeteria."

Once Gram and the nurse had left the room, Aunt Ginny picked up her purse. "Coffee?"

"I never say no to that."

Kenzie followed her great aunt down the corridor to the elevators. Aunt Ginny had a shuffle to her gait that had come on over the last couple of years. Sleeping in hospital recliners surely wasn't a help.

They took the elevator to the first floor where it opened up across from the entrance to the cafeteria. The scent of bacon and maple syrup erased the institutional smells from this hall.

Aunt Ginny pulled in a long breath. "I'm going to need pancakes, eggs, and hash browns to go with that coffee."

As if understanding the situation, Kenzie's stomach growled.

"My treat." Aunt Ginny hobbled into the large open room.

They procured trays and worked their way along the commissary, picking the items they wanted from the buffet.

Kenzie chose a table near the window. The hospital sat on the top of a hill, giving a beautiful view of the blues and greens that painted their valley.

Aunt Ginny grabbed Kenzie's hand and offered up a simple grace. After saying "Amen," she gave her hand a warm squeeze. "Clara will be okay, this time."

The bite of egg Kenzie had been chewing grew rubbery in her mouth.

"What I'm trying to say is we're getting old. Okay, Clara and I, we are old. We're not going to be here forever."

"But I'm not ready to be without either of you."

Aunt Ginny dumped an abundance of sugar into her coffee cup, then topped it with three creamers. She stirred the concoction with a wooden stick. "Clara doesn't like to talk about everything that happened with Bristol. She thinks by not mentioning the hard things, she can live in a world where none of it happened." She took a sip, then added a bit more sugar. "If there was one gift I could give to my dearest friend, it would be the truth. We both need it more than I can say. We need to know what happened to Bristol that day."

Breakfast sat like a swarm of bees in Kenzie's stomach. "I've done something."

"What's that?"

"I've been looking into Grandpa's disappearance. A friend of Sophia's is helping me. We met with one of the detectives from the Betty Campbell case."

"The hot one or the old grouch?"

Kenzie drew a blank. "I'm not sure."

"Well, I guess it would have to be the hot one. The other guy has got to be dead by now." She took another drink of coffee, this time smacking her lips with pleasure. "Betty's case was all the talk that year. And the gossip around Bristol being involved was insane. And there was Daddy's illness. It wasn't long after they found her that he went terribly downhill. Not a day goes by that I don't thank the Lord for sparing me from dementia."

"I didn't know about that."

"It's all in the videos, my dear. The neighbor boy is putting them in the clouds. He told me he could give you access to them."

Kenzie's nose tickled with restrained laughter. "Thank you. I'm sure that will be helpful."

Aunt Ginny reached her hand across the table and squeezed Kenzie's. "Do whatever you can to find out what happened to my brother. Clara is counting on a beautiful reunion in Heaven. If for some reason my big brother wasn't the man I knew him to be, and he's spending eternity in

Hell, well, I'd like her to go into the great beyond knowing the truth. She's been waiting for him for over fifty years."

Chapter 21

CLARA

When we arrived at Bristol's parents' house, we walked into a scene much like a family reception after a funeral. Patricia sat in a wingback chair, her gaze out the window as if something horrible were happening in the branches of the old oak tree.

Uncle Albert paced up and down the dark hallway that led to the bedrooms. Each time he came into view, he glanced at his sister, huffed, and began another lap.

I found Ginny in the kitchen with Aunt Marnie. When trouble arrived, you could usually find women in this room making coffee. This was not the occasion to pull out the Sanka in anyone's cup. I busied myself by lining up needed dishes and utensils on the counter.

Sidling up to Ginny, I pulled a wisp of hair away from her face. "Where's your dad?"

When she looked my way, it was clear she'd been crying. Red rimmed her eyes and the delicate skin below had swollen. Without speaking, she pointed toward the only room in this house I'd never been in, Patricia and Hubert's bedroom.

She tipped her head onto my shoulder, and I pulled her into a full embrace. My dear friend, the one who was always so strong, shook me with her sobs.

I'd been so wrapped up in my list of woes, I'd neglected to look at this year from Ginny's perspective. Her only cousins were off to fight a war on the other side of the world. Her brother was likely to follow at the whim of the government. And her father was slipping away. Seeing him physically attack her mother had to break Ginny's already fracturing heart.

None of this was fair. How could a war thousands of miles away take so much from a decent family in Oscar's Creek, Oregon?

I rubbed my palm over Ginny's hair, smoothing the wayward pieces that had escaped her ponytail. "It's going to be alright. I promise you. We'll get through this together."

Aunt Marnie busied herself with designing a tray of cheese and crackers. I couldn't remember when she'd failed to interject her perspective into a conversation, but I was grateful for the reprieve. Yet, I had no words of wisdom to share with my friend. More than likely, the family would need to accept that the time for Hubert to move into a place where he could be cared for around the clock had come.

I led Ginny from the kitchen to the living room and sat beside her on the couch. There was nothing I could say to make the situation better. My only experience with senility was with a great aunt, but that had looked very different from what I was seeing with my father-in-law. If anything, she'd grown quieter over the years of slippery memories, becoming content to sit and watch the unfamiliar faces around her as if taking in a picture show of everyday life. Each day she'd spent more time sleeping than the one before until one day she didn't wake.

I remember asking my grandmother why she didn't put her sister into an institution. I'd heard my parents talking and knew little about what that really meant. With a tear in her eye, Grandma told me what we contributed to the world was sometimes just being there. Having her sister near gave her peace.

When years later a man at church put his wife in an institution for senility, I judged him harshly. I knew so little about the ways in which life could hurt the heart. I'd go back to correct that foolishness if I had the choice.

Patricia rose from her chair, heading toward the hallway.

"Where are you going?" Uncle Albert held both hands out as he blocked her way.

"I'm going to check on my husband." Though her words were strong, her chin quivered. "He could be hurt."

"I'll see to Hubert." He turned to walk away, but Patricia grabbed his arm.

"You're not going to be here forever, Al. He's my husband, in sickness and in health."

I'd never seen Bristol's uncle angry like this before. His jaw shifted back and forth as if he'd taken a physical hit. "There's nothing in those vows that condones hitting a woman."

The back door knocked open, and Bristol walked in with firewood stacked from his hand to his ear. It took more than a family emergency to stop my husband from keeping his mother's wood stack full. He glanced at the scene then dropped the pile into the box near the woodstove. "What's going on? I was only gone for a minute."

My mother-in-law used the distraction to skirt around her brother.

A moment later, a scream cut through the house.

Chapter 22

MATTY

"Captain?" I tapped on the frame of the open door. "Could I talk with you for a minute?"

The captain tipped back in his office chair, producing a squawk that seemed to echo through the room. "Come on in. Have a seat."

Two chairs sat on the company side of the desk. I took the one farthest from the door, hoping Morgan wouldn't see me talking to our superior without his consent or inclusion.

The captain was a rounded man, a man who'd worked his way up from beat cop to where he sat now. Though he had me by at least thirty years, his head was densely covered with dark hair unblemished by gray. I'd had very little interaction with him since joining the force at Oscar's Creek, but the few times our paths had crossed, I felt he was a decent kind of guy.

"I'm surprised to see you in here without Morgan." He wrinkled his nose, making his glasses bob. "Is there something I can help you with?"

"I hope so, sir. I'm concerned about the way the Campbell investigation is going."

"That's interesting. Morgan was in here this morning with a glowing report. He said you're closing in on the killer, and you've been a real asset. Is that not true?" He pulled a sheet of paper from the inbox at the side of his cluttered desk and slapped a hand over it.

I had to conclude this was the latest report. I did most of the paperwork, but the report that went to the captain was completed only by Morgan.

"In the past, in other jurisdictions, it has been the policy to interview all the members of the deceased's family." If there was one thing I'd never been good at, it was speaking up to people in authority. This trait kept me out of my father's way and in the good graces of the ranking officers in Vietnam, but it often left me reconciling situations I didn't agree with.

"And you haven't done so?"

The air in the office grew heavy, and I started to sweat. I couldn't lose this job. "No, sir, we haven't yet."

"Yawl, get to the point. I'm six months away from retirement, and I don't want to spend the entire time waiting for you to answer a simple question. Why haven't you interviewed the family?"

The floorboards creaked behind me.

"Because there was no need for both of us to press questions on a grieving mother and her children right after their loss." The booming voice came from behind me. Morgan.

My stomach soured—first at being caught in the captain's office and second because Morgan was flat-out lying.

"In fact, I was looking for this rookie so we could head over to the Campbells' house and remedy that gap in our paperwork."

I rose from my chair, not about to try the tattletale method. "Thank you, sir." I dipped my head as if I were bowing to a Chinese dignitary. Shame was a weight I couldn't shed.

Morgan didn't say a word to me as we gathered our things and headed for the door. On the way out, Connie gave me a look that could only be read as pity. I was in deep trouble, and she knew it.

We got into the car assigned for use by the three detectives. I still hadn't been behind the wheel of the bronze sedan, and I doubted I would as long as I was working alongside Morgan.

I was ready to think I'd made up the additional tension when we'd gone two blocks from the station and Morgan yanked the steering wheel, throwing us into an awkward park at the curb. "Don't you have a lot of nerve?" I stared out the window as Morgan spat out a series of insults.

At some point, the words started picking at the cords in my jaw. Blood pulsed behind my ears, and my face grew hot. I threw open the heavy door and jumped from the parked car, pacing back and forth on the sidewalk. I pictured my wife preparing the nursery for our child, the small yard and the cozy home we'd purchased in the middle of Oscar's Creek, the rave reviews our neighbors gave the school district.

When my lungs relaxed enough to take a full breath, I looked back at the car. Morgan was still sitting in the driver's seat, but his face had returned to its normal ashy tone.

I gave my neck a final stretch, then climbed back in. Rebuttals to his tirade ran through my mind, but I clamped my mouth closed, thinking of my future.

At the Campbells' house, I shook out my arms as we waited for the doorbell to be answered.

"I'll take the mom." Morgan's words were another demand, but after this case, I wouldn't have to work side by side with him again. I'd be done with my probationary period, and there would be a buffer between me and this pompous creep. "You can interview the kids."

Mrs. Campbell opened the door, a young child on her hip. I'd known there was an age gap, but I hadn't realized the youngest was only a toddler. I glanced at Morgan, who returned my look with an expression of triumph.

Inside, Mrs. Campbell led us to a sitting area with a matching loveseat, sofa, and two high-backed chairs.

I ran my hand over the velveteen fabric. "This is lovely furniture, Mrs. Campbell. My wife would adore this set." I always preferred to enter hard conversations with a small bit of trivial talk. It made people feel at ease, and they were much more likely to share information with me when they'd opened up about something of no real importance.

"We recently purchased this set down at Flanigan's. I'm sure she could find something she likes there." The smile she offered was weakened, I assumed by her grief, but even in a time like this, Mrs. Campbell remained a gracious host. "Could I get you gentlemen coffee? I have a plate of cookies from a family at church."

Morgan waved her off.

"Oh, please. If you don't eat some of them, the boys will. It's so bad for their teeth."

"We would love some cookies," I answered for both of us, knowing Morgan would get around to accepting the offer sooner or later.

I sat on the loveseat, giving it a little bounce. The frame was sturdy, solid.

Morgan shook his head. "You got a kid coming, and I know how much you make. Don't fool yourself into thinking you can afford to live like the Campbells."

As much as I wanted to be angry, I knew he was right.

A boy about ten years old walked into the room, his gaze seemingly fixed in a scowl. He looked from Morgan to me, not saying a word.

Mrs. Campbell returned with a tray that she set on the coffee table. "Help yourself to coffee and treats, detectives." She looked at the boy. "Have you been introduced to Benjamin?"

The younger child lifted his arms to his brother who picked him up.

"No, ma'am," I said before taking a bite from an oatmeal cookie.

"Detective Morgan and Detective ..." Her mouth twisted.

I quickly swallowed. "Yawl. Detective Yawl, ma'am."

"Yes, Detective Yawl. That's an unusual name." She wet her lips. "This is our son, Benjamin. Benjamin, these fine men are doing all they can to discover what happened to ..." She covered her mouth with her hand. "Excuse me, please." Mrs. Campbell disappeared into the kitchen.

I looked to Morgan, finding him content to eat cookies. "Should I follow her?"

His reply was more growl than words, but he stood and ambled through the kitchen door.

Benjamin's neutral stare hardened. I couldn't say he was glaring at me, but there was a venom in his eyes that made me sit up straighter.

I pulled out my notepad. "Benjamin, what can you tell me about Betty's death?"

"Ben."

"Excuse me?"

"My name is Ben. My friends call me Benny. Only my mom can say Benjamin." He scooped a cookie from the tray and placed it in his brother's chubby hand.

"Okay, Ben. I understand this is hard, and I want to make it as simple as possible. Tell me about the last time you saw your sister."

"She was in her room, not doing anything, really."

"What time was this?"

He shrugged. "I don't know. I didn't pay any attention."

"Was it dark or light outside?"

He scratched the top of his head as if he was thinking. "Probably dark."

That didn't tell me much. The sun would have set early this time of year. "Was it before or after supper?" A boy his age would be well aware of mealtimes.

"After."

"Did she seem upset?"

His forehead crinkled. "She's a girl. She's always upset."

I made a note that he still used the present tense when referring to Betty.

Morgan came through the kitchen door. "You about done here, rookie?"

"Ben, do you have anything else to add? Any ideas about who would hurt your sister?"

"Nope."

"Thank you for your help." The sarcasm would be obvious to an adult, but I doubted this kid would pick up on it.

Morgan grabbed another cookie and headed outside.

Chapter 23

KENZIE

Kenzie studied the photograph of Betty Campbell's necklace, as if by staring at the image, she'd know where to find it and what happened the night of Betty's death. She stuck the paper onto the bulletin board in her dining room and pierced the surface with a tack. Beside that, she added a photo of Betty Campbell she'd found online.

Gram would be horrified if she saw what was beginning to look like a murder board. Giving Gram and Aunt Ginny closure was the top priority, but more questions were growing from the mystery. Kenzie had developed a need to understand what had happened in her family background. She needed the truth of what had caused nearly every relationship between a man and a woman to be doomed since the day Bristol Danes disappeared. Was she just as likely to wind up alone—a third generation of a Danes woman without a man to share her life with?

Kenzie pulled her laptop from its bag and set it on the chipped countertop. She reviewed the tabs she'd left open from her last search for information. She'd combed search engine results with her closest result being Bristol the Great Dane's Instagram page. If her grandpa was alive and using his legal name, she expected she'd have found some trace of him, or if he was dead, at least an obituary, but nothing existed, not even a reference to his original disappearance.

If Sophia hadn't called in a favor with Frank, she'd be nowhere. Would that be so bad? At least she wouldn't be living with the possibility that her grandfather was more than a runaway husband and father; he could be a murderer too. Had he run to avoid jail? That didn't seem right. Today's murder statistics said only 49 percent ever got solved. These numbers had to be far better than they'd been in 1970. If he was guilty, he very well may have gotten away with it.

Another look at Betty Campbell's photo had Kenzie wondering about the family she'd left behind. And the people—children, grandchildren, great-grandchildren—who would never exist because Betty was stolen from this world.

Kenzie ran a brush through her hair and splashed water on her face before grabbing the flyer. She'd stop by the twenty-four-hour print store on the way to work. That would allow her time to breathe some fresh air and come up with some next steps. It was still possible that what happened to Betty Campbell had nothing to do with Bristol Danes.

At the bottom of the stairs, Kenzie froze, staring out the door at her car parked along the curb.

Something fluttered in the breeze, her windshield wiper holding it down.

Again.

Her stomach turned to solid rock in her gut. She looked back and forth, confirming that she was alone on her small side street. The sun had risen, but the day was still in its newest phase, casting orange light across the sidewalk.

Before she could take a step, a jogger came around the corner, and Kenzie lunged back into the door of her complex.

The woman continued as if not noticing the odd reaction.

Okay. Kenzie shook out her hands and stretched her neck. She was being ridiculous. It was likely an advertisement for a local restaurant, yet she'd immediately created a story in which she was being stalked, and the perpetrator was watching from the shadows, ready to spring forward and kidnap Kenzie, keeping her captive in a torture chamber until she finally succumbed to malnutrition.

She had to stop listening to true-crime podcasts.

Without looking, Kenzie tugged the paper loose and shoved it in her pocket.

She managed to drive two blocks before pulling to the curb and retrieving the offending flyer.

Do you think you can ignore me?

Cold flushed her, leaving goose bumps along her arms. Kenzie removed the first note and set it beside the new one. She wasn't a forensic specialist, but she'd bet a week of meals they were written by the same unsteady hand.

Closing her eyes and breathing deeply, she struggled to get her heart rate under control. Seven scribbled words and her whole life felt as if it were balanced on a tenuous edge.

Her eyes popped open. What if he was watching her? It had to be a man. It was always a man in her mystery novels. And they were always watching.

The little car was like a fishbowl with Kenzie as an easy target. She stuffed the papers under her purse and pulled away from the curb, checking her mirrors in rapid succession, alert for any sign of a follower, but the street was nearly empty, no one giving her even a glance.

A mile down the road, she'd calmed to the point of embarrassment. She wasn't stalking material. Maybe she had a car that looked a lot like someone else's. The creep would sure be surprised when he caught a look at her, a plain thirty-something with hair that did nothing but lie flat as if she were a wannabe hippie.

Even so, she decided to skip the print store for now. She'd go on her lunch break when it was busier—less chance of running into creeps.

The great thing about arriving at the courthouse over an hour early was the availability of parking spaces. Kenzie parked then got out of the car. From down the block, a woman raised a hand and waved.

Squinting, she could just make out the teal and black of Sophia's running attire. How anyone could subject themselves to that kind of pain and exhaustion at the beginning of the day was unknown to Kenzie.

At a pace that looked Olympic, Sophia arrived at her side. "Hey. Did you decide to run with me? I've only gone a mile or so."

Kenzie's hand shot up, forming a stop sign between them. "You have to know that's not why I'm here. If I ever do show up for a run at this insane time of the morning, please have me committed until I'm back in my right mind."

Sophia jogged in place as if she needed a restroom. "The exercise clears my head. I think it will do you a lot of good."

"Interesting jab, but I'll stay foggy, thank you very much."

Sophia's feet slowed. "If you're not here to run, what's got you up so early?" Worry lines creased her forehead.

"Something woke me, then I had a plan to make copies of Betty Campbell's missing flyer, but ..." She moved her gaze to the giant oak that grew near the courthouse.

"What?" All Sophia's motion stopped.

"There was another note."

Sophia whipped her phone out of some hidden pocket and started texting.

"What are you doing?"

"Come on." She started for the courthouse. "Let's get inside."

"What about the rest of your run?"

"Forget that. You are far more important to me than my mental stability." She looked over her shoulder and smirked. "Move those legs, girl. I'll feel a lot better when you're inside."

"You haven't even seen the message." Kenzie's feet clopped along behind Sophia, trying to keep up the pace. How could her friend ever dream that she'd be able to manage a run?

At the top of the steps, Sophia rapped on the door. "It's Judge Lancaster," she called through the door.

The large oak barrier creaked open. "That was a quick one, ma'am. Everything okay?"

"Officer Travis, it most certainly is not." She ushered Kenzie through the door. "I want eyes on Ms. Danes at all times. No one comes near her without a reason. Am I clear?"

"Perfectly. Is there a circumstance I can share with my captain? We'll need to bring in an extra officer."

No one was even looking at Kenzie. She had rights. "Not a chance. I'm fine, and I don't need a detail." Clearly Sophia really did need that morning run.

Sophia's hand reached out. "Let me see it."

When Kenzie didn't move, Sophia's eyebrows rose. "Okay." Kenzie dug the quarter sheet of paper out of her pocket, bringing the old one with it.

"And I suppose your fingers have been all over this?"

"I do tend to hold things with my fingers, yes." She handed it to Sophia who motioned toward the desk.

"I'm calling Frank."

"No." Kenzie's face flushed with warmth. "I mean, there's really no reason to bother him, especially this early."

"It's not all that early anymore, and Frank seems like the kind of guy who would be up with the sun." She made a few selections on her phone, then held it to her ear. "Good morning, Frank."

Kenzie stood at the window, staring down at the people who freckled the sidewalks below, each one with a plan for the day that had nothing to do with Kenzie or her family. They weren't the sort of family who incited stalkers or had deep dark secrets. It had always been Gram, Kenzie, and Kenzie's mom. Three women who liked to read and didn't go out much. They didn't party, commit crimes, or even travel to exotic places.

When Kenzie ran through the years, the only interesting thing that had happened was the disappearance of her grandfather and the uncertainty she had about her own dad, though she doubted that story held any shocking details.

The DNA test results were still sitting in her email. So many answers held in the tiny deposits of microscopic threads.

"Frank is on the way."

Kenzie turned, leaving the possibilities to weave their own stories. "There's nothing he can do."

"We'll let him be the judge of that." A smirk twisted Sophia's lips. "See what I did there?"

Shaking her head, Kenzie let out her first full smile in days. "You have the strangest humor."

"Sometimes it's hard to tell the difference between strange and brilliant."

Chapter 24

CLARA

I stood against the wall, frozen, as my husband and Uncle Albert rushed to Hubert and Patricia's bedroom. It wasn't until I heard my father-in-law's accusing voice chanting "Killer!" over and over again that my feet were able to move from their anchor in the shag carpeting.

Once inside the door, I wished for the moment before when I didn't have this image in my mind that would likely haunt me until my last day.

Bristol held one of Hubert's arms while Uncle Albert had the other. A razor blade was held in his grip far too near to Albert's neck. "You're a killer!" His screams shot off the walls unaimed but hit Bristol square in the heart.

My husband's jaw was defined by the tension it held, veins throbbing visibly below the surface.

What kind of bitter disease would have a father throwing horrible accusations at his beloved son? It made me fear for the future, the uncertainty of old age when not even the mind could be trusted to tell you the truth.

It wasn't until Ginny and Aunt Marnie came into the room and dropped to the floor that I even noticed Patricia.

She was pushed up against the bed, her knees to her chest. One hand clenched the other, and blood seeped from between her fingers.

I rushed to the bathroom, flipping through washcloths until I found one that wasn't stark white. Returning, I handed it to Aunt Marnie who pulled Patricia's hand apart, gasped, and wrapped the sliced palm with the cloth.

My stomach wobbled, and I sat back on the mattress.

Hubert continued his rampage, but the razor blade had landed on the floor. Now I could see the blood on the blade—the blood that had come from his wife's hand. She'd been cut by the person she should have been able to trust with her safety. But Hubert wasn't there anymore. Only the body of the strong man I'd once known remained, and it had turned fragile and thin. Inside, he was someone else, a stranger.

Finally, drained from the struggle, Hubert lost all the fight within himself. Bristol and Uncle Albert guided him to the chair in the corner of the room, each man keeping a hand on one of Hubert's shoulders.

"You're going to need stitches." Aunt Marnie helped Patricia to her feet. "It's deep."

"I'm fine. I can't."

Ginny wiped a tear from her mother's face. "Mom, you have to go in. That cut will not heal on its own."

"I can stitch it up. My mom used to do it all the time on the farm. Remember, Albert?" Her gaze held her brother's. "Remember how Mama stitched up your arm that time you got cut so bad? I could do that now."

He shook his head. "No, Patty. Mama did that because she had to. We were out in the middle of nowhere, no doc around. You need medical attention."

"But they'll take him away." Her shoulders jumped with sobs.

Uncle Albert gave Bristol a look, and then he came to the bed where he sat next to Patricia. "Little sister, I understand you want to take care of him." Albert took her uncut hand in his, ignoring the drying blood. "He needs more than any of us can provide at home. It's for his good as much as yours."

Hubert's glassy eyes looked into the room as if seeing something no one else could. He'd fallen into another reality, drifting away on a current that would never shift directions. My father-in-law, for all intents and purposes, was gone.

Chapter 25

KENZIE

"Why didn't you tell me about the threat?" Frank's words beat him through Sophia's office door.

Kenzie stood, taking a defensive stance. "There was nothing to tell. At the time, I'd received one silly note on my car. How was I to know it wasn't an unfortunate prank?"

"Because all threats will be taken seriously until proven otherwise." He leaned against Sophia's desk, his arms crossed tight across his broad chest.

She stepped closer. "This isn't the military. I'm an average-looking court reporter in a small county courtroom. Why would I ever assume someone would come after me?"

"There's nothing average about you, including your looks." He raised his eyebrows.

"Are you calling me ugly?"

Sophia stepped between them. "Girl, he was saying you're pretty. What is the deal with the two of you?"

Plopping down in a chair, Kenzie kept her face turned away from the others while she willed the warm flush to dissipate.

"I get it." There was laughter in Frank's voice, and it brought rage back to Kenzie. "You assume the best of everyone else but the worst of yourself. What is that about?"

"Oh, my goodness." Kenzie popped back to her feet. "We aren't here to do a mental health assessment on *poor Kenzie*. Can we talk about the notes and move on, please?"

"Fine. Let's see these notes." Frank took a seat by the table.

Sophia laid them out. "One was on her car at her grandma's place, and the other was right outside her apartment."

Frank looked up at Kenzie. "Do you have somewhere else you could stay for a while?"

"No. I'm fine where I am." She took the seat across from him.

"Do you at least have a roommate?" Frank rubbed a palm across the top of his head.

"Yes. I do." She kept her gaze away from Sophia.

"She does not." Sophia could be such a tattletale. Leave it to a judge to be particular about the truth. "Guinea pigs do not count as roommates. You can both stay with me."

"Hector is not a fan of change."

Sophia rolled her eyes. "Hector will adjust. It's you I'm concerned about."

Frank rubbed at stubble that looked perfectly trimmed to a five o'clock shadow. "Okay. I'll swing by at five and follow Kenzie back to her place. If we go in separately, I can sneak her out to my rig later, then bring her to your house."

"Wait. What about my car? And how do you plan to *sneak* me out of the building with Hector?"

"How big is a guinea pig?"

"Too big for your pocket." Kenzie caught herself mid-glare and softened her expression. But really, who didn't know at least roughly the size of a guinea pig?

"Maybe he could go into a purse or something?"

Sophia stepped forward. "He needs his cage." She wasn't Hector's biggest fan, so this level of care was a true testament to the depth of her friendship.

"We can take a couple trips. The key is getting Kenzie to your place without whoever this is"—he motioned to the crumpled notes—"seeing where we've gone."

Kenzie dropped into Sophia's desk chair. "This is all ridiculous and unnecessary. I'm a grown woman, perfectly capable of caring for my safety."

"I wonder if Betty Campbell thought the same thing." Frank's remark poured a soberness over the room.

Kenzie ached to protest, to say that was 1970; women were different back then. But were they really? Betty must have been as capable as the next person, even if society deemed her weak and dependent. Yet, like so many others over all the years of humankind, her life had been stripped away before she'd had time to truly come into herself.

A loud knock on the solid wood door had them all swinging their gazes toward the sound.

"Come in." Sophia brushed her skirt as if they had just been crawling around on the ground.

A young man—he couldn't have been long out of college—with hair cut short on the sides and curls at the top stepped into the room. "Judge Lancaster. Court is ready to proceed upon your entrance."

Kenzie jumped from her seat. If Sophia was late, so was she. "We can work this out later." Without looking back, she hustled from the room, nudging herself past the new clerk whose name she didn't yet know. With each step, the echoes of creaking wood seemed to grow louder until she arrived at the double doors leading to courtroom number two.

Inside, all eyes turned her way.

Margaret, the officer assigned to this courtroom, scanned Kenzie as if taking an inventory of every flaw past, present, and future, that Kenzie brought to her well-controlled domain.

It occurred to Kenzie that if these notes really were from someone who wished her harm, Margaret could be her only defense during work hours. It would be important to stay on her good side. She forced a smile and waved at the officer, who huffed in response.

Kenzie caught a glimpse of a familiar form in the back of the room.

Frank.

She would never admit it to him, but his presence allowed her muscles to relax and her heartbeat to slow to a more casual rhythm.

The clerk, Billy Owens, dropped a set of papers onto Kenzie's desk. "There's been a change." His eyebrows rose as if he were spilling all the tea.

Kenzie flipped over the top page and inhaled. They had Solomon Stockdale coming in to be arraigned on murder charges. It made sense—the crime had happened in this county—but Kenzie couldn't get her mind around the husband's arrest. She hadn't heard a thing. Flipping through the pages, she saw that he'd only been arrested that morning. Money could buy just about anything, and that man would want out on bail as soon as possible.

The volume in the room rose as the press shuffled in, news of the arrest had surely leaked. Every once in a while, Judge Daniels heard a case that brought in the local paper, but this was the big time. Reporters from local television stations entered—people Kenzie recognized from the news. She overheard a man in a suit asking Billy about the press section, an accommodation they'd never had need of prior to this hearing.

From the side door, Solomon Stockdale entered, flanked by officers on each side. The business attire he was known for had been replaced by the jail-orange pants and a shirt—no buttons, drawstrings, or zippers. On his feet were a pair of matching Crocs.

The job of court reporter came with regular opportunities to practice a blank face. Inside, Kenzie chuckled. The great and mighty fall harder than the humble.

Solomon Stockdale didn't seem prepared to stumble. He held his chin high, not bothering to make eye contact with the press.

"All rise. The honorable Judge Daniels presiding."

There was one thing Kenzie knew that could get under the judge's skin, and Stockdale was displaying it.

Smugness. He dripped with the indulgent expression of a man used to winning every battle set before him. The rich had that way about them, always sure they were above consequences paid out by the rest of humankind.

Kenzie bit her lip, holding back the disgust. The death of Brooklyn Stockdale had shaken up the entire state only a couple weeks earlier. She'd been the kind of rich everyone could get behind, presenting herself in a humble way that she backed up with action. Each Thursday afternoon since Covid had taken their tiny homeless population and turned it into a community of its own, Brooklyn served a meal, supplied needed hygiene items, and built personal relationships with men and women on the very fringe of life.

She'd even approached Uncle Denny about buying the furniture store. It was directly across from the area where tents and lean-tos had become commonplace. She'd wanted to turn the store into transitional housing.

A wave of disgust wove through Kenzie. How could he stand there as if he was above prosecution for the murder of such a generous woman, someone he'd vowed to love and cherish? Had he even loved Brooklyn?

It was unusual to see a team of defense attorneys at an arraignment, but that's what stood behind the defense desk. They offered a litany of motions until finally the judge read the charges and asked for Stockdale's plea.

No one blinked when Solomon declared himself not guilty.

Within thirty minutes, the creep was wrangled out of the building. He'd produce the bail and be out in time for an afternoon jog.

This trial might be the thing that finally got Kenzie back in school. She'd been on the path toward law school when she'd let it all go and settled for this spot on the sidelines—with no power to influence justice. There were moments in time that changed a person, that built confidence where only a sprout of hope had been. Kenzie could honestly help people as an attorney, and she would.

Judge Daniels tapped his gavel to bring the murmurs of the courtroom into submission. "I'm setting bail at three million dollars."

The corners of Solomon Stockdale's mouth rose in a slight smile.

Chapter 26

CLARA

Ginny and I were the ones who took Patricia to the clinic. Aunt Marnie stayed behind to make arrangements while Bristol and Uncle Albert stood watch over Hubert, who had gone into a deep sleep as if nothing unusual had happened.

The door to the examination room swept open, and Dr. Campbell walked in.

I ducked my head, moving my gaze to the linoleum. Our town was small, but we had two doctors. I'd never considered that Dr. Campbell would even be here. His daughter had been gone just over a week.

My memory shot back to Betty's little brother outside the window of the hardware store. The hatred etched into his small face touched on frightening.

"Well, good afternoon, Mrs. Danes. I understand you have quite the cut." Dr. Campbell swiveled on his stool, a clipboard in his hand and a pen tucked behind his ear. "Do you mind if I take a look?"

Thoughts spun. This man had the strange ability to disconnect. If it were me who had lost a daughter, and the mother, wife, and sister of a potential suspect sat in my office, I'd go crazy. Maybe that was a skill doctors had to master, disconnecting from patients in order to share the worst of news, breaking hearts over broken bodies.

Patricia held out her hand still wrapped in green terry cloth.

With gentle movements, the doctor peeled away the fabric.

It appeared as if the bleeding had stopped until he stretched her fingers flat, reopening the wound. "You really did a good job here. How did this happen?"

The room stilled in the silence as none of us offered an answer.

Dr. Campbell raised his chin. "Anyone?"

"I was slicing a muffin." Patricia turned her face to the right. "I guess I wasn't paying attention, and the knife cut into my hand."

"This is a deep cut. Are you sure that's what happened?" He crossed his arms against his chest.

My heart pounded. We weren't breaking any laws, I didn't think, but the events of the day along with being in this tiny room with Betty's father was getting to me. Did the man in front of us think my husband was a killer too?

"Well, that's exactly what happened. Do you expect I would make up a story for a silly cut?" Power seemed to have refilled in Patricia. She sat straighter and stared directly into the doctor's eyes.

"I'll just chart this as inflicted by a distracted housewife. We get at least one of these a week."

"My word." Patricia's face flushed. "If men were in the kitchen, you'd have one a day. Can we get this taken care of in a jiffy, please?"

The room was nearly silent as the doctor got to work. Twenty minutes later, we were stepping out of the clinic that had felt like a glimpse into prison.

"I can't believe that man." Ginny huffed as she dug around in her purse for the car keys. "His daughter is dead, and he didn't seem at all bothered by the loss."

Patricia held her hand to her chest. "Everyone experiences grief differently."

I wasn't sure about that, but my only losses had been a distant grandparent and our neighbor. Maybe it was normal for Dr. Campbell to pour himself into work instead of staying home mourning his lost child. But, even so, shouldn't he be with his wife? I couldn't imagine Mrs. Campbell having the cold resolution of her husband. Who was caring for her and her remaining children, especially the youngest who was still quite small?

"I've heard things about the doctor." Ginny stopped near the Buick and turned back toward us. "Mrs. Miller next door to the Campbells says he's a violent man. She says she's heard him belittling both his wife and Betty on many occasions. And Mrs. Miller has seen bruises on them both."

I covered my mouth.

"That's enough." Patricia tucked loose hair behind her ear. "We shouldn't be out here gossiping about a family who just buried their only daughter."

"I'm just saying that instead of looking at Bristol"—Ginny shot a look at me—"who is obviously innocent, maybe the police should investigate the *good* doctor."

Chapter 27

MATTY

As we left the Campbell home, I felt as if I could finally take a full breath. Grief was heavy inside those walls. It radiated off the older boy like hot angry coals, while Mrs. Campbell seemed weighed down by an invisible chain.

Morgan huffed out a breath. "Mrs. Campbell had nothing relevant to add. Betty was home for supper, then went out sometime after that. She never saw her again. She didn't know of anyone who would want to hurt her daughter. Anything from the kid?"

"Not a helpful thing. He last saw her in her room the night before her death." How do people come out of that kind of sorrow?

Dr. Campbell had been at work. At first, I had inwardly questioned why he would return so soon, but after an hour, I could understand the need to get away and pretend life was still okay.

When I was a boy, a girl from up the block died. Her father started traveling more and more for work, then one day, he stopped coming back at all. I might not have noticed it myself, but one night while I was having trouble sleeping, I overheard my parents in the kitchen discussing the situation.

I couldn't understand back then how a man who had lost his daughter could walk away from his wife and son. It seemed as if he was voluntarily losing everything.

As a man, I've had the chance to see death, to watch my friends and fellow soldiers destroyed in front of me. Running begins to look like the only way to safety, as if turning away might protect you from another loss, the one that would break you into pieces that could never mend.

We drove away in silence, even Morgan seemed impacted.

Without a discussion, Morgan made the decision for lunch, pulling into the drive-up.

I'd heard this place used to have waitresses on roller skates, but eventually the concrete became too cracked, so they'd switched their wheels for more sensible shoes.

"You know what you want?" Morgan unrolled his window while looking at me.

I nodded.

Reaching out, he flipped the small silver switch. A moment later a feminine voice scratched through the speaker.

We placed our order, with Morgan ensuring the woman knew we needed separate checks. Then he flipped the switch to the off position.

"Are you happy now that you've met with the family? Did it solve the crime for you?"

I loosened my tie and unrolled my window. Outside, the air was warming as if we were finally ready for a real spring. "Oh, come on now. We had to interview Mrs. Campbell and Ben."

"There was fire coming off that boy. I imagine we'll be dealing with his shenanigans now."

"What do you mean?"

Morgan laid his head back on the headrest. "I didn't want to say anything, out of respect for the doc, but Betty had a reputation." He lifted both eyebrows and shot me a knowing look.

"What kind of a reputation?" It was juvenile, but I wanted to make him say it.

"You know what I mean. She wasn't such a good girl with the boys."

"And maybe they weren't so good with her?"

He looked up at the ceiling. "You get how it is."

"No. I'm sure I don't."

"Boys will be boys."

Two women approached the car, both wearing the burnt orange dress and white apron uniform. They carried matching trays.

The taller lady came up to my window. "Which one of you got the onion rings?"

"That would be me." I leaned out of the way, and she hooked the tray onto the open window. "Thank you." I felt an impulse to be extra kind to make up for the chauvinist who sat in the car with me.

I sunk my teeth into a burger so juicy it dripped onto the napkin in my lap. Nothing could compete with an all-American burger.

The radio squawked. "Morgan, Yawl, you out there?" Connie didn't bother with the police radio etiquette, and no one around the office seemed brave enough to broach the subject with her.

I picked up the handset. "We're here."

"We got a call from the gas station on 12th. Grover says he had a stranger come through just after closing the other night. Thinks it was the same night Betty was killed. The guy is back there now."

"Thank you. We'll check it out."

Morgan honked the horn, and the servers came running out of the small building. As soon as the trays were removed, he pulled out. "Looks like we've got a lead."

We parked behind a blue Chevy sedan, the only car at the filling station. A man with an army jacket stood outside his car door. Brown curls came to his shoulders, and a mustache curved from one side of his lips to the other. "Listen man, you've already washed my windshield twice."

Grover took one more swipe over the glass with his squeegee and stepped back.

"Excuse me, sir." I approached the man with one hand on my gun while Morgan came at him from another angle. "We were wondering if we could have a word with you."

The man held his hands up, alarm shining in his eyes. Above a patch with the name Banning was another non-military label which read Veterans for Peace.

I'd heard of this group, traveling the country and marching all the way to Washington, D.C. They were men who'd come home from a violent war only to be called "baby killers." Instead of hiding their service as I did, these soldiers took the fight to the country, waging a new kind of war against a government who continued to send young men to their deaths.

"Banning. You got a first name?"

"It's Fred. I got my identification in my back pocket."

"Go ahead and retrieve that, but do so slowly."

The man's hand shook as he reached around his body for his wallet. It continued shaking while he opened it and fumbled at the card, finally pulling a Washington State driver's license free.

I pulled my notepad from my shirt pocket. "What brings you to Oscar's Creek?"

His gaze drifted to the ground. "I'm just looking for somewhere no one knows me. A buddy got me hooked up with the guy from the furniture store. He needed someone to haul stuff around." He shrugged.

"You ever heard of a girl named Betty Campbell?"

His head bobbed. "Mr. Flanigan told me what happened to her before I went to the house."

Morgan's eyes were wide over the shoulder of Banning.

"I delivered a bunch of stuff there."

"Where are you staying?"

"My aunt and uncle live off Benton Avenue. I'm staying with them." His shoulders dropped. "Hey, man, do you harass every new guy in town this way?"

"Can you tell me where you were last night?"

"I rolled in around ten, and I went straight to my aunt and uncle's. Aunt Caroline had a bed made up for me. I ate supper, then I crashed."

I wrote down all his contact information, but this lead felt as pointless as every other one we'd located. I made a mental note to ask Dr. Campbell about his interaction with Banning when he delivered their furniture.

Chapter 28

KENZIE

When Kenzie came out of Sophia's guest bath, she found Frank still checking the windows for security. "You act like you're in the Secret Service, and I'm the president's daughter."

He turned; his left eyebrow crinkled the way it tended to when he evaluated his words. "I will bet you are far more important than a presidential daughter to many people."

She swallowed down the rising embarrassment and stepped into the kitchen. Sophia had picked up some extra veggies for Hector on the way home. Could you ask for a friend better than that? "Oops. It's time to get Hector his dinner."

In the crisper, she found one of Hector's favorite treats—carrots. She pulled out a cutting board and knife and started chopping them into pieces that were too small for the little critter to choke on. He'd had a crazy day, and he was wired—a lot like Kenzie. He also had a habit of taking his stress out on his dinner.

As she opened the cage, he scampered over, sending a spray of fresh shavings onto the end table where Frank had set him.

"Settle down. We need to be good guests." Kenzie dumped a handful of carrots into the dish, then started to sweep up the mess.

"I've got a question for you." Frank settled into the sofa as if he were preparing to stay.

"What?"

"Why do you deflect when you're given a compliment?"

"I don't do that." She pressed her fists into her sides.

"Yes, you do." Sophia's voice traveled down the hall from her office.

Kenzie opened her mouth to argue but couldn't come up with an excuse.

"It really gets under my skin." Frank crossed his legs, one ankle resting on the opposite knee. "Granted, I've only known you for a short time, but I've seen no evidence that you're as unworthy as you seem to think." He dropped the leg back to the floor.

Kenzie reached in and stroked Hector's coarse fur. "Like you said, you haven't known me for long. I could be a serial killer or some kind of closet narcissist."

He joined her at the cage, his presence bringing with it that spicy scent of whatever kind of soap he used and a lot of tension. "I doubt serial killers or closet narcissists give this much love and concern to guinea pigs." He reached into the cage and patted Hector's head only millimeters from Kenzie's hand.

She pulled back. "Shouldn't you be out searching for evidence that proves Solomon Stockdale is innocent?"

Frank gave Hector a scratch behind the ears, then stepped back. "I'm not on that case." He shifted his weight from one foot to the other. "I will get back to your apartment though. I want to hang out and see if the guy was stupid enough to leave another note on your car."

"I can't pay you for this." She ventured a glance toward him, then thought better of it and returned her stare to the safety of the guinea pig.

"So you've said." He picked up his jacket and flung it over his arm.

Sophia came down the hall, dressed in an old T-shirt and flannel pajama bottoms. She plopped onto the couch and removed the bookmark from a bright red novel, *The All-American*.

Kenzie looked between the two of them. "And if she's paying you, well, you'd better not take it. I'm fine looking after myself. I'm sure the police won't let anything happen to me."

"Hmmm." Sophia flipped a page. "I wonder if Betty Campbell thought the same thing."

Kenzie placed her palms in the curve of her back and twisted, disguising the shivers that ran through her when thinking of Betty's last moments. "You can't keep using that." As far as anyone knew, Betty hadn't been threatened prior to that night. Maybe her murder was nothing more than a random attack by a stranger who happened to see a young woman out in the night. Such a callous act—taking the life of another person for one's disjointed pleasures.

"That reminds me." Frank pulled a padded book out of his bag. "I *borrowed* this yearbook from the high school."

"You stole!" Kenzie's heart rate rose. She'd always been the girl who followed the rules, never pushing against the line of what was right and what was wrong. Even the thought of taking a yearbook without authorization made her nervous.

"It's not stealing because I'm planning to return it." He set the book on the coffee table.

"Soph?"

She kept her gaze on her book. "Still stealing, though it would be a pretty minor charge."

"The size of the charge shouldn't matter as much as the moral implications." Now she had the attention of Frank and Sophia, both staring at her as if she'd said something akin to the Unabomber's manifesto. "What? If society didn't abide by the rule of morality, can you even imagine the implications?"

Frank scratched at his beard. "Hm. Like maybe there would be murders and missing people and all that? What a horrible thing to think about."

She tipped her head to the side. "Fine, but you need to take that back as soon as possible."

"Don't you even want to know why I borrowed it?"

Sophia placed a bookmark between her pages and set the book aside. "Of course we do."

"It's the Oscar's Creek yearbook from 1969. You'll find Betty Campbell in there." Frank opened the book. It's binding creaked with age. "Your job," he looked up at Kenzie, "is to make a note of anyone who's in a photo with Betty. We'll start with those people. If we don't have any luck there, we'll work our way through the class. Understand?"

Kenzie sat on the couch near the open book. "We're going to contact these people? See if they remember anything from the night Betty was killed?"

"More than just that night. We want to know if anything unusual happened in Betty's life leading up to her murder."

"What if they don't want to talk? Or they've died?"

His shoulders drew up then dropped. "Then we keep looking. Someone knew something. We need to pray that the someone is still around, and that they're ready to share." He raised a hand in goodbye. "I'm out. Text me the list. I'd like to get started first thing in the morning."

Kenzie stood, walking toward the door behind Frank. "Don't you have other cases that require your attention?"

"You'd think so, but my business is new, and I haven't taken on many clients yet." With one hand on the open door and the other on the frame, he twisted back to see her. "This one is important to me."

A chill swept in from outside, wrapping cold around Kenzie's body. She hugged herself, rubbing her palms up and down her arms. "I want to do this with you. It's only fair since you're not getting a paycheck."

His face brightened with a lopsided grin. This man was actually kind of handsome in an ex-military sort of way. But handsome didn't mean he was any different than all the other men out there.

Chapter 29

CLARA

I pulled the pot roast from the oven and set it on the stove. The entire house held the warm scent of rich beef juices, simmering carrots, potatoes, and onions. This was what Bristol would come home to.

It took three weeks to get Hubert admitted to a nursing home. Three weeks that felt like a lifetime stolen from me. I was a selfish woman, but who wouldn't be? Bristol and I were approaching our first wedding anniversary, that day on the calendar that would change our status from newlyweds to married. *Just* married. Those fifty-two weeks should have been filled with quiet whispers, late mornings snuggled in bed, planning for our future. Instead, Ginny was with me more than my husband, who stayed the night at his parents' house often to monitor his father.

Business at the hardware store had picked up a bit, but most customers seemed disappointed to see Ginny and me manning the place, as if we couldn't point the way to the three-inch nails. Or maybe they were hoping for a bit of gossip we were unwilling to provide. Land's sakes, this family was full of enough tidbits to fill the mouths of every woman at a Sunday luncheon.

When I complained to my mother, she reminded me to count my blessings and then added something about hungry children in Africa.

For a minute I felt guilty for not being grateful that the police had left us alone for the time being. But instead of relief, the lack of contact felt like the next layer of dread spread on top of Hubert's senility and waiting for Bristol to be called up for service in Vietnam.

I could never be the kind of housewife my mother was, pretending all was well when nothing really was. How had I not noticed before the resemblance between my mom and the mannequins in the window of Meier & Frank?

Yanking off my apron, I pulled two plates from the cupboard and began setting the table.

The cuckoo clock squawked six o'clock, dinnertime, yet still no Bristol. Part of me wanted to throw myself onto the bed and weep that my husband didn't seem as excited to be reunited as I was.

I shook out my hands, closed my eyes, and took a couple long breaths. This situation was not going to turn me into a weeping woman, unable to manage under the pressure cooker. As bad as it was for me, it was far worse for Bristol.

My thoughts shifted to Carmen Colter. She'd been a year ahead of me in school. Her son was two weeks old when her husband shipped off with the Navy. Carmen didn't even have a mother or a mother-in-law to help. Her own mom had passed away during her pregnancy.

Maybe that was the way to count blessings when times were tough? At least I wasn't in Carmen's position. That was a blessing for me.

The car engine growled into our short driveway and cut out. A minute later it was followed by the slam of the door.

I threw off my melancholy and stood, ready to embrace my husband. Maybe there was a bit of my mother in me after all.

The door opened, and Bristol met me with a smile that didn't light up his eyes. He was playing the same game.

My smile dropped away. "Are you okay?" I wrapped my arms around his waist.

"Nothing to worry about." His voice was a low rumble above my ear.

I pushed back. "I don't want us to have a marriage like our parents' generation. You can be honest with me about anything. We'll bear each other's burdens, okay?"

He blinked away moisture. "You are a rare find." With a hand on both sides of my head, he kissed me, warm and soft, the scent of the hardware store clinging to him like a familiar cologne. "I had a couple visitors at the store."

My body seemed to anticipate that this was not a good kind of visitor. My breath held in my chest as I waited for him to go on.

"It was the police again. They wanted to run through my story from the night Betty ... you know."

I stared into his crystal blue eyes. Bristol couldn't even get the word "murder" past his lips. How could anyone think that my gentle husband was capable of that kind of terror? "They've already asked you all about that. This is such a waste of time. There's a killer out there, and those two are messing around."

"Let's not allow it to ruin our evening." He tipped his nose into the air. "It smells absolutely wonderful in here. Pot roast?"

That brought a smile to my face. "With chocolate cake for dessert."

"It's so good to be home."

I wrapped my hand in Bristol's before pulling him toward the dining room.

He said a blessing but remained quiet as we dished our plates and started eating.

When I could no longer take the sound of silence only interrupted by chewing, I let my fork clatter down. "Let's talk about it. All of it. To start with, how is your mom?"

"I'd assumed you were getting updates from Ginny on that front." He took a long drink of milk. "I've never seen her so ... vulnerable. Do you understand what I mean?"

"I think so. Your mom is the kind of person who can handle anything, or at least she's always seemed that way. She's strong." I scooped another potato onto Bristol's plate.

"Thank you." He sliced it into eight pieces with his knife and fork. "It's like she's shrinking before my eyes. And I can't figure out how to help her. This thing with the police, she must have heard the rumors, but we don't mention it. My whole life, I've looked up to my parents. They were the people who kept me safe. How am I supposed to take care of them now when I don't have any idea what my own future holds?" He wiped his face with one of the rust-colored cloth napkins we'd gotten as a wedding gift. "I thought Vietnam was the threat, but I'm beginning to wonder if being called up will be my saving grace."

"Don't say that." I tossed my napkin onto my half-full plate. "It's a misunderstanding. Nothing more than that. The police will get their man, and it's not you." For a flash, my mind betrayed my heart and flipped to the image of blood on Bristol's shirt. I had to believe in my husband. He'd never given me a reason to doubt him.

Somehow, the topic of conversation hadn't dampened Bristol's appetite. He plunged his fork into the wedge of beef I'd left behind and began slicing and eating.

"Maybe we should hire a lawyer. You know, just to be careful." I pushed my chair back and stood.

Bristol finished chewing and wiped his mouth. "That would only make me look like I had something to hide. Besides, we can't afford the fees. The store hasn't been doing well since this whole thing started."

"Eventually, people will get over the rumors. They can only go so long without supplies."

He pushed his plate away. "Don't count on it. I heard Merv has started stocking small building needs in a corner of the grocery store."

"The nerve." My fists punched into my sides. "And that man calls himself a Christian."

"Don't blame Merv. He's doing right by his customers."

"What about his friends? We've known him since we were in elementary school. My mother said no good would come from him taking over the store. Boy, did she have that right."

"When all this is over, you and I will think about starting over in a new place."

A verse from the book of Ruth ran through my mind. *"For wherever you go, I will go; And wherever you lodge, I will lodge; Your people shall be my people, And your God, my God. Where you die, I will die, And there will I be buried."*

But that would mean leaving Ginny and my parents. It would mean raising our family without the support of our extended family. How could I leave everyone behind? Yet, there was Canada. And Canada could mean keeping my husband safe.

"Why wait? Bobby knows a guy who helps people escape the draft. We could go to Canada and there'd be no more police questioning, no more waiting for the government to call you up for service."

Bristol cupped my cheek in his hand and pulled it to his chest. "And no more dignity. I can't leave my family, and I promised Detective Yawl that I'd stay in town." His heartbeat pounded in my ear. "You deserve so much better than this."

"Wherever you are, is where I'll be content."

Suddenly, the front door shook with the force of someone hammering on the other side.

Chapter 30

KENZIE

Thursday mornings were always chaotic in the courtroom. They started the day with hearings, most of which covered trial readiness for trials that would never happen due to plea bargains. It made her rethink law school for the hundredth time. Every single job that surrounded her seemed lost in piles of paperwork.

On this Thursday morning, the Stockdale case was front and center.

Solomon Stockdale made his way to the front of the room, his head held high as reporters scribbled notes.

Once Judge Daniels was seated and court was in session, the room's volume dropped to a level unusual for even a typically slow day.

A man from Stockdale's defense team stood, straightened his already perfect tie, and stepped around the table. "Mr. Stockdale and his team are ready to proceed to trial. My client would like to assert his right to a speedy trial and move the date up on the calendar. Mr. Stockdale's business has been unduly impacted by these false claims, and he is eager to clear his good name."

The judge tipped his head to the side. "Does the prosecution have anything to say about his request?"

"We do, Your Honor." The district attorney cleared her throat. "We would like to maintain the schedule already in place. It's the state's opinion that the time between now and our trial date will be essential to present our case fully."

"Your Honor, the state issued the charges against my client with the understanding that they had a case. If that is not true, I'd like to move for a dismissal."

Daniels rubbed his pointer finger and thumb into his forehead. "That won't be necessary. I'm granting the defense's request to move the trial date up."

The DA stepped forward, but Judge Daniels held up a hand. "Mr. Fathington is correct. You started this process, and his client has the right to a speedy trial." He turned toward the clerk. "What do we have available, Billy?"

Billy's chin raised. He handed a sheet of paper to the judge.

Judge Daniels nodded. "Thank you." He looked directly at Solomon Stockdale. "I'm setting your trial to begin in two weeks. Is that acceptable to the defense?"

"Thank you, Your Honor." The attorney shuffled back, sitting himself behind the table again.

In a higher humidity setting, steam would have risen from the prosecutor's head.

When the judge dismissed for a long lunch break, Kenzie blew out a long breath of relief. She needed to get outside and into the fresh air. The atmosphere in the courtroom had turned toxic.

Billy and Margaret ushered the crowd out of the room, with Billy waving jazz hands as if that would hurry the reporters along. Most were already in a rush to try for a statement from Stockdale or his team.

"Kenzie." Billy's eyebrows lifted as he jogged up to her desk. "This was on one of the benches." He handed her an envelope with her name written in neatly squared letters.

"Thanks." She stuffed it into her bag. Billy knew everyone's business, but she wasn't going to give him a hint into the nightmare she was dealing with.

"Secret admirer?" He tipped his head.

She continued gathering her belongings. "Doubtful."

The door creaked open, and Billy turned to shame whoever dared to enter.

"It's okay." Kenzie came around the desk. "He's with me."

Frank stood as if ready for inspection, his hands held behind him and his shoulders back. If it weren't for the smile, he'd be downright intimidating.

"I see." Billy's tone said she was about to be the newest line of gossip in the courthouse. "I'm guessing I know where that note came from."

She opened her mouth to correct him but then thought better of the idea. Let Billy think whatever he wanted. Kenzie would rather he thought she and Frank had something going than know she had a stalker.

Kenzie hustled toward Frank. "Well, we'd better get to lunch. I'm starving." She gave him a look she hoped he would understand.

"Right this way." Frank pushed open the door and stood aside for her to exit. As it shut behind them, his face broke into a full grin. "What was that all about?"

"Billy. I don't like that man knowing my business. He's ..." She hesitated, looking for the right word. "Annoying."

"Isn't that what you say about me?"

"This is different. And you're not so annoying. You're just, I don't know, always around." She shrugged.

"My last girlfriend complained that I wasn't around enough."

"Well, I'm not your girlfriend." Heat flushed her cheeks. Why was she having this response? Kenzie turned away and headed toward the back doors. "I'm getting lunch at the food trucks. Are you coming along?"

"Why, thank you for that generous invitation. I'd love to."

"That." She shook her head. "That's what's annoying."

"You'll learn to love me." A deep rumble of laughter emanated from his chest. "I'm dying for a burger."

They walked down the sidewalk past rows of parked news vans with reporters and camera people packing up.

"Looks like you had an interesting morning."

Kenzie reached into her bag and pulled out the envelope. She tore it open before handing it to Frank in case it wasn't from the creep. She *could* have an admirer.

Looks like you've made your choice, but I'm a very generous person. I'm going to give you another chance to let it go. Consider this your final warning. And if you're getting any ideas about bringing in the police, well, I know where your precious grandmother lives.

She nearly tossed the page to Frank, feeling its volatility in her grip.

Frank's hand slid around her upper arm as he read the words. He pulled her toward the corner of the lot where the food trucks were parked. A stand with doggy bags and a garbage can took up space here. Frank snagged a sack from the roller and dropped the page and envelope inside.

"What are you doing?" She looked around as if someone were watching them.

"I'm preserving evidence. There could be fingerprints."

"He said no police." Kenzie pulled back from him. Before she could think, she'd yanked the bag from his hands and pulled the paper out, crumpling it in her fist. "My grandma and Aunt Ginny are all I have."

Frank pulled her to his side. "They are not your only people. You have Sophia, and you have me."

"I barely know you."

"That's on you." He shuffled her toward the hamburger stand. "I'd really like to get you back inside, but I do know you, and I know you'd rather take your chances with a killer than miss lunch."

"Who said this guy was a killer?"

"Who said he was a guy?"

A shiver ran over Kenzie's skin. "It could be anyone."

"That's right." His gaze ran over the people in line. "Is there somewhere your grandmother and aunt could go for a while?"

"Aunt Ginny has family in Chicago. Maybe they could visit." Kenzie raised her hands and let them drop. "Gram won't go. She's worried about money. It's all she can do to keep the house right now."

"Then we purchase the tickets for her. Nonrefundable."

Kenzie thought about her own nearly maxed out credit card and her student loan payment. Then she thought about Gram. She was worth everything. Kenzie would gladly live in a cardboard box if that's what it took. "I'll buy the tickets. You're right about one thing."

"What's that?"

"Gram will not waste nonrefundable tickets."

Chapter 31

CLARA

All the words that were being spoken around me swirled like Bristol's shirt had in the washing machine.

Detective Yawl was the one who handed over the warrant for Bristol to see as what felt like an army of policemen tramped into our home and started tearing apart our privacy and security.

Outside, the night was crisp with the chill of winter still hanging on. Bristol took me toward the car to get out of the cold, but another officer stopped us, explaining that the warrant also allowed them access to our vehicle.

I looked to our neighbor's house across the street in time to see Mrs. Heilman closing the curtain. A minute later their porch light went out.

Nothing made sense. My husband was the man whom everyone in town could count on to help, yet when an allegation arose, the same folks who'd once sung his praises quickly turned their backs.

I slipped my hand into Bristol's. "We're going to be okay."

He nodded.

I felt a hand on my arm before I knew Mr. and Mrs. Pauling were there. "Come along. You two don't need to be out in this cold. I'll make you a cup of cocoa and something to eat."

My stomach wobbled at the thought of food. At the same time, I filled with gratitude for this couple we hardly knew.

Bristol looked to Detective Yawl, who gave a nod as if offering his permission to leave the premises.

The Paulings ushered us two houses down and into their front door. We walked through the small house—very similar to our own floor plan—and into the dining room.

Mr. Pauling pulled out a chair at the end of the table where a pipe sat, ready to smoke. "I think I've got another around here if you'd like."

Bristol shook his head. "No thank you, sir."

"Goodness that makes me feel old. Call me Bill. And the wife is Elma." He tipped his head toward another chair. "Take a seat."

My husband sat, but I entered the kitchen where Elma busied herself pulling milk from the refrigerator and pouring it into a saucepan. From there she unwrapped squares of chocolate that she dropped into the liquid.

"Why are you doing this?" I twisted my finger around a loose strand of hair.

"Honey, we've been there." She turned her face toward mine, giving me a knowing look. "It's been nearly twenty years now, but I remember it like it just happened. Our little boy, our Benjamin, went missing the night of July 4th. He was five years old. We searched all over the place, assuming he'd gotten lost among the neighborhood crowds. Around midnight, we called the police."

A knife stabbed through my heart, stealing my air with the slice. "I'm so sorry."

"Thank you." Her eyes filled with tears. "It wasn't long before we realized the police suspected one of us had killed our boy."

I looked back at Bristol, finding both him and Bill silently listening.

After a long puff on the pipe and a smoky exhale, Bill opened his mouth to speak. "We were fortunate. Our son was found a week later. He'd been kidnapped by a woman who'd had some kind of nervous breakdown. She truly believed Benjamin was her son."

"If the worst had happened, I have no doubt I would have lost my son and my husband would have been put away." She pulled four mugs from the cupboard, lining them up one after the other on the counter, not one of them matching. "Bill and I understand how hard it can be to have wrongful accusations thrown at you. We just felt like this was our chance to turn our experience into something good."

"Oh, Elma, I don't think your words are saying what your heart means." Bill lowered the pipe to the table. "We don't want you feeling like you're alone in this mess, like we did. If you need something, we're here."

For a moment, the doubts came back. It was that shirt. The blood on the sleeve. I couldn't make it go away, make it stop popping into my imagination. What if the police found something else, something that led them to Bristol, something I should have taken care of?

I marveled at the way Elma and Bill took us in, not questioning my husband over guilt or innocence. They had more faith in the man I'd vowed to love and respect till death do us part than even I had shown. Bristol deserved so much better than what our community was handing him.

Chapter 32

KENZIE

Kenzie folded the printed airline tickets in half; if Gram and Aunt Ginny had trouble with the cameras on their cell phones, they'd hate having their flight information on an app. She entered the front door of Gram's house. It would always be Gram's house, even though Aunt Ginny had moved in years ago when her husband died.

Once, Aunt Ginny had made a joke, calling the house the widows' cottage. Gram had not taken it well.

"Hello?" The house was quiet as if no one was home, yet the car they shared sat in the driveway. "You all forgot to lock the door again." A chill wove up Kenzie's spine. "Gram? Aunt Ginny?"

What if she was too late?

Her chest pounded, and her breath grew short as she searched one room after the other, finding no one. In the kitchen, she turned in circles as if they were just out of her reach. "Gram." Her voice echoed through the room.

"For heaven's sake, what's all the yelling about?" Gram entered through the back door, her garden apron smudged with soil. Pulling off her gloves, Gram gave Kenzie an assessing look. "Are you okay?"

Tears rushed to Kenzie's eyes. She did her best to blink them away. "I was worried when I couldn't find you."

"That's ridiculous. We're in the backyard putting in the garden. Is this all because of the TIA?" She wiped her forehead with her wrist, leaving a streak of dirt behind. "The doc says I'm as healthy as could be. I've made all the changes they suggested, and I'm taking my blood thinners. This Dr. Ness, she seems to really know her stuff. Not like the guy we had when I was your age. Dr. Campbell was nothing short of a quack."

Kenzie's lips tingled. "Dr. Campbell—wasn't that Betty Campbell's father?"

Gram's face paled. "What do you know about Betty Campbell?"

Instinct had Kenzie looking for an escape route. "Nothing. I mean, I saw a flyer about her. It's a cold case. That's all." She was lying to her grandmother, the woman who'd protected and loved her all her life. Kenzie hoped the outcome would make the transgression worthy. "Hey, I have a favor to ask."

Gram's features remained stony. "What's that?"

"Could I stay here for a couple weeks?" She forced her face to portray the request as fully benign. "The landlord is finally updating, and he also needs to fumigate. You know, the whole thing. It's a mess." *Stop talking.* She did this when she was nervous, spewing unneeded details—in this case, lies. "Would you mind?"

"We don't have another bedroom."

"I am happy to sleep on the couch."

"Okay. You and Hector are always welcome here." Gram pulled an orange pitcher from the refrigerator and poured lemonade into three glasses.

"And there's something else."

"Do not tell me you're bringing a man with you. I can deal with that little pig, but I'm not going to be party to any premarital canoodling."

Kenzie bit her lip to hold back a laugh. "No, Gram. There's no man." Though her mind immediately turned on her and provided an image of Frank. "I got you and Aunt Ginny a surprise."

Muffled claps came from Aunt Ginny's gloved hands as she entered the kitchen. "I love surprises."

"I know how excited you've been about becoming a new great-grand-ma."

Aunt Ginny clapped again.

Gram tipped her head. "For goodness' sake, take those filthy gloves off before we have so much dirt in this kitchen we can plant our garden here."

Kenzie held the papers out. "I've arranged for the two of you to spend a week in Chicago."

"We couldn't do that." Gram waved a hand in the air.

Stepping forward, Aunt Ginny snagged the pages with her still-gloved hands. "Look at that." She tapped the paper. "Nonrefundable. We couldn't possibly let Kenzie's hard-earned money go to waste."

Looking between Kenzie and Ginny, Gram shrugged. "Okay, but Kenz, don't be spending your money on us like this again. You have a whole life in front of you. Save what you can and use the rest for some fun."

"Look who's talking." Ginny squeezed Gram in a side hug. "You never spend money for fun. You're as frugal as an old miser, but I love you dearly."

"What about the garden? We've only just set out those seeds."

"I'll look after everything." Kenzie crossed her arms and took in a calming breath. Everything was falling into place. Gram and Aunt Ginny would be flying to Chicago in the morning, and she'd have two fewer worries breaking into her every thought. "Can I help you get packed?"

Gram tugged the papers out of Ginny's hand. "Tomorrow morning?"

"It was a special deal." They didn't need to know that the ticket price had been outrageous and had completed her race to fill her credit card to its maximum.

Kenzie passed out the glasses of lemonade. "To new babies and adventures." She held out her cup, and they all clinked. A well-played plan was in action.

Chapter 33

MATTY

As a detective, I was trained to follow leads, but a great deal of my job also depended on trusting my gut. And my gut told me we were looking at the wrong man.

Morgan slapped the warrant on my desk only minutes before quitting time. "Head home and get a meal with that beautiful wife of yours. We'll meet at the Danes' house at 7:30. I've got a whole crew ready to rip that man's place apart."

My stomach soured thinking of what we would put the young couple through in the name of investigation. "Why not wait until morning?"

"In this town, rumors spread like fires. If we wait that long, one of the guys will spill the plan to his wife, she'll call her mother, her mother will call the neighbor, and before we can take a look, the entire town, including Bristol Danes and his wife, will know our plan. We meet at 7:30."

Gretchen knew something was up when I walked in our front door and removed my hat. She'd laid out a lovely meal for the two of us, likely one of our last before the baby arrived, and I had to cut it short with more work. But, by golly, I married one of the best ladies on the planet, and she didn't shame me for my commitments outside our home. It made me even more determined to get the mower out this weekend and trim our lawn before it overtook the sidewalk.

I arrived at our meeting place just up the street from the Danes' residence with an uneasy feeling and a warm cookie wrapped in a napkin in my pocket.

Morgan was already there when I arrived. He climbed out of the car and gave a tip of his chin toward the home we were about to invade. "I've been keeping an eye on them. No one's left the house. I've radioed the team. They're on the way."

As if hearing our discussion, three marked police cars pulled up to the house, one blocking the family car from exiting the driveway.

Morgan motioned me to follow.

As we approached the front door, my mind continually replayed visions of Clara Danes, her eyes so full of shock and confusion on our first visit. It hurt my heart to think of Gretchen in that position.

The sound of Morgan's pounding on the door was enough to garner the attention of the neighborhood.

I stood back as he informed the couple of our right to search the premises.

The spring evening had turned chilly by the time Bristol and Clara Danes exited the house. He held his wife close with her body tucked under his arm.

It was a relief when an older couple ushered them away.

Inside, the house buzzed with officers opening and rifling through every drawer and cubby. They removed sofa cushions, digging deep into the grooves where spare change loved to reside. They felt under desks, went through the washer and dryer, and checked the contents of Bristol's shaving kit, as if our murder weapon could have shrunk to fit in the small black bag.

Morgan shone a flashlight on a statue of some Greek figure, checking every detail for a hair or sign of blood.

By morning, the entire town would have Bristol Danes tried and convicted of Betty Campbell's murder. Playing a part in the social demise of a man who, on the outside, seemed to be as clean as a bar of soap made me feel like I was perpetrating a crime myself.

An hour later, we'd gained nothing but a shirt with a tear on the sleeve and a blonde hair pulled from a scarf in the entryway.

We already had the shirt Bristol claimed to have been wearing the night of the attack, but Morgan insisted we take this one too as there wasn't much difference between the two styles.

I did my best to set the house to rights, but there wasn't much to be done in the minutes before Morgan bellowed that we were returning the home to its owners.

Outside, I saw the couple returning. I lifted my hand in a greeting that was not returned.

Bristol Danes stared back at me with eyes darker than the night. A chill ran across my skin. For the first time since Betty Campbell's body had been discovered, I thought I could be looking at the eyes of a killer.

Chapter 34

CLARA

We returned home to a war zone. Drawers had been pulled from cabinets, furniture moved, and vent covers pulled from their holes in the floor.

I pulled my sweater tighter over my chest as if the thin knit could protect me from the feeling of vulnerability and the invasion of my privacy. Until now, I'd thought I was the kind of person who would do whatever it took to help another, but this was too much. If our justice system was built on the principle of innocent until proven guilty, what was this?

Bristol returned from our bedroom. "It's a mess."

I nodded. There were no words that could encompass the feeling that weighed me down at this moment.

A loud knock at the front door drew a scream from deep in my lungs. I slapped a hand over my chest. "Who could that be?"

"I have no idea." Bristol stepped toward the door, his shoulders slumped in defeat. "Maybe they've returned to make an arrest."

I gasped. "Don't open it."

He looked my way. "And what would you have me do, run?" Bristol pulled the door open without checking the peephole.

My mother and father stood on the step. Mom pushed her way past Bristol without waiting for an invitation. A moment later, I was wrapped in her arms, and the tears I'd been holding back flooded from me.

The boom of my father's voice snapped me back. "Son, let's take a look at the damage in the shed." Dad placed his beefy hand on Bristol's shoulder and moved him toward the back door.

Tingles prickled my face. I knew that tone. It was the one my father used when Billy or I had come to a point of needing fatherly discipline. "What's Dad doing with Bristol?" I couldn't stop the alarm that came with my words.

"Don't you worry about them. Daddy wants to have a man-to-man talk with your husband." She brushed at her skirt as if being in my now-cluttered home had dirtied her clothing. "We wonder if you would be better off staying at home for a while. At least until this whole thing blows over."

I stepped back. "This is my home. I can't leave my husband when he needs me the most."

"It's only temporary. I'm sure Bristol will get this all worked out and then you can come back." She pushed the sofa back to its original position, parallel to the television, and then did the same with the coffee table. "Let's get this place tidied up. You don't want anyone coming by and seeing it in such a state."

"Who is going to come by unannounced at this time of night?" Until tonight, the answer had been easy. No one. But now we'd already had the entire police force followed by my parents.

I followed Mom to the kitchen and started putting away spices, as if there was something hidden behind the oregano. Anger pulsed in my chest. We were good people, not criminals. What could possibly link my husband to a crime like murder?

And what was my father saying to Bristol?

It was too late to revoke his blessing on our marriage, wasn't it?

"There's no time like the present to wipe out these drawers." Mom filled a bucket with water and poured in a generous amount of ammonia.

I coughed as the gases filled my kitchen. "It's nearly ten o'clock. I'd rather not get into a deep clean."

She huffed and continued with her task of turning my kitchen into a space where surgery could be done without worry of germs.

By the time Dad and Bristol returned, flashlights in hand, Mom was preparing to mop. "Get on out of here. I don't want dirty feet in here after I mop."

I wondered if she was preparing my home to be shut up for a season, as if I would return to my life as their child, living in my old room while Bristol headed off to prison.

Throwing down the rag in my hand, I stepped to my husband's side. "Mom, Dad, I'm not leaving here. And I think it's time for you both to go home. Bristol and I have a big day tomorrow, and we need our sleep."

"Well." My mother's eyes were as round as the plates I'd just re-stacked in my cupboards. "I think you're making a big mistake, young lady."

"I disagree." My dad reached for his coat. "Clara belongs with her husband. Edna, let's leave them be."

Dad gave me a hug, a gesture that was uncommon for him.

Though Mom was making her disagreement very evident, she followed him out the door.

When they were gone, Bristol closed the door and engaged the locks. "It stinks in here."

His wrinkled nose brought a smile to my face and took some of the invisible weight from my shoulders.

Chapter 35

KENZIE

There was something comforting about the airport—the way the planes came and went, the rumble of their engines and all the traffic closely controlled and in order. Kenzie sat in her car and watched as another flight rose into the sky, gliding toward the clouds.

Could there be a future in which she had a career that didn't bring trauma and unrest into her daily life? She could be a flight attendant, but her height would likely be an issue. She couldn't see her hand in front of her face without glasses or contacts, so pilot might not make the list either.

In truth, she loved the law. She loved the order in the chaos, the rules and procedures. What she didn't love was wondering every time there was a stranger in the gallery if they were there for the proceedings or there to watch her.

Her cell buzzed with a text from Frank.

Are you okay?

Yes, why do you ask?

You haven't moved for twenty minutes.

Kenzie's mouth fell open. She tapped the call icon.

"Hey." Frank's voice came through with complete calm.

"Are you watching me? Where are you?" She twisted around in her seat, scanning the parking lot.

"Relax. I'm at your gram's house. I have the cameras to install."

"You're tracking me." A growl started in her belly and shoved its way up. "I can't believe you're tracking me."

"You'd feel very differently about that if you were kidnapped."

She hopped from the car, looking under the vehicle. "Where is it?"

"It's not on the car."

"You *are* watching me."

He had the audacity to chuckle. "No, I can hear you huffing and puffing and the sound of planes."

"Did you inject a tracker into my body while I was sleeping or something?"

Now, he completely lost it. "This isn't Star Trek or Wars or whatever you're thinking of. I dropped a tracker into that bag you always carry around. Listen, I wasn't trying to be creepy or anything. It was actually Sophia's idea to do it without telling you. I had doubts."

"I'm going to kill both of you."

"No, you're not. And more importantly, no one is going to hurt you on my watch."

"I thought you were an investigator. This sounds more like bodyguard duty." She sat down in the car again, shuffling through her bag.

"I've had that job too."

"I'm hanging up." She smashed her finger onto the "end call" icon and tossed her phone toward the passenger seat. Rummaging further in her bag, Kenzie's fingers ran over something round and smooth. She pulled it out and stared at the small device. Instinct told her to position it under her tire and flatten the little privacy invader, but Gram had raised her to be frugal. Who knew how much something like this cost?

She dropped the tracker into her cupholder.

Ten minutes into the one-hour drive back to Oscar's Creek, Kenzie's nerves started to calm.

Kenzie pulled to the side of the road and dug the list of names from her bag. The first was Barney Douglas. He'd been pictured with Betty twice, both times in an academic setting. She punched in the number she'd scrawled beside the name and tapped the record button on her phone.

Sophia had given her a rundown on the laws in Oregon. She could record through her phone without letting the other person know, but in-person conversations required consent.

"Hello."

"Hi. Is this Barney Douglas?" Kenzie pulled back onto the quiet country road.

"I'm not buying anything." The voice was as gruff as it was frail. She thought back to the photos from high school. Barney had been a slight boy with dark glasses and a nose that curved across the bridge.

"I'm not calling to sell you anything. Are you the Barney Douglas who attended Oscar's Creek High School in the late 1960s?"

"I am. But that's all you're getting out of me. I'm not sending you a cent."

"Please don't. I want to ask you some questions about Betty Campbell."

Kenzie passed a herd of cattle grazing on spring grass as she waited for a reply.

Finally, he spoke. "I haven't thought about Betty in years. She was a beauty. I had a bit of a crush on her, I'm embarrassed to admit."

"Why are you embarrassed by that?"

"Oh, well, she was out of my league, a real beauty. I even carved our initials into a tree once: B.D. + B.C. I dreamed of showing it to her someday, imagined her running into my arms. I must have looked ridiculous following her around like a pet."

"I'm sure she thought you were very nice."

"Yes. Like one of her little brothers." A touch of laughter lightened his words. "I was never a prospect for a girl like that."

"She had two brothers, right?"

"Yes, ma'am. I'd see her traipsing around town with the boys. They were both quite a bit younger than her. A spread between the two of them as well. I guess the doc and his wife liked to really space them out."

Kenzie turned her blinker on and passed a tractor. "Do you remember who Betty hung around with?"

"See, I was only in Oscar's Creek for my senior year, so I can't speak to anything prior. I remember she seemed sad and didn't do much socializing with the other girls." He blew out a breath. "It's been a real long time, but this conversation sure takes me back. Why are you asking about Betty after all this time?"

"I'm working with some people to bring closure to her case. Do you remember anything that happened after Betty died?"

"I'd left town for college. In fact, I didn't hear about her death until months after it happened. What did you say your name was?"

"It's Kenzie Da ... Duncan. Thank you for your time." Kenzie disconnected the call. She bit back tears. There'd been no good reason to lie about her last name, but at that moment, talking with someone who had cared for Betty, she couldn't admit to being Bristol Danes' granddaughter.

The next name on her list wouldn't need to ask her name. She would meet with Uncle Denny in person. She'd have to let him know that Gram and Aunt Ginny were out of town anyway. Gram had said to wait until they'd left. Uncle Denny would have wanted to take them to the airport, and she couldn't abide the way he drove like every street was a racetrack.

Chapter 36

CLARA

I wandered through the IGA, filling my cart with essentials for the week. I wasn't immune to the stares and whispers of the women who passed by me, but I was strengthened in my convictions. Not a soul in this town knew Bristol the way I did. They hadn't felt the way he touched me with hands so gentle it was as if he were caressing a baby bird.

These people with their judgments and assumptions would not take away a minute of the time I had with Bristol before they called up his number and stole my husband from my home.

I added a can of pineapple rings to the growing stack of items. If I wasn't careful, I'd go over my weekly grocery budget, but my desire to give Bristol everything the world was taking away from him overrode my frugality. I'd make an upside-down cake for our dessert to follow his favorite meal: meatloaf and mashed potatoes. I even picked up a couple bottles of root beer.

Tonight we would celebrate our blessings.

The cashier was a girl I'd gone to school with—a year or two younger than me. I think she was in Betty's class. With a whispered prayer, I pushed my cart forward. "Good morning, Sue. How are you today?"

Sue's mouth fell open, then she snapped it shut and scratched at a spot behind her elbow. "Clara. Good morning. I didn't realize it was you." She didn't make a move toward my groceries.

"How have you been?"

"I'm good."

A woman behind me cleared her throat.

"Oh. Sorry. I don't know where my mind went." She lifted the first item from the cart.

I knew exactly what had taken Sue's attention, but I wasn't going to do what everyone seemed to think I should—cower at home as if either Bristol or I were guilty of a crime.

"I understand you're seeing Fred Wilder." My face began to ache with the effort of maintaining a smile.

Sue punched numbers into the cash register. "We've been going steady for a month now."

And just like that, I'd taken her thoughts off condemning my little family. Her eyes grew dreamy as she unfolded the story of her romance with a guy I only remembered as a scrawny kid on student council. Fortunately, I'd listened to Ginny's tale of the odd couple being seen at the drive-up last weekend. Sue with her perfectly manicured nails and long sleek hair, and Fred with glasses so thick they could have been made from pop bottles. The heart wants what it wants, my mother-in-law always said.

When we were finished, Sue handed me my receipt and the bag boy hefted my two grocery sacks back into the cart. "Where to, ma'am?"

I hated being called "ma'am." I was still a newlywed. The magazines said that title was good for the entire first year, yet all over town, people insisted on referring to me in the same way they would greet my mother. "It's the blue Ford." I started to lead him outside. As soon as the double doors swished open, my heart skipped a beat. Betty's brother leaned against a pillar, one leg bent, his arms crossed tightly across his chest.

"Ma'am?"

"Sorry." I forced my legs to carry me past the boy, not making eye contact.

A long whistle followed me across the parking lot, injecting fear into my quickening steps. What was wrong with me? He was a child, no more than twelve or thirteen, but the look in his eyes … it was empty. And when I looked back, those vacant eyes were staring straight at me.

At the car, I thanked the bag boy, then hopped in behind the wheel, closing the door and pressing down each of the four locks. The car bounced as the trunk was shut, and I waved my thanks through the window.

I wasn't the kind of woman who jumped at her own shadow. Scolding myself for letting the look on a grieving young man's face frighten me, I peered over my shoulder and backed up from the parking spot. When I turned to drive on, the Campbell boy stood only ten feet beyond my front bumper. He held his bike at his side, his eyes unblinking.

I swallowed hard as I drove around him, anxious for the comfort of my relatively safe home.

Chapter 37

MATTY

I had no doubt that Fred Banning wasn't involved in Betty's murder, but leads must be followed, and I was the man without seniority.

The bells jingled as I stepped into the furniture store. Before I could get my bearings, a rounded man with a swirl of hair covering an obvious bald spot lumbered toward me.

"Good afternoon. Can I interest you in a man's best friend?" He pointed to a row of recliners.

"I thought dogs were a man's best friend."

"Only to the man who doesn't have a good Barcalounger in his home." He slapped his hand on the leather arm of a cushioned chair. "Go ahead, have a seat."

I pulled my notebook from my pocket. "Actually, Mr. Flanigan, I'm here to ask you a couple of questions." I held out a hand. "I'm Detective Matteo Yawl with the Oscar's Creek Police Department."

He seemed hesitant but shook my hand. "Oh, yes, my wife, Marnie, mentioned you the other day. Says you have a very nice wife who's about to add to your family. We have a great selection of cribs and changing tables on our second floor."

"I'm sure you do. We're actually all set with baby supplies." This was a white lie, but we really did have a crib, a hand-me-down from my older sister's kids. "I'm here on official police business."

Albert's voice dropped in tone and volume. "Does this have anything to do with Betty Campbell's murder?"

"Yes, sir. Did you observe anything unusual that night?"

With two fingers, Albert smoothed back hairs that were working their way from behind his ear. "That entire night was unusual. We gave a party to wish our boys well. You're new around here; you might not know that we have twin boys who recently left for Vietnam."

My face tingled. Having been to Vietnam, I never knew what to say to parents who had sons over there. The truth of the things I'd seen would only cause them pain and worry, but I wasn't an actor. I couldn't put on a patriotic face and congratulate them on their children's bravery when I knew the boys that returned home would be forever changed by the horrible things they'd witnessed.

"Floyd and Denny enlisted." His back straightened as if he were standing at attention. "Their mom is a mess, but we're proud that they chose to serve. That night, we had friends and family here to the store. We had a crowd of hippies across the street waving signs and singing a bunch of their flower-power songs. It was downright disrespectful." A vein pulsed in his neck. "You ought to be looking into that group. They don't care about the laws of this country one bit."

I made some notes, mainly to give Albert the feeling that I was taking him seriously.

"I understand you've hired a new guy." I pretended to check my notes. "Fred Banning."

"Yes, Fred has been a great addition, unlike Charlie, whom I hired at the same time. I'm going to have to let that boy go. This generation."

"When did Fred start work?"

"That would be the day Betty's body was found. I know because it was the day the boys left. Fred took over for Floyd and Denny. I couldn't afford to not make deliveries."

"I understand Fred delivered a new set of furniture to the Campbell family."

"Yes, he and Charlie did."

"Were the pieces ordered before Betty's death?"

"No, the doc came in and asked me to personally see that his wife got the very best living room set and matching rug." Albert shrugged. "I think he didn't know what to do, so he bought her something. My wife was appalled when I told her, but she doesn't understand the pressure on a man to keep his wife happy."

I thought about how my wife would respond to such an action. Gretchen would be flabbergasted. A gift of new furniture would almost always be a big win, but any gift in order to staunch the grief over losing a child was nothing less than futile.

"Fred came into work on time, ready to get to it?"

"He did. I was impressed, as his uncle had warned me that Fred would be driving much of the night before, but he showed up with more energy than I've been able to muster in years."

"Thank you. This has been helpful. I'll be in touch if I have any more questions." I tucked my notebook back into my pocket.

Albert raised a hand. "I sure hope you find the guy."

My hand stopped on the cold metal handle of the door. "One more thing. Was Betty at the party?"

Albert shook his head. "She didn't hang out with the same crowd as Floyd and Denny."

I nodded my thanks and stepped into the cold rain.

Chapter 38

KENZIE

T he furniture store looked as if it were closed, but the open sign still
hung on the front door. Upon her entry, the bells rang, a set of
Christmas bells strung together with silky red rope that was tied to the
long metal handle. As a child, Kenzie had loved to pet the soft strands
while Gram helped with Uncle Denny's bookkeeping.

"Uncle Denny?" She walked past the rows of recliners, an item that
seemed meant for another generation. "Uncle Denny, are you here?"

Footsteps pounded up the steps to her right.

Denny appeared with sweat dotting his brow. "Kenzie. What brings
you by?"

She looked around again. "Don't you have anyone working today?"

"Business has been slow. It seems you young folks like to buy your
furniture in kit form rather than invest in pieces that will last a lifetime."
He picked up a dish of candy from the front desk. "Have a sweet."

Kenzie lifted a hand. "No. But thanks. I was hoping we could talk."

"Is everything okay with your grandmother?" Creases formed between his eyebrows.

"Yes. In fact, she and Ginny are off to Chicago to visit the new baby."

"Well, isn't that something? Do you think it's safe for her to be traveling?"

"The doctor said she can go back to living her life the way she desires."

He crossed his arms over his round belly. "I don't feel too good about the two of them traveling without assistance. I wish you would have told me about this trip. I may have been able to go along for safety."

Kenzie bit back a smile. Uncle Denny wasn't in the best shape himself. There was a kind of wheeze that followed each exhale, and he seemed out of breath more often than not. "Don't worry. They promised to call as soon as their plane landed."

Denny plopped into one of the recliners. "I'm sure that's not what brought you to see me. Spill the beans."

"I have some questions about Betty Campbell."

Faster than Kenzie expected for his age, Denny was out of the seat. His face glowed red. "I thought I told you to leave that alone."

"I know. But I think this is important. If we can prove Grandpa didn't have anything to do with Betty's death, that would give Gram so much peace. It might even be enough to convince her to have him declared dead." She tucked a loose strand of hair behind her ear. "There's an insurance policy and social security. Gram could really use the money."

"I've told her a thousand times that I'd help out."

Kenzie looked around the empty store. Sold merchandise had not been replaced, no employees were in sight, and a layer of dust had settled over the desk. "How's business been?"

"What's that got to do with anything?" The way his chest bumped up and down with each puff of air concerned Kenzie. He wouldn't have a heart attack because she'd brought up a sore subject, would he?

"It seems like you'd want to retire one of these days. You could get out and golf or join Aunt Ginny's bridge group."

He tipped his head to the side. "No changing the subject."

She grinned. "You caught me."

Denny flared his nostrils, then a small smile replaced the scowl. "Your grandmother should have put you over her knee and given you a good licking when you were small."

"You never would have let her do that."

He pushed her words away with a wave of his hand. "There's nothing more to know about Betty Campbell than she was a mess. Don't get pulled in by all the kind words spoken about the dead. That girl was trouble. She brought it everywhere she went." He dropped back into the recliner, staring off at the far wall of the showroom. "I don't think for a moment that Bristol was responsible for her death. My cousin was one of those guys who would make a full stop at an intersection in the middle of a ghost town. It's a pretty big leap to go from goody two-shoes to murderer."

"Then why was he a suspect?"

Denny shrugged. "I don't really know. Floyd and I shipped out around the same time. We didn't get word about Betty's death for weeks after it happened. To be honest, we didn't give it much thought. In Vietnam, death was everywhere." He went silent, his eyes gazing off to another time. "Then we lost Floyd." He shook his head. "The world had bigger issues back then."

Kenzie had never heard Uncle Denny speak about Vietnam. It was a subject that wasn't to be mentioned, much like talking about her grandfather. For the first time, Kenzie wondered what would have happened to Bristol Danes if he'd made it to the draft office that day. Would he have come home, or would Gram have still waited a lifetime to be reunited with the man she loved?

Chapter 39

CLARA

I bolted up in bed, my mind still swimming between the dream world and the frightful world of reality. There was a sound—I was sure I'd heard something. Reaching my right hand over, I felt for Bristol, finding his hip angled up as he slept on his side. With all my might, I gave him a shove, nearly pushing him over.

"What?" He made a sound somewhere between a yawn and a growl. "Clara, what is it?"

"I heard something."

Bristol sat up, rubbed his eyes, and blinked.

The two of us were silent in the dark, listening.

There was only the sound of crickets and the hum of the bedside clock preparing to flip the next number.

Bristol shifted, dropping his legs over his side of the bed.

"Shh. They'll hear you."

His feet wedged into the slippers waiting on the floor. It sounded like a sandpaper block working a rough piece of wood.

My pulse pounded behind my ears, and I pulled the covers up to my chest. There was a chill in the air. Had someone opened a door—a window? "You have to be quiet. They're going to hear you."

"That's what you keep saying, but I haven't heard a thing. Are you sure you didn't dream this sound?"

I pulled the blankets higher, refusing to respond because now that I was more awake, I was not actually sure. I strained my mind, trying to find the gossamer thread of my interrupted dream, but it was gone. Maybe that was better. The dream I'd just had would haunt me forever.

Deep in some sweaty jungle, I watched as my husband was shot and pushed into a bush to die. With everything I had, I tried to get to him, my legs bound by the gripping reach of vines. Then finally, I broke free. I lunged into the brush, only to find Betty Campbell's lifeless body.

Our bedroom door creaked as Bristol pulled it open, not even a bat in his hand for protection.

"What are you doing?" I whispered.

The streetlight shone through our curtain, creating the shadowed silhouette of my husband, one hand on the door frame. "I'm checking it out so we can claim the last hour of sleep before the alarm goes off."

Minutes passed without a sound. I stood, easing myself closer to the door for a better listen. A crash somewhere in the living room had me jumping back. I ran to the closet, my feet cold on the bare floor, and retrieved a tennis racket. For the first time, I wished with all my heart that Bristol had been a baseball player.

With the racket poised over my head, I made my way down the hall to save my husband from our intruders.

The light snapped on.

Bristol stood by the door, his expression blank and one slipper missing.

I swung my gaze from one side of the room to the other. "Are they gone?"

"Who?"

"Whoever was out here."

"The only invader in this house was our very own furniture, which you have rearranged again." He leaned on the back of the sofa and pulled up one leg, rubbing at his exposed toes.

"Did you stub it?"

His look spoke louder than his words could have.

"I'm so sorry." The situation was getting to me. Since the police had searched our home, I hadn't been able to regain my sense of security. He was right. I had rearranged the furniture at least three times this week. So few things in this new world of ours left me with any control.

"I suppose there's no reason to go back to bed now." He found his missing slipper and pushed it onto his foot. "No time like the present to start on inventory. Business has been steadily growing, though I'm sure it's just to get a gander at the town killer."

"No one believes that."

He dipped his head, giving me a questioning stare.

"It's still relatively fresh. Once they've really thought it through, there's not a soul in this town who would convict you." I stepped close to my husband, running my hand through his mussed hair. "You are a good man. Our friends and family understand this about you."

I tipped my head onto Bristol's chest. My complete understanding of the law was from Perry Mason. From what I'd seen, this case would make a terrible episode. No evidence, no witnesses, no way that Detective Morgan could bring a case against my husband.

"I'll make bacon and eggs. Will that make up for getting you out of bed?" I leaned up and kissed his cheek.

"You know how to get to my heart—bacon. Crispy bacon." His grin told me all was forgiven.

Honestly, a man like that could never kill another human being.

And then I remembered Vietnam. Young men from all over this country, men who were not killers, who wouldn't normally harm a fly, were being made into soldiers with the task of eliminating the enemy. It wasn't fair. Did communism really create such a threat to our way of life that we must sacrifice our husbands, fathers, and sons?

Tears flooded my eyes as I entered the kitchen.

My heart had always ached for the families left behind, but I was only just beginning to understand what must happen when a man was drafted into a war he didn't choose to be a part of.

I yanked open the refrigerator harder than I intended. A bottle of ketchup tumbled to the floor, the lid flying off on impact, and a stream of bright red shot across the linoleum.

My stomach lurched, and I lunged for the back door in time to be sick all over my flower bed.

From back there I could hear the garage door being pushed open. What was Bristol doing? The sun was only just tipping over the mountains, casting a blue light across the yard.

I breathed deep, telling my stomach to behave and thanking God it was so early that the backyard neighbors wouldn't have seen my dramatic display.

Stepping back inside, I kept my gaze away from the mess that looked far too much like how I imagined the spray of blood from a gunshot would appear.

I picked up the jar and mopped the mess with my gaze just above my target.

Bristol came into the kitchen, a bucket in one hand and a brush in the other. His work clothes were mostly under a pair of coveralls. He rummaged under the sink, coming out with one of my harshest cleaning products, which he poured into the bucket as it filled with hot water.

"What on earth are you doing?" I anchored my fists into my sides. "That seems like a bit much for a ketchup spill."

He looked at me, his expression a twist of confusion. "Ketchup?"

"On the floor." I lifted the mop still in my hand.

"It's for something else. There's a mark on the garage door. I want to get it cleaned up before I go to work."

The set of his jaw told me there was something more to this than the words he was sharing.

"What kind of mark?"

"It's nothing, really." The way his eyes stayed focused on anything but me told me my husband, the man who'd always treated me as an equal, was lying.

It didn't take much to make my mind spin with concerns. Were there other lies I wasn't picking up on? Was my entire life built on the insta-bility of untruths?

I threaded my hands into rubber gloves and pulled a scrub brush from under the sink. "Let's go."

"It's not that big of a project. I can handle it. You stay inside where it's warm."

I set my jaw and tipped my head.

The sigh that whistled from his lips sounded like forfeiture. "Is there anything I can say to stop you from helping?"

"No."

"Okay, then." He walked toward the door, his shoulders rounded with resignation.

For a moment, I considered staying behind and letting him keep whatever secret he desired to hold, but this was a marriage based on the concept that we shared each other's burdens. I wasn't ready to give up just yet.

Outside, the cold bit at my exposed cheeks.

Bristol set the bucket at his feet.

Steam rose from the water, creating an eerie mist in the dawn light.

I let my gaze go to the garage door, knowing whatever I saw would be a shock.

A KILLER LIVES HERE

I swallowed down my emotion, forcing my tears to settle in my chest, then I dunked my brush into the bucket and began to scrub at the bright red paint.

Chapter 40

KENZIE

Kenzie pulled up to Gram's house only to find Frank was already there, his phone pressed to his ear. He waved her toward him—a move that made Kenzie all the more irritated with the man who'd had the nerve to track her location.

"Do you remember any difference in Betty after they returned?" Frank's free hand hovered over a notepad with a pencil poised to write. "I see. That's interesting. Tell me more about that."

Curiosity replaced Kenzie's frustration. She took a seat next to him, straining to hear the person on the other end of the call.

"I understand. Would you mind if I called you again if any other questions arise?" Frank smiled and nodded as if the other person could see him. "Thank you." He set the phone on the step.

"Well?" Kenzie rubbed her palms together. "Who was that?"

Picking up the notepad, Frank flipped a few pages back. "That was Sue Wilder."

The name was familiar. Sue had been in the choir photo with Betty. "I take it Sue had information."

"She mentioned something I certainly hadn't come across."

"Why do you do this?" She leaned back on her hands.

"What?"

"You know what." For reasons outside of Kenzie's conscious thought, a smile tried to spread across her face. "You drag out information. You're like a soap opera—the way they give you only enough information to make you crazy for the next day's episode."

"You watch soap operas?" His voice held a tinge of amusement. "That surprises me."

"My mother watched them, and what makes you think you know me so well?" She sat up now and wriggled on the step, her backside tired of being sat on after a day of driving.

"It's my job. I pick up on clues—information people share without realizing they're laying out a part of themselves for inspection."

That took Kenzie to her feet. "You're kind of creepy."

"I am not." He shifted his weight, leaning against the porch railing. "Do you want to hear what I learned?" His eyes sparkled the way a kid on the playground might when he's about to stick a worm under your nose.

Crossing her arms, Kenzie put her weight on her left foot and tilted her head to the side.

"Betty was known to 'run with a wild crowd.' Those are the exact words she said. Sue described her as a lot of fun, always ready for a dare."

"That doesn't justify what happened to her."

"Of course not. But Sue also mentioned the time when Betty was gone."

"Gone? You mean after she died?"

"Nope. Betty and her mother left town during Christmas break of her junior year. They were in Madison, Wisconsin, where Betty's great aunt lived alone. From what Sue can remember, the aunt had taken a fall, and Betty and her mother went to stay with her while she recovered."

"When did they return?"

He raised his eyebrows. "Not until school was out for the summer."

Kenzie stretched her neck with slow circles. "At that time, wouldn't it have been expected for Betty to stay back and care for her brothers and father?"

"Exactly. I asked that too. Sue couldn't remember the circumstances. But she did say that Betty was quieter when they returned." He stood, stretching out his long legs. "That could be a result of maturity, but we know she was drinking at least the night she died, so I have to imagine whatever changes that took place didn't completely calm Betty."

"How old were her brothers when this happened?"

Frank pulled an orange notebook from a backpack at his feet. Scanning pages, he came to one and looked up, tapping his finger in the middle of the sheet. "The youngest brother was born in 1968. I don't have the exact date, but that information won't be hard to attain."

Pulling a section of hair over her shoulder, Kenzie began to braid as her mind spun. "That's a tight timeline." She ticked off months on her fingers. "Betty's mother had to have been pregnant when they left for Wisconsin. If not, maybe her husband visited at some point, but if she didn't conceive until they came back to Oscar's Creek, the baby would have been born in 1970."

"Mrs. Campbell could have taken Betty along to help because she was pregnant, had an affair in Wisconsin, or ..."

"The baby was Betty's."

"You do watch soap operas."

She gave him a shove. "You have to admit, it's possible."

"If the youngest Campbell brother was born while they were out of state, I think we've found something that could play into why Betty Campbell was the only girl murdered." He dropped the notebook onto the step and paced the short walkway. "That's been bugging me. I couldn't find another case like Betty's anywhere near Oscar's Creek in 1970 or any year near it. That tells me that Betty's murder was personal."

A shiver washed over Kenzie. "What if my grandfather was the father of Betty's baby? That would be a solid reason for killing her."

He stopped next to her. "Don't let your worries lead your investigation. We have no evidence to that fact. We don't even have a birth date for the kid yet."

Kenzie's hand shook as she unwound the small braid. "I might." Dread seemed to take the warmth from the spring sunshine. "I took one of those DNA tests a while back. I have a relative I couldn't identify."

"Where?"

She shook her head. "I don't know. They have privacy settings that keep me from viewing any information outside of their birth year, gender, and relation. He's a second cousin with only 3.125 percent shared DNA."

"Was the birth year 1968?"

Kenzie raised her gaze to Frank's eyes. "Yes."

Chapter 41

CLARA

Ginny met me at the door. "Thanks for coming by. Mom is still a mess. She just sits on the sofa and crochets. At this rate, we'll be able to provide throws for every house in Oscar's Creek by next winter."

"I had hoped it would be better by now." I rubbed my hand up and down Ginny's arm.

"I haven't mentioned a thing about Bristol's trouble. I don't think she could handle it."

I cringed at Ginny's use of the word trouble. It was so much more than that—the issues coming down hard on my husband's shoulders. He had more than any one man could handle with keeping the family business afloat, preparing for potential deployment to Vietnam, and now wondering each day if he faced murder charges.

Inside, we found Patricia as Ginny had described. She lifted her chin to me in recognition, then returned to wrapping, inserting, and pulling mustard-yellow yarn in a steady rhythm.

I followed Ginny to the kitchen, where we'd planned to bake Nestlé Toll House cookies. It was a weekly tradition with us, but in the past, we'd always baked at my house, taking a bite of raw dough without *adults* there to warn us of potential dangers.

Ginny slid the flour canister across the countertop.

For the first time, I noticed the lines of gold that wove across the surface of the white Formica. This time with Ginny each week was like those threads; they gave my heavy life moments that shimmered above the dullness of my fears.

I reached for the butter, already at room temperature, and unwrapped the sticks, tossing them into our bowl while Ginny clicked the beaters into the hand mixer.

"Bristol went to visit your dad yesterday."

Ginny nodded. "How did that go?"

I scooped sugar with Patricia's Tupperware measuring cup. "He didn't say much about it. Have you been?"

Ginny pressed the beaters into the butter and flipped the switch. "I can't. I just can't see him that way."

"I know it's hard, but he still needs you both."

"He doesn't even know who I am." Ginny held the bowl with one hand, deftly moving the beater around the edges. "It's like visiting a stranger who's stolen my daddy's body."

"I'm so sorry." There were times I felt so alone in my grieving over the loss of the newlywed life I'd planned, yet I'd left my best friend to fight through her own suffering while I stayed fixated on my own losses.

And yet, there was still joy. We still had our cookie Wednesdays, even if they'd begun to look different from how they had been in the past. I still had warm nights snuggled next to the love of my life, while my mother-in-law faced a lonely bed at the end of the day. And the Campbell family faced each day without Betty.

I blinked back tears. My world may be crumbling, but I wasn't alone. The year 1970 was proving to be a beast for Oscar's Creek.

The doorbell rang just as I pressed the brown sugar into a cup.

Ginny wiped her hands on her apron. "Don't go dipping into this while I'm gone."

I smiled. We were far from the place where the dough looked appetizing.

Mrs. Walden's shrill voice etched through the air. "I brought a casserole."

My shoulders slumped. I couldn't leave Ginny and Patricia to handle that woman on their own.

Ginny held a Pyrex baking dish covered with loosening plastic wrap over what looked like a pile of cheese.

With one hand on the door frame, Mrs. Walden pressed her ample body through the opening, pushing Ginny toward the wall. "Well, there you are." She waddled toward Patricia before anyone could stop her. "You have been in my prayers, dear." She dropped onto the sofa, lifting Patricia up by an inch or two. "I'm so sorry to hear about Mr. Danes. It's such a shame when the mind leaves us like that." She patted Patricia's arm. "At least it's spared him from living through the trouble with Bristol."

My mouth fell open, and my body froze to the spot where I stood, unable to stop the avalanche that was about to fall on my mother-in-law.

Patricia still hadn't spoken, but she tipped her chin toward me as if looking for answers.

Mrs. Walden leaned back, folding her arms over her large stomach draped in a floral-print dress. "Now, I don't think you have a thing to worry about."

"Mrs. Walden, can I get you anything? Did you come to borrow something?" Ginny's words were desperate, and to anyone willing to understand, her message was clear—change the subject.

"No dear. I'll only be a few minutes." She turned back to Patricia. "As I was saying, they'll never be able to prove Bristol did a thing to that girl. He's a good boy." Her gaze shifted to me as she shook her head in pity.

"Barbara." Patricia's voice was weak with lack of use. "I think it's time for you to get going. We're very busy here. As you can see, the girls are baking, and I'm busy with this afghan." The set in her jaw left no room for discussion.

Mrs. Walden gave a huff and then hoisted herself up. "Good afternoon to all of you ladies. I'm sure I'll be seeing you at church on Sunday."

At the mention of church, my body tightened. Going anywhere in public was becoming uncomfortable, but nearly half the souls in Oscar's Creek were members of our congregation.

I'd managed to feign a headache last week and stay home. It wasn't a complete lie. There'd been pain brewing behind my eyes almost daily since the night of the draft lottery.

This week, I'd need to straighten my spine and accompany my husband to worship. We were a team, after all.

As I followed Ginny back to the kitchen, my thoughts shifted to the men in Vietnam. I'd heard a returning soldier on the news chanting, "No man left behind." I would live those words in my marriage, never leaving my husband to fight this battle on his own. We were a team—a battalion of two.

Chapter 42

KENZIE

F rank finished the security installation as Kenzie used his laptop to trace information on Betty Campbell's family. There was a Theodore Campbell born in Madison, Wisconsin, on April 26, 1968. His parents were listed as Dr. Charles and Amelia Campbell.

Kenzie wondered how Frank had all this information at his fingertips and if it was through legal means. A month ago, the way in which he investigated and the ethics he used to find information would have been important to her. Life had changed.

She continued browsing Theodore Campbell's vital information, wondering how a baby could be passed off as the mother's when she saw the name of the doctor who'd delivered Theodore. It was his own father, Dr. Campbell.

She jumped up, racing to the side of the house where Frank stood at the top of a ladder. "You know you're not supposed to use that rung. It's not safe." She grabbed ahold of each side, wondering if she had the strength to keep the mechanism from tumbling.

"I've almost got it." He snagged a drill that hung from his belt and tightened a screw. "There it is. The final exterior camera." Placing his hands on the ladder, he climbed down. "What did you find out?"

"His name was—*is*—Theodore Campbell, and he was born in Wisconsin. Guess who delivered him? It was Betty's father."

"You sure don't give a guy much time to guess."

"That proves it, doesn't it? Betty must be the biological mother of Theodore." A buzz of excitement kept her body moving.

A dog barked.

Kenzie waved at one of the neighbors, who responded with a nod but kept a leery eye on Frank.

"It's not proof, but it seems more than likely true. Even so, it may have nothing to do with her murder."

"But it could have everything to do with it. What if the father killed her to keep his secret safe?"

"Her parents still knew."

"They may not have known who fathered Theodore." Kenzie collected tools from the ground near the ladder and placed them back in their box. "Even the threat of outing the father to her parents could have been enough to make him angry. It was a different time back then. People don't even flinch when a man walks away from his child now, but in 1970, I would bet there was a higher standard."

Frank collapsed the ladder and leaned it against the house. "You really don't like men, do you?"

She paused. "I wouldn't say that." Biting at her upper lip, she gave the question a minute's thought. "It's more that I don't trust men to follow through. They don't seem capable of the same level of connection that women have."

"Ouch." He slapped a hand over his chest.

With her arms crossed, Kenzie gave him her best challenging stare. "Prove me wrong."

"And how am I supposed to do that?"

"Are your parents still together?"

"No."

Kenzie held one finger up. "I bet your father was the one to leave."

"He was."

"There you go."

"He died of cancer when I was eight."

Kenzie cringed. "I'm sorry, but you know what I mean."

Clouds rolled in, buffering the light from the sun and dropping the temperature.

"I know that the way we experience life is through a lens we create with our experiences." He lifted the ladder under his arm and started for the garage. Rain pelted the driveway moments after they'd stepped through the single-car entrance. "I'd venture to guess you didn't grow up with a lot of men around."

"My Uncle Denny. Aunt Ginny's husband died when I was very young, and I've never met my dad, so yes, men have been scarce." Her jaw began to throb, reminding Kenzie to release the pressure on her back teeth.

"It's kind of a family dynamic you have. Your grandfather was missing, your father left before you were born, and even a potential father-figure died while you were too young to understand the difference between walking away and passing away."

"Aren't you supposed to be an investigator, not a shrink?"

"You'd be surprised how much the two professions intersect." He held open the door to the house, and Kenzie walked through.

Inside the air was much warmer, with a coziness that always made Kenzie feel loved and comforted. She took a seat on the couch and pulled one of Aunt Ginny's crocheted blankets over her legs. "I'm a court reporter. There's not much that surprises me."

"There's another thing. How often do you see happy marriages at work?" Frank set Gram's puzzle book on the end table and took a seat, his gaze on Kenzie as if unwilling to let this discussion die until they'd come to a resolution.

"Never." She rubbed her fingers over yarn stitches. "We see custody disputes, marriage dissolutions, domestic assault. It makes me feel a lot better about my eternal singleness."

Frank laughed. "Eternal singleness? That's a new one. What makes you think you'll always be single?"

"Why would I think anything else? My mother and grandmother both chose men who walked away. And I'm horrible at relationships."

"Maybe you just need to date a man with the patience to show you what a good relationship looks like."

Kenzie opened her mouth, just catching herself before she replied with a sarcastic statement about if Frank wanted to fill that role. "Maybe someday."

Chapter 43

CLARA

Sunday morning, I was up before the sun, dressed in my finest skirt and blouse, my hair curled and sprayed before Bristol even stirred.

He wandered into the kitchen, still wearing his loose striped pajamas, and plopped into a chair at the table. "No headache this week."

At that moment, I knew he'd been on to me the week before, but all that was in the past. "Not even a tiny twinge."

He raked his hands through his tousled hair. "Maybe I could get one this week."

Setting the bowl of cracked eggs on the counter, I went to him, standing over his slumped form. "God knows the truth about all this. He sees what's coming down the line for you and me. And He sees your innocence. I think that deserves some praise, don't you?"

His head tipped back, and a small smile spread across his whiskered face. "When you put it that way."

"It's easy to forget that we're not going to church for the people in the building. I could do without most of them."

He reached up and touched my cheek with his rough hand. "Marrying you was the best thing I've ever done."

Leaning down, I kissed the top of his head. "You'd better get yourself together. Breakfast will be ready shortly."

The chair fought against the linoleum as Bristol pushed back from the table. "You've got it, Captain."

It took all my self-control to hold back the shiver I felt at the military reference.

***

We sat together in the parked car, watching parishioners filing toward the church doors. I clutched my purse in my hands and took a deep breath. A few weeks ago, these had been our friends. There was no reason to think they'd all turned their backs on us because of false rumors.

Bristol's door popping startled me, and I said my first prayer of the day thanking God I hadn't screamed.

He came around and opened my door before reaching his hand for mine.

Pastor Thomas greeted each person as they entered through the tall double doors.

I looped my arm in Bristol's, letting his strength move us up the steps.

"Well, there are the newlyweds." Pastor Thomas gave my husband a firm slap to the shoulder. "I'm glad to see you both looking so connected this morning." His gaze landed on our linked arms. "I get that this is a tough time, but I have a great deal of faith in the truth, and that truth will be uncovered."

"Thank you, sir."

Inside, the room was darker than the brightness my eyes had grown accustomed to. I blinked as they adjusted, bringing faces and figures into clarity.

Standing before us, staring directly at me while Bristol talked fishing with a friend from high school, was that boy, Betty Campbell's brother. This was not the church his family attended. Looking around, I didn't see other Campbell family members.

I clung to my husband's side until I saw the spark of satisfaction my discomfort gave Benjamin.

With a deep breath, I released Bristol's arm and crossed my own over my chest. If this boy wanted to battle, I was in it. I could sympathize with his grief, but I would not be intimidated by a child.

Benjamin Campbell didn't blink. If anyone near us noticed the stares between us, they made no mention or move to help.

I was about to turn my back when I saw the most frightening thing I'd ever witnessed.

With a slow smile accompanied by the flare of his nostrils and a look of evil in his eye, the boy walked out of the building as if he'd only come to show me he could be anywhere I was.

Kelly Wilder came up beside me. "Wasn't that Ben Campbell?"

"I think so," I said, knowing it was.

"I hate to say it after all that family is going through, but he's a rotten scoundrel. He's in the same grade as my sister, and he torments her."

I looked at Kelly. "He's Angela's age? I thought he was younger."

"He's shorter than average, but he's got a mean streak that makes up for it."

Realizing that boy was more like fifteen rather than thirteen gave my fears permission to expand. He was nearly a man. A very angry man who seemed to point that anger toward me.

The piano started to play a hymn, ushering us all to the sanctuary.

Bristol took my hand, and we walked up the aisle to the row where we sat each week beside my parents. My brother refused to attend until the church took a stance against the war.

When we were seated, Bristol put his arm around me. "You're shaking. Are you okay?"

"Just a chill," I lied because I couldn't bring myself to tell Bristol that Ben Campbell scared me. My husband didn't need another thing to worry about.

Chapter 44

MATTY

One blonde hair was not enough to convict a man of murder, especially when it could have been the hair of a hundred women within the community, including his own sister. But for Morgan, he was satisfied that he'd found his man, even if we couldn't make an arrest with the evidence, or lack of evidence, we'd gathered.

Gretchen set a plate of tuna fish sandwiches on the TV tray beside two glasses of milk. She dropped onto the sofa and rubbed her palm over the bulk of her rounded belly. "I don't think I can manage much longer. I haven't seen my own feet for so long, I've forgotten what they look like."

I flashed her a smile. "They are as beautiful as always." Though the truth was they'd grown swollen over the ankles and looked about as done in as my poor wife. She was a trooper. Watching her manage through this pregnancy had made me grateful to be a man.

"I saw the Danes couple at church today. I understand that we're not supposed to discuss it, but everyone in town knows you're investigating him for Betty Campbell's murder." She stretched her back then reached for her glass.

Before I answered, I took a bite of my sandwich. I always loved the way Gretchen chopped up celery to just the right size to provide a crunch without making the sandwich lumpy. I took a gulp of milk to help the bite down. "This doesn't go beyond this room, but I don't think it was him."

Her mouth hung open for a moment. "Then how could you allow the town to condemn them the way they are?"

"It's not that simple. Morgan has it in his mind that Danes is the guy. He's my superior. I've stated my disagreement, but until he decides to take this case in another direction, we continue to look through Bristol Danes's life."

"That makes me sick. What you're telling me is any family at any time could face this kind of scrutiny for no reason?"

"His name wasn't randomly picked out of a hat." I peeled off the crust from another half of sandwich and placed it back on the plate. "There was reason to make him a person of interest."

"I'm sure you're not going to share that reason with me." She cocked her head to the side.

Shoving a huge bite into my mouth, I mimed that I couldn't speak because of the food.

"Cute." Gretchen finally took her first section of sandwich. After a small nibble, she returned it to the plate. "I'm not feeling great." She rubbed at her lower back. "I don't know how I'm going to do this for another three weeks. Could you help me up?"

Standing, I moved the tray to the side and took her hands in mine, pulling Gretchen to standing.

She moaned.

I wondered how *I* was going to manage another three weeks of watching my wife in such agony.

"I'm so proud of you. This hasn't been easy."

Her eyes went round.

"What is it? Are you okay?"

A flush ran up her neck and into her cheeks. "I think my water just broke."

A dark patch was growing in the carpet at our feet. "What do we do?"

"I think we go to the hospital."

"Yes. Of course." I took her arm and started leading her to the door, but she stopped me.

Three deep breaths later, I was wrapped in a ball of fears. I'd made it home from Vietnam. I had worked as a police officer, then a detective. I was a man, for crying out loud. And right then, I was petrified.

"Get a towel from the bathroom for the car and call the doctor. The number is by the phone." She held the edge of the sofa with one hand and waved me on with the other.

In the bathroom, I pulled the entire stack of bath towels from the cupboard, not knowing which one she'd want, then took them all to the car, setting the stack on the passenger seat. As I rushed back through the living room, I stopped to check on Gretchen, but she gave me another wave, her face pinched with what I assumed was pain.

It took three tries to dial the correct number on our rotary phone.

A woman answered.

"I think my wife is in labor."

"Can you give me her name and due date please?"

"Gretchen." I fumbled for a moment, almost giving her maiden name. "Yawl. She's due in three weeks."

"Sir, a lot of the time women will have false contractions prior to going into real labor. There's nothing to worry about."

"There's ..." I searched my scrambled mind for the right words. "Water or whatever all over the place. It kind of gushed out of her." My face flushed.

"I see. I'll contact the doctors and have them meet you at the hospital. Congratulations."

That was it. No instructions other than go to the hospital? I slammed the receiver onto the cradle.

In the living room, Gretchen had made it to the door where she was now bent over, a mournful sound coming from somewhere in her chest.

Putting one arm around her back, I took her hand with my other and tried to move her toward the car.

"I can't do this."

"Sure you can." My heart pounded. "We'll get you to the hospital and they'll help."

When she looked up at me, it was clear she thought I'd lost my mind.

"I'm proud of you." I repeated the one thing that kept playing through my mind. "You're the strongest person I know."

We shuffled toward the car.

I'd never felt so helpless in my entire life.

Chapter 45

KENZIE

Theodore Campbell still resided in Oscar's Creek.

He was only fifty-five, so young it made Kenzie question whether they'd found the right person. If Betty Campbell had been still alive, she would be seventy-one. It seemed like a lifetime could take place between those ages.

Frank drove them to Theodore's home, a trailer on a couple acres of land south of town. He parked the truck beside a beaten-up Honda, then used his key to unlock the jockey box at her knees. Inside, he retrieved a pistol, checked it, and fastened the weapon to a holster at his hip.

Kenzie's chest tightened. "Do you think that's necessary?"

"I hope not, but I'd rather have it and not need it than not have it and wish I did." He popped his door open.

A dog shot out from the backside of the house.

Kenzie watched in horror as the rust-red beast came at Frank, stopping only ten feet before him and showing sharp teeth as he growled his displeasure at the intrusion.

With slow movements, Frank reached into his chest pocket and pulled out a hunk of something. He tore it into small pieces, tossing the first at the dog's feet.

Drool dripped from the canine's jowls. He sniffed the treat, ate it, then stepped a couple feet closer to Frank.

Four pieces later, and Frank was scratching the beast on the top of the head. "Come on out. He's friendly."

Kenzie wasn't sure she agreed with his assessment. She came around the truck, keeping Frank between her and the dog. "Give me some of that stuff."

"Are you jealous of the dog?" He chuckled low in his chest.

"No. In case he decides to eat me, I'd like to have an alternative to offer."

Frank reached back into his pocket and handed Kenzie a hunk of something that smelled like beef bouillon cubes and felt like pureed liver.

"Is that part of the detective kit?" Movement behind the curtain of the mobile home drew Kenzie's attention. "Someone is in there."

"Let's hope it's Theodore."

They approached the door, the dog panting at Frank's side. At the top of a set of rickety wooden steps, a door jolted open.

"Kujo, you good-for-nothing mutt, get in here." The man slapped his leg, and the dog obeyed, his head hanging low. "What do you want?"

The man before them looked like a shadow of the driver's license photo they'd seen. His skin had a sallow appearance, more gray than pink. Dark eyes seemed to sink into his face, and his teeth were discolored and uneven.

Frank put a hand on the stair railing. "Are you Theodore Campbell?"

"Who's asking?"

"Just a couple of people from town. I'm Frank, and this is my friend Kenzie."

"I don't owe you nothing?"

"Not a cent."

"All right then. What are you doing here?"

"Mr. Campbell, can I call you Theodore?" Frank gave the man in front of us his full respect.

"It's Teddy to those who care to call me anything."

"Well, Teddy, we've got a few questions we thought you might be able to help us with."

Teddy lifted his chin in response.

"You had a sister, Betty, is that correct?"

Teddy's eyebrows raised. "Do you have information about what happened to her?"

"I'm sorry. We don't, but we're looking into her case."

"You're not cops though, right? 'Cause you have to tell me if you are."

Frank waved a hand in the air. "No, sir, we're just citizens like you. Teddy, do you have any family here in town?"

The man stepped outside for the first time. He spit into the grass and looked at the clear sky. "I ain't got no one 'cept maybe the good Lord if He hasn't given up on me yet."

"I'm sure He hasn't." Frank nodded his head. "What about your brother—Ben, is it?"

"That no good waste of breath has been in the state pen since not long after he quit high school. Our parents were so ashamed, they moved us to Albany to get away from the gossip."

"But you came back?"

He nodded. "I got into my share of trouble too. Nothing like Ben, but I needed a fresh start. I decided to come back here. I've always wondered what it was like in my family before Betty was killed. I thought, maybe if I came back to the last place she was alive, I'd find peace."

Peace. Wasn't that the thing everyone was looking for? Peace, security, the knowledge that there was love around you.

Kenzie's heart broke for the man in front of them. "Have you found any of that peace?"

He looked off to the side and spit again. "I'm still looking." The rough exterior crumbled under the show of vulnerability. "A weird thing happened a few months ago." Teddy eased himself onto the top step. "A man came by here, a lot like the two of you are now." He raked his hands through graying hair. "He claimed to be my boy."

Kenzie's mouth fell open. "Was he?"

Teddy shrugged. "I got no reason to doubt him. I knew his mama, if you know what I mean. She was a good person, I assume she still is."

"What was the man's name?" Frank had his notebook out and ready.

"William."

"Last name?"

Teddy looked up, tears in his eyes. "I was neck-deep in a bottle at the time. I'm ashamed to say, I don't recall. It wasn't the one I knew his mom by. She'd married, and they both took that guy's name." He shook his head. "That day he came by, the way I handled it is my deepest regret. I've been trying my best to get sober since. I'm on ten days right now. It's the longest so far."

Frank squeezed Teddy's shoulder. "That's good work. You've got something to be proud of there."

Teddy's dull eyes grew shiny.

How long had it been since this man received a genuine compliment? Gram always said that every person on earth was a child of God, and that no matter how deep they'd fallen, there were still arms waiting to catch them.

Working in a courtroom had allowed Kenzie to forget that principle. The callousness with which she saw the world had grown slowly, too slowly to see until the shame of her judgment on Teddy washed over her.

"If you come across my boy"—Teddy looked back at the mobile home as if something were calling him back—"tell him I'm sorry."

"You've got it, friend." Frank held out his free hand and shook Teddy's, pulling him into a brief hug. "We'll do our best to get him back here."

"I'd appreciate that."

"One more question before we leave you be." Frank dug his hands into his pockets. "Have you ever taken one of those DNA tests?"

"Sure." He let out a long whistle. "I'd sure like it if this information didn't go any further than us."

Kenzie nodded. "We don't want to pry into your private business, but it's important."

"I did one a few years ago, after I heard about familial DNA matching. I wanted all of Ben's victims to have justice. The test helped, but not as clearly as I'd hoped. As it turns out, Ben and I aren't even brothers."

A tingle spread down Kenzie's arms. "Can you tell us what you found out?"

Teddy's gaze drifted to his feet. "Betty was my mother. I've never known my father."

"When was the last time you checked your account?" Kenzie wrapped her arms tightly against her discomfort.

"It's been years."

Frank handed a business card to Teddy. "You might want to take a look."

They thanked Teddy for his time.

As they walked to the truck, Kenzie had a thought and spun around. "What was the name of William's mother when you knew her?"

Teddy turned back from the doorway. "Elisabeth Willows."

Chapter 46

KENZIE

Kenzie gathered her belongings, sorting out the remains of the days work. What she needed now was a long, hot shower, a meal with not a single vegetable on the plate, and a good snuggle with Hector. But when she straightened, Frank stood in front of her desk.

He didn't have to utter a word. Her night's plans had changed.

"We got the okay. Benjamin Campbell will see us, but we have to hurry." He waved her forward in a way that made her want to move slower.

"It's an hour to the penitentiary."

"Exactly. Let's get moving." Frank turned his body toward the door with his face still cocked in her direction.

This gave her distinct memories of middle school: being woken up probably more than a few times, then finally rushed from the house unprepared and only half aware that she'd overslept and was in danger of another tardy.

She trailed after him.

In the parking lot, Kenzie found Frank's mother's car rather than the truck. "Are we undercover?"

"Ha. You're funny." His words and tone did not match. "Mom needed to borrow the truck. She's building a gazebo in her backyard and needed lumber."

A made-up image of Frank's mother popped into her head as she climbed into the car. It was essentially a picture of Frank with long gray hair.

"What are you smiling about?" He turned the key, and the engine started.

"I was just wondering what your mother is like."

"You're welcome to meet her. She's pretty cool." He pulled out, not hesitating to get on the road. "So, you're interested in my family, huh? I'm growing on you."

Kenzie tipped her head back. "You have got to be one of the most confident men I've ever met, and not in a good way."

"Ouch."

She rubbed her stomach as it growled. "Do we have time to get food?"

"I've got you covered." He pointed a thumb over his right shoulder. "Grab that insulated bag."

A blue-and-yellow pack sat on the seat behind Frank. She pulled it onto her lap and unzipped the top. Kenzie placed the bag between her feet and pulled out containers of sliced veggies, hummus, and some kind of flat bread sliced into triangles. "Did your mom make you a sack dinner?"

He darted a quick glance her way. "I made that myself. I figured you'd be hungry. You usually are."

"So many veggies." She forced a smile as she inventoried the assortment of carrots, peppers, celery, and something white. She held up the last container with a questioning look.

"Jicama. It's delicious."

"I'll take your word for it."

"Try it. There should be some cheese in there too."

She reached into the bottom and found a baggie of cheese slices next to two cans of flavored sparkling water. "Are you trying to kill me?"

"More like the opposite. Give it a try. Who knows? You may like real food."

She peeled open the lid from the red peppers and took a slice. "I'm not much of a raw vegetable person."

Frank flipped on his blinker then merged into the left lane on the freeway. "You're not much of a vegetable person at all. Try it. You're making me feel like that guy in the *Green Eggs and Ham* book. Try it, try it, and you'll see."

Kenzie took a breath, opened her mouth, and bit off the end of a pepper stick. It was juicy and crisp with more flavor than she had imagined. She shrugged, then ate some cheese.

"I don't understand how you eat junk all the time and still look like ... so fit."

Kenzie stopped chewing, the cheese forming a lump of goo in her mouth.

Frank reached over and snagged a carrot, dipping it in the hummus.

When she was uncomfortable, Kenzie liked to snack. It soothed her. Veggies would have to do.

They arrived at the prison with thirty minutes of time remaining.

Inside, they placed all their belongings, including cell phones, into lockers. A guard took them down a long hall, past an area where men were getting haircuts, and into an open cafeteria.

A woman sat on a high stool near the door, watching over the prisoners and their visitors. She pointed to an empty table. "Have a seat over there. Your inmate will be escorted to you in a moment."

Ten minutes later, a man with deep wrinkles and broad shoulders lumbered into the room. He was short, but wide, and the hatred on his face seemed to come from the marrow in his bones—all-consuming and foundational.

A guard gave him a shove toward the bench. "No problems from you."

The man sat down. "What do you two fancy folks want with me?" He crossed his arms, placing them on the table between them.

"Betty Campbell was your sister, correct?" Frank asked.

"What's that to you?"

Kenzie leaned forward. "Mr. Campbell, I'm Kenzie Danes. Do you recognize my last name?"

A slow grin spread across his face. "I remember Clara." He let out a soft whistle. "She was a beauty. The kind of woman a man can ... enjoy."

A shiver washed over Kenzie.

Frank rested a hand on her knee. "We're not here to discuss Clara Danes."

"So, she's still kicking?" He waggled his eyebrows.

Frank's grip grew tighter. "What do you know about your sister's death?"

"You mean her murder?" Benjamin rubbed a hand over his jaw. "I know a lot about it. More than anyone, I'd guess."

"What can you tell us?"

Benjamin's eyes grew dark. There was something broken in this man, a place in his soul that had been crushed and beaten, leaving him without the heart he needed to care. "What's in it for me?"

Frank leaned back, removing his hand from Kenzie. "Justice for your sister, for one thing."

"There's no justice for Betty. And what's the point of all that, anyway? The dead are dead." His gaze shifted to the far wall.

"I'll tell you what I believe. I think that Betty is at peace, but the living, they are the ones who need justice, and you're telling me you have information that could give them that. What's in it for you to keep it hidden?"

"Please," Kenzie said. "If there was something I could do for you in return, I would, but I have no control over your sentence. What else is there?"

He tapped a finger on his chin. "I've been a bit low on funds in my commissary. Let's see, I think a thousand bucks will do it."

Kenzie's mouth fell open. "A thousand dollars?" She shook her head. "I don't have it."

"I'm messing with you. Four hundred will get me what I need." He placed his palms on the table and stood. "Come back after the money is in my account, and we'll have another chat."

Frank stood.

"How do I know you'll keep your word?" she asked.

"He won't. This is ridiculous. We're not paying you for information."

Kenzie put her hand in front of him. "Do we have your word that you'll tell us what happened to Betty? The truth?"

"Of course. My word is good." He turned and walked out of the room with a guard.

Chapter 47

CLARA

After church, we went to see Bristol's father in the nursing home. I'd avoided every visit, but my luck had run out. Ginny and Patricia pulled into the parking lot behind us. It was to be a family time, like the days of my engagement to Bristol when they included me in Sunday supper.

I clutched my purse tight in my lap, preparing myself for sights I'd never forget, when I was again reminded of the boys in Vietnam. They returned with images in their minds. I'd heard many of them woke screaming in the night, their dreams taking them back there. I prayed that would not happen to Bristol. If he had to go, I wanted the same man who left to be the one who returned.

As if sensing my unease, Bristol's hand came to rest on my arm. "Are you ready?"

I tipped my head onto his shoulder. "I don't think I will ever be ready for this."

"I understand. It's hard. Try to remember we're doing this for Mom. She needs to see us all together even if Dad is only here in body."

I wondered if the pep talk was solely for me, or if he needed the words himself.

Bristol's door opened with a pop and squeak. He stepped out, then came around the car to open my door. I stepped out and took a moment to situate my hat, pressing the bobby pins in so hard I felt them scrape against my scalp.

Patrica looked a little like Jackie Kennedy in her plum-colored dress with the short-cut jacket and matching shoes. Her hair was pinned neatly at the nape of her neck, and a string of pearls hung against her collarbone. But her face couldn't hide the grief that seemed to invade her like a virus. New lines had formed in the skin that was sallow and loose along her jaw.

Beside her, Ginny gave me a small wave. She scooped her arm into her mother's, and we all walked toward the entrance as if we were heading to a funeral service.

Inside, the air was thin with the scent of urine and body odor.

I covered my nose with a gloved hand, trying to be discreet.

Patricia didn't seem to notice. "We're here to see Hubert Danes. I am his wife, and these are his children."

I moved my hand down to my heart. It touched me to be referred to as a full family member.

"Mr. Danes is in the dining room. You are welcome to join him there." The nurse was young with her blonde hair tucked into a tight bun and her uniform crisp and clean as if she'd just come on duty. "Do you know how to find it?"

"I do. Thank you." Patricia nodded, and we followed her down the hall like little ducklings trailing after their mother.

The halls were white from the walls to the flooring. Everywhere I looked seemed to be designed for ease of cleaning rather than to please the eye.

The dining room wasn't much different. Square tables were surrounded by metal chairs. At one end was a cafeteria-style lineup, much like the one we'd had in high school, but the people who went through the line seemed to be mainly employees.

While I'd found the smell in the entry to be repulsive, the scent in here wasn't much better. It reminded me of canned peas, but gallons of them set out for days.

A woman on the other side of the buffet slopped mushy food onto plastic yellow plates which were delivered to men and women who sat blankly at the tables in front of them.

We found Bristol's father at the far end of the room. He sat in an armed chair facing the window. His tall frame hunched over as if the life were leaking from him, leaving only bones and flesh where a vibrant soul had once resided.

"Hello, Honey." Patricia ran her fingers through his hair, which had grown longer over his time here. "We all came to see you."

He didn't move, his gaze seemingly stuck on the glass between him and the rest of the world.

Bristol came around the front of the chair and squatted to his father's eye level. "Dad, Ginny and Clara are here too. Would you like us to sit with you while you eat? It looks like one of the nurses has brought you a plate full of supper." My husband looked to his mother and shrugged. He'd gotten no response.

"Bristol, help me turn him toward the table." Patricia tugged on one side of the chair while Bristol pushed it into place.

Maybe there hadn't been anything of interest outside the window. His stare didn't change with the movement. Now he faced a woman in an orange robe, her hair a frizzy mess.

She noticed Hubert. "Hey, buddy, what are you looking at?" Her words were slurred, and some kind of creamy vegetable hung from her chin. "I'm not looking for a man." She flung her hand around in the air.

"Well, I daresay"—Patricia turned his head away—"my husband wouldn't be looking at the likes of you for company either."

"Mom." Ginny put her hand on Patricia's shoulder. "That lady doesn't know what's happening. She's here just like Dad because she's gone addle-minded."

Patricia turned, raising a hand in the air as if she were going to strike her daughter, but she lowered it before taking a swing. "Your father is not addle-minded. You watch your mouth."

Ginny had stepped back out of her mother's reach. "I'm sorry. What I meant was the other lady is confused. She didn't mean to upset you. Neither did I."

Patricia covered her face for a few breaths. "I'm sorry. I overreacted." She took a seat next to her husband. "How about we try some supper?" The table had been set with a fork and spoon. No knife, but there wasn't anything that would require cutting.

With the spoon, Patrica scooped up something green, which looked like canned peas run through a blender, and held it to Hubert's slack mouth.

He didn't make a move until the food was on his tongue, then he opened and closed his mouth a couple of times and swallowed.

Ginny leaned close to my side. "It's the medications they have him on. They keep him calm. I can't stand coming here. This is not how Dad would want to live."

I laced my fingers with hers. "I know. We can pray that his time comes soon."

I realized my words were not as quiet as I'd thought when Patrica's head turned my way, a scowl condemning me without need of words.

"I'm sorry. That's not what I meant." But it was. Hubert wasn't here. We had come to visit the body he'd once lived in. If there were any bit of him left, I hoped he could see that we still loved him and that we would be fine. He'd raised solid children who would take good care of their mother. He could go on to Heaven and wait for us there.

Chapter 48

KENZIE

If Kenzie didn't already recognize Solomon Stockdale, picking him out from his legal team would be difficult.

They stood around the defense table like a team preparing an attack. Five men and one woman, all dressed as if this were a New York City courtroom.

For all intents and purposes, the location didn't matter much to Stockdale. His life was on the line.

Billy leaned on the edge of Kenzie's desk. "I can't believe this is actually happening here in our little town."

"You read my thoughts." Kenzie tried to get a good look at Stockdale without making it obvious. While the jury was tasked with keeping an open mind, she was not. Men who killed their wives should be punished. If Stockdale walked free from this crime, she would tender her resignation and leave this kind of work behind her.

Billy's phone buzzed. He looked down and then nodded to Kenzie. "Time to get started."

The courtroom of people rose to their feet as Judge Daniels entered. When all were reseated, a grim mood fell over the room.

The prosecution took their turn first, bringing witness after witness to the stand to outline the case against Solomon Stockdale. Just before noon, Kevin Logan, the county district attorney, called Janet Farner to the stand.

"Mrs. Farner, please tell the court what you do for a living."

She cleared her throat. "I'm a realtor, mainly working with commercial properties."

"Was Brooklyn Stockdale a client of yours?" Kevin paced in front of the witness.

"She was."

"Could you tell the court what kind of business you were doing with Mrs. Stockdale?"

"Objection." A man from the defense was on his feet. "Relevance?"

Judge Daniels tipped his head back. "Let's give Mr. Logan a minute to get there."

The defense council sat.

"Mrs. Farner, please tell the court about the business you were doing with Mrs. Stockdale."

"Brooklyn, Mrs. Stockdale, wanted to purchase Flanigan Furniture down on Second Street."

Kenzie's spine straightened. This was the first time her own family had had any connection to a case, even this tiny of a connection.

"And what did Mrs. Stockdale plan to do with this space?"

The witness looked down, pulled a tissue from the box on the table, and dabbed at her eyes. "She planned to make it into a shelter for the unhoused. It broke her heart to see all those people out in the cold."

"Was Mr. Stockdale on board with his wife's plan for the store?"

"No." She shook her head. "Mr. Stockdale thought she was wasting his money. He forbade her from taking the funds from their joint account."

"How did she finance the plan?"

"She sold off everything she could, including her private jewelry, and then she went to anyone who would listen and laid out her plan. Of course, all of it was for naught."

"Why's that?" Mr. Logan crossed his arms.

"We couldn't get the owner to sell. He was so adamant about it, I had to wonder if Mr. Stockdale was paying him off."

"Objection." The same defense attorney jumped to his feet.

Judge Daniels shook his head. "Sustained. Please refrain from giving the court your opinions and assumptions. We're only interested in the facts here."

Mr. Logan stepped toward the prosecution's desk. "Mrs. Farner, based on your professional experience, was it unusual that the property owner did not accept the offer presented?"

"Yes. It was a generous offer, and the business has been failing. The rejection was highly unanticipated."

Kenzie's feet fidgeted beneath her desk. Why would Uncle Denny make such a poor decision? She'd been in the store recently. Business was nonexistent, and she hadn't seen any sign that Uncle Denny had an influx of cash from other means.

The doors opened in the back of the courtroom and Frank appeared, his expression serious.

Judge Daniels dismissed for lunch. Before the jury had even made their way out, Frank was at her side. "Come with me."

"What are you talking about?"

"Just do what you need to do, then come with me."

The set of his jaw was enough to start a fire of fright in her chest. "Okay. Give me a minute." She rushed through her procedure for securing her desk then let him usher her from the room and down the hall.

"Head to Sophia's office."

"What happened? You're scaring me."

Frank tapped on Sophia's door.

Sophia swung it open and motioned them to come in.

"What is happening?" Kenzie's pulse was pounding.

Frank leaned against Sophia's desk. "I found William."

"And?" Kenzie dropped into a chair.

"It's Billy."

Chapter 49

CLARA

I woke on Monday morning with a dry throat and nausea. It had become a routine feeling this last week but always resolved after I had a piece of toast with jam. If I hadn't been taking the birth control pills the doctor prescribed, I might have taken these signs as symptoms of pregnancy.

Regardless, I had an appointment to see Dr. Swift this morning.

Bristol was in the shower while I suffered through the toast, one nibble at a time. The smell of his cooking eggs nearly sent me to my knees, but like every other time, my stomach settled.

When he walked into the kitchen, I caught my breath. Bristol was always handsome, but first thing in the morning, his hair wet and combed back, his face freshly shaved, and his shirt still untucked, I would swoon at that sight for the rest of my life.

"I could use a very stiff cup of coffee this morning." He moved to the percolator, still cold on the stove.

"I'm sorry. I haven't even started it yet."

"No problem. I'm capable of a few things in the kitchen. Coffee is one of those things." He started the process while I scooped his eggs and put them on the plate next to bacon and toast.

"Here you go." I set his breakfast on our small kitchen table.

"Aren't you eating?" He eyed me with concern.

"I've already had some toast, and I'm not very hungry this morning." I pulled two coffee cups from the cupboard and set them beside the stove.

"You said the same thing yesterday. Are you feeling okay?"

I shrugged. "I'm seeing Dr. Swift today, but I'm sure it's nothing. Probably a bug going around."

He took his seat, reached for my hand, and said a quick blessing over the food. "This looks amazing."

The percolator started to hiss, filling the room with the vibrant scent.

In the living room, I heard the mail slot squawk open and the thump of envelopes hitting the hardwood floor. "I'll get that." I went over to collect the stack then started to look through each item as I reentered the kitchen.

My breath stilled when I saw the official-looking missive from the Department of Defense.

"What is it?" Bristol ran a napkin over his face.

I handed the letter to him.

Deep lines creased his forehead. He slid a finger under the flap and tore open the envelope. After a deep breath, Bristol pulled the paper out and flattened it on the table. He nodded. "It's my draft notice. They want me to report to the draft office in Salem."

I covered my mouth, holding back a sob.

Bristol stood, pulling me into his arms. "It's okay. I still need to pass the physical and a few other things. Who knows, maybe Uncle Sam will find me unfit for service. Or the war could end before I even get to

Vietnam. We are not without hope. Even if I do get shipped out, I will return home, and we will go on with our lives as if it never happened. I promise you this." He kissed the top of my head, and for a moment, I believed that everything was going to be okay.

"You really think so?"

"I do. Don't you worry." He held me back, smiling. "If I have to go, I'll be thinking of you every day while I'm gone. And when I return, we'll start a family. We'll fill this house with kids, and then we'll buy a bigger place and fill it."

I laughed. "Easy now."

"We'll live the American dream."

"Right now, your eggs are getting cold, and the store needs you there to open it." I kissed his cheek and went to the stove where I poured steaming coffee into our cups. There was still hope. There was always hope.

***

I stepped into the office of Dr. Swift and Dr. Campbell to find it buzzing with displeasure.

At the front desk, I gave the woman my name.

"I'm afraid we're running a bit behind schedule. Dr. Campbell is out unexpectedly."

My stomach rolled with a wave of nausea at the mention of Dr. Campbell. "My appointment is with Dr. Swift. I made sure of that when I scheduled."

"I understand, Mrs. Danes, and I assure you that is the doctor you will be seeing, but Dr. Swift is trying to take on the job of two doctors today.

You'll need to be patient. He will get to you as soon as possible. Now, please take a seat and wait for a nurse to call you back."

A toddler ran through the room, tripped, and burst into loud cries.

His mother scooped him into her arms and bounced him up and down until his tears dried.

I snagged an old copy of *Time* and leaned against the wall until a man stood, offering me his seat. Inside the cover I found images from Vietnam—soldiers bandaged and bleeding, jungles, and explosions. It was nowhere for my husband, nowhere for any man to find himself. I wondered how Denny and Floyd were faring, having heard nothing aside from Aunt Marnie's worry.

At least they had each other.

I was near tears when a nurse called me, yanking me from where my mind had taken me: to the middle of a country I would never step foot in.

My legs were shaky when I stood. It took a moment to get my bearings.

The nurse's eyebrows raised in frustration as I took my time to tuck the magazine onto the shelf where I'd gotten it.

"Follow me." She led me down a hall, stopping outside an examination room. "We'll have you wait in here. The doctor will be with you shortly."

As soon as I stepped over the threshold, she shut the door, leaving me like a prisoner waiting for judgment. I really didn't feel bad now. Maybe whatever was making me ill had passed, and I was taking up the doctor's valuable time.

I stopped with my hand on the knob. Voices were just beyond the barrier.

"Poor Dr. Campbell," a young female voice said. "He's had such a hard time of it. First losing his daughter, and now all the trouble his son's been into."

"If you ask me," said an older woman's voice, "Mrs. Campbell hasn't been doing her job. Those children need a firm hand. They've spoiled them all, and it's led to one dying and another running wild. I can't stand to imagine what will happen to poor little Teddy."

Slowly, I lifted my hand and stepped back from the door.

I wasn't sure if I should be relieved that Ben Campbell was getting in trouble more than his harassment of my little family, or if I should feel a greater level of concern for our safety.

Taking the seat intended for patients, I fiddled with my purse strap, digging my fingernails into the leather.

The way the older woman had spoken about Betty made my nerves crawl. Did it matter who she hung out with or even if she'd been a bit wild? No one deserved to be murdered and dumped by the river.

The door swung open, and Dr. Swift entered the room. I'd known this man since my elementary school days. He had a fatherly presence that made me more than a little uneasy when the conversation turned to women's issues.

"Good morning, Clara, or should I call you Mrs. Danes?" His jovial smile etched away a layer of my stress.

"Let's stick with Clara, Dr. Swift. You've earned that right with your years of keeping me healthy."

"Well, I hope I can continue a good record today. What seems to be the problem?"

I went on to describe my issues, letting him know that I wasn't concerned about pregnancy due to the pills he'd prescribed, but I'd been under a lot of strain in the prior weeks.

By the time I'd been through the gauntlet of examinations and blood draws, I was feeling hopeful that the virus was something that had passed, and I was as good as new.

Outside, the sun shone, and the air smelled of new plants bursting from the earth. I inhaled, choosing to thank God for the time I had with Bristol at home and praying that the battles in Vietnam would end before my husband joined the ranks of men shipped over there. How many other wives and mothers must have said that same prayer, yet the war had gone on for nine years with no real sign that the end was near.

I stepped off the curb without seeing the car that swerved to miss me.

From the passenger side, Ben Campbell smiled an evil grin.

Chapter 50

KENZIE

"Billy? Billy Tucker?"

Frank nodded. "I think he's the one who's been leaving the notes too. Think about it. How easy was it for him to *find* the note left in the courtroom?"

Kenzie's stomach swayed. "I thought he liked me. I don't understand this. Why would Billy want to hurt me?" Her mouth fell open. "Billy is related to me."

Frank and Sophia nodded.

"My grandfather? Was he the father of Betty's child?" She shook her head. How could she ever share this information with Gram? "It can't be."

"It's a pretty solid reason for Betty's death. If Betty had threatened Bristol with revealing his identity as Teddy's father, there's no telling what he might have done to stop her."

"It can't be." She stood again, walking circles around the room. Thoughts spun. Billy was her second cousin, and he hated her. Maybe life hadn't been perfect for Kenzie growing up, but she'd always had family around her, people who kept her safe and assured her that she was loved and worthy. What had Billy had? Whatever had caused him to feel such animosity for her must have been serious.

"I'm going to ask Daniels to dismiss court for the day." Sophia lifted the phone receiver on her desk.

Kenzie raised a hand. "No. I won't have Solomon Stockdale running around free for an extra day because of me. Billy doesn't know that we know. There's no reason to tell him until we need to, and we can't prove that he's the one who's been threatening me."

"I don't like the idea of you in the same room as that guy." There was a protectiveness in Frank's tone. "We can't be sure of what he's up to."

"Security has been tight with the Stockdale trial in session." Sophia set the phone back onto its cradle. "He'd be an idiot to try something now."

Frank's head cocked to the side. "You're saying he's not?"

"I am." Kenzie looked from Frank to Sophia. "I've worked with Billy for months. He's not a fool."

Soft folds appeared on Sophia's forehead. "I think it's safe to say you didn't know Billy as well as you thought. With that in mind, we can't be sure what he'll do."

The room grew silent.

This took Kenzie's poor judge of people to a new level. She'd picked horrible men to date, skipped around groups in high school, never finding the right friends, and once moved in with a woman who treated her like a housekeeper rather than a roommate. None of that compared to working alongside a man who was stalking her and leaving her threatening notes all while she thought they had a friendly relationship. In her mind, Billy was still the harmless man with the over-the-top drama and love of gossip. She hadn't even noticed a family resemblance.

The alarm on Kenzie's phone buzzed. "That's my ten-minute warning. I've got to get back to the courtroom."

"You didn't even have lunch." Sophia fumbled around in her giant purse like a mom at a soccer game, unaware that she too hadn't eaten. "Here you go. Eat this." She handed Kenzie a granola bar.

Kenzie took the offering, but her stomach was a mess of knots that would never allow her to swallow a bite.

"I'm going with you." Frank flung his bag onto his back.

"The courtroom is full. I don't know how you got in earlier, but the deputy at the door is supposed to stop anyone else from entering."

"Cory and I go way back." He winked.

Every time he did that, it gave her a strange feeling, but she wasn't about to ask him to stop. Something told her that would give him that same strange feeling, and he'd like it.

Moving toward her, Sophia opened her arms. They didn't often hug. Before Kenzie was even in her friend's arms, she felt the prickle of tears behind her eyes.

Kenzie laid her head on Sophia's shoulder, absorbing the comfort. When she inhaled, a spicy male scent filled her nose.

"Can I join in here?"

Sophia released one arm from Kenzie and pulled Frank close.

His nearness was like standing on the edge of a rooftop with the odd temptation to let herself go and fall free, but the other part of her brain screamed to step away from the precipice.

When they broke apart, Kenzie was less confident than she'd been before. Even though she was grateful to have Gram and Aunt Ginny states away, her heart longed for the reassurance they always provided.

Frank and Kenzie walked side by side down the stairs and back to Judge Daniels's courtroom. The media had returned from lunch, their chatter filling the tall room with a buzz of excitement.

Kenzie had nearly forgotten about the testimony from that morning. Uncle Denny had refused to sell the store to Brooklyn Stockdale.

Kenzie pulled out her cell and typed in a text:

> *Are you free for dinner?*

She couldn't think of a time when she and Uncle Denny had shared a meal without Gram and Aunt Ginny, but Kenzie wanted to check in with him and be sure he was really doing all right.

Billy walked up and down the gallery aisle, his arms crossed and head swinging from one side to the other as he doled out stink-eye to reporters eating at their benches, leaving crumbs and wadding up paper wrappers. "Hey, you in the hideous green polo."

A man who'd just shoved the last chunk of his sandwich into his mouth turned toward Billy, his cheeks bulging. He pointed to his chest in question.

"Yes, you. Do you really think I'm not going to notice that soda pop you've hidden under the bench?" Billy stood in a power stance that contradicted his thin body. "Sealed beverages only in the courtroom. Get that out of here before I revoke your spot and give it to someone with more respect for the institution of law."

Even as he raged at the shamed reporter, Billy looked nothing like a homicidal stalker. Of course, Solomon Stockdale didn't appear like the kind of guy who would murder his wife either. The human mind had an uncanny way of placing people in boxes that restricted their skills and desires, while in truth, the world was filled with people who were even unpredictable to themselves.

Chapter 51

MATTY

I paced myself mad in the waiting room outside labor and delivery. On the way to the hospital, it had seemed as if the baby would arrive any moment, yet I still paced this small room eight hours later.

Every hour or so, a kind nurse popped her head in to tell me all was well. Her efforts to relieve my discomfort only left me feeling more and more useless, knowing somewhere down that hall my wife suffered to bring our child into the world.

Outside the single large window, the sun dipped behind the Cascade mountains. I could no longer make out our car in the parking lot or the lines on the road that led here. It was claustrophobic the way the entire world seemed to close in on this room.

A tap on the door startled me.

"Hello, again, Mr. Yawl." The nurse entered the room with a blanket and pillow in her arms. "Since you've decided not to go home and get some rest, I brought you a few things to help with your comfort. Feel free to lie down on the sofa. It's not much, but you might be able to get a bit of sleep."

"How much longer do you think it will be?" I could hear the desperate edge in my tone, but I didn't care. I needed to see that Gretchen was alright.

Her sticky-sweet smile made me want to rush through the door and find my wife.

"Babies come in their own time. This is normal. Nothing for you to be concerned about. Dr. Campbell has an excellent record with deliveries."

My body stilled. "Dr. Campbell?"

"Yes, sir, he's your wife's physician."

That seemed like the kind of thing I should have known. "I thought Dr. Campbell was on leave."

Her eyebrows rose. "I assure you, he is not." She handed me the bedding. "Now, I suggest you get some rest."

When she was gone, I picked through my coat pocket and found my notebook. Sure enough, Mrs. Campbell had said he was working when we'd been by for the interviews. I'd done one of those things a good investigator should never do. I'd made an assumption. I'd thought he was merely doing the minimum required to keep the office going.

It seemed like Dr. Swift could have taken over some of the workload while Dr. Campbell saw to his family.

Maybe I was being overly protective, but I didn't like the idea of a doctor delivering my baby while he was certainly distracted by his own grief. What if he made a mistake?

I tossed the blanket and pillow at one end of the sofa and resumed pacing.

We knew Betty had been drinking that night. According to Dr. Swift, she was intoxicated.

A witness saw Bristol Danes with Betty that evening. Betty was stumbling. It looked like more than a friendly neighbor helping out.

Bristol led us to believe he'd only been in contact with Betty for a few minutes.

A blonde hair was found in the Danes residence.

Even so, it wasn't enough to push aside my doubts. Something was still missing—some clue that would either condemn or exonerate Bristol Danes. And I had no idea where to look.

I must have dozed for a moment, because the sound of the nurse coming into the room made my head snap up.

"Mr. Danes. I have news."

I jumped to my feet, running a hand through my hair.

"You have a baby girl."

I blinked away tears as I pictured my daughter—hopefully with all of Gretchen's beautiful features and none of my sharp ones. "Can I see her?" Not even knowing which of my girls I wanted to see more.

"There's more."

My smile dropped. "Are they okay?"

"Yes, but you also have another daughter. Twins."

I stepped back until my legs touched a chair, and I dropped into it.

"I understand it can be a shock, but your wife and daughters all did very well. The babies are cleaned up and in the nursery if you'd like to take a look at your daughters."

I nodded. "Yes, please."

She held the door open. "Come along then."

My legs were weak when I stood again, and I followed the nurse as if I were sleepwalking. We came to a huge set of windows. On the other side were two tiny bassinets, each with a tiny baby bundled in pink-and-blue blankets.

"You stay right here." The nurse tapped my arm, and then she went through a door and appeared next to the babies. She deftly lifted them into her arms and came to the window where I could get a good look at them.

Maybe it was my new-father eyes, but they were both a picture of perfection. I looked from one baby girl to the other and back again, trying to find a difference, but my daughters matched down to the tiny dimples in their chins. How was I supposed to know which one was which?

Did we have room in our little home for two children?

What about cribs and clothes and all the baby stuff? We'd planned on bringing one baby home. Did we have what we needed for two?

"Mr. Yawl?" The nurse's voice was muffled through the glass. "Don't you go passing out. Take a breath."

I did as instructed, feeling the prickling sensation along my arms start to ease.

Those little girls were completely reliant on my ability to provide for my family—a family that had doubled in size. I still had a month in my probationary time on the Oscar's Creek force. No matter what the circumstances or who I had to work with, I couldn't lose that job.

Another nurse approached, a slip of paper in her hand. "Mr. Yawl, a Mr. Morgan would like you to contact him when you're available."

Chapter 52

CLARA

The doorbell rang when I was searching through my Betty Crocker cookbook for something new to fix for dinner.

On the other side of the door, I found Detectives Morgan and Yawl. "Can I help you, gentlemen?" I chose my most polite and benign voice.

"We have a few questions for you, ma'am." Morgan was so much broader than Yawl, I couldn't help comparing them to Abbott and Costello.

"I believe I've given you all the information I have."

"Again, it's just a few questions. We'd be more than happy to take you down to the station if you'd rather play it that way." There was a note of superiority in his voice that made my jaw tighten.

"Come on in." I stood back and let them enter my home. "I'm in the middle of something, so I'd appreciate you making this brief."

Morgan eyed the sofa, as if expecting me to invite them to sit.

I did not oblige.

Detective Yawl brought a notebook out of his breast pocket. "When your husband arrived home on the night of the going away party, did he seem at all upset or uncomfortable?"

I anchored my hands to my sides. "His cousins were leaving the next morning for Vietnam and his father was experiencing a serious health concern, of course he was upset."

Detective Morgan lifted his chin. "So, your husband was under a great deal of pressure. When a man is pushed too hard, there's no telling what he will do."

"You don't know Bristol. He's a good man. He wouldn't and didn't hurt Betty Campbell."

Morgan crossed his arms, a slow smile curving up his round face. "Then why didn't he give us the shirt he'd been wearing that night?"

"He did." I looked to Yawl for confirmation. "I saw him hand you the shirt right here in my own living room."

"You know that wasn't the one he'd been wearing." Morgan pulled an envelope from his pocket and retrieved a photograph. "See this?" He indicated the image of Bristol at Denny and Floyd's party. "The shirt he's wearing here has a hole near the cuff. It's small, but you can see it."

"So?" My face burned, and I hoped the color wasn't blazing red. "I'm not sure what that has to do with the price of tea in China." Though I did get it. It was the same thing that made me aware that he'd given them the wrong shirt that morning when they'd first come looking for answers.

"The shirt Bristol gave us did not have a hole in the sleeve." Yawl's tone was calm, the kind of voice that could get you to say things you shouldn't. "We're just wondering if there was some kind of mistake. Maybe he grabbed the wrong one, and we could get the other one now."

"Well, I'm not sure. I've mended that hole, you see."

"That's fine."

"And I've washed it."

"We understand. We'd just like to get the right one into evidence."

I let my arms fall loose at my sides. "Oh, dear. I don't think I can give you that one." I bumped a palm against my forehead. "I've donated it with a bunch of other old clothes. You see, I couldn't get the mended area to lay flat. I'm no good with a needle and thread." I shrugged.

Morgan rolled his eyes like a teenage girl. "Do you really expect us to believe that?"

I gave him my best stare down. "Did you see it when you were ripping my house apart?"

We stood in silence for what felt like a minute.

"I didn't think so." I lifted my chin. "I have no reason to lie to you or to keep some silly shirt from you. If Bristol gave you the wrong one, well, accidents happen. His work shirts are all very similar to each other. You have no reason to keep harassing us."

"Do you have an explanation for the blonde hair found on his jacket?"

Yawl's head dipped.

"Have you seen Bristol's sister? There's never been a blonder girl. I suggest you compare it to Ginny's hair. I'd put down a bet that it will match, and I'm not a betting woman." Anger burned in my belly. "I think it's time you men headed out. I have things to do that are of actual value."

Morgan turned first, opening the door with his beefy hand.

Before he left, Yawl gave me a long look. I couldn't be sure, but it seemed like sadness or maybe an apology in his eyes.

Chapter 53

KENZIE

They were seven days into Solomon Stockdale's trial when the defense took over.

Kenzie had thought herself immune to the sway of the attorneys, but the Stockdale team presented its case at a level she hadn't seen before.

"Your Honor." A slim man with a smooth face and hair that looked professionally styled stepped to the center of the room. "We would like to call Chance Calloway to the stand at this time."

Calloway had a familiar face. It was plastered all over the county and beyond. He was the realtor used for high-end sales and commercial properties. He also had a reputation, though unproven, of dirty dealings.

Once on the stand, Calloway was sworn in and prepared for testimony. He leaned back in his seat, a look of utter boredom on his face.

"Mr. Calloway, what is your relationship with Solomon Stockdale?" The attorney's words were presented toward the audience as though this were a play and he was projecting his lines.

"I purchase and sell local real estate for Mr. Stockdale."

"Did Mr. Stockdale ask you to make an offer on any property within Oscar's Creek this year?"

"Yes. There have been a few that we've looked into."

"What about the building on the corner of Buchanan and Second Street? Did Mr. Stockdale have interest in that property?"

Calloway yawned as if this court proceeding was interfering with his scheduled nap time. "Yes. The furniture store. I was asked to purchase the property at any price."

Kenzie looked up from her work. *Any price?*

"Did Mr. Stockdale mention why he wanted this particular property so badly that he was willing to pay well beyond the market price?"

"It was a birthday present for his wife." Calloway nodded. "I remember because I thought it was a strange thing, buying a furniture store as a birthday present. My ex-wife wouldn't have been impressed, but what do I know? Maybe she wouldn't be my ex if I'd done things differently."

The district attorney groaned, earning a scowl from Judge Daniels.

"Were you able to obtain that property for Mr. Stockdale?"

"The old man wasn't interested in anything I'd offered, but I wasn't done negotiating when Mrs. Stockdale ... died."

"I see." The attorney paced in front of the jury. "Mr. Calloway, do you think it's odd for a man who wants his wife dead to attempt to purchase an entire building for her?"

"Objection." The district attorney was on his feet. "Mr. Calloway had no way of knowing Mr. Stockdale's motivation."

"I'll withdraw the question." Stockdale's attorney turned his gaze on the jury and lifted his eyebrows as if mocking the DA. "Mr. Calloway, did Mr. Stockdale ever say an unkind word about his wife in your presence?"

"Quite the opposite. He told me this building was important to her, and he felt bad about not taking her desires seriously."

The attorney gave a slow nod.

Jury number four crossed his arms as if placing a barrier between himself and whatever the district attorney had to say in rebuttal. He was one for the defense, and they only needed one.

Kenzie surveyed the audience, curious if Stockdale's team was winning them over as well. Everyone seemed entranced by the proceedings except for Frank. His eyes were trained on Billy, as if by looking away, he would allow the court clerk to go all homicidal maniac.

With all the questions about the furniture store and the motivations behind the desire to purchase it, Kenzie started to wonder if Uncle Denny would be subpoenaed to testify. He wasn't on the current list of witnesses, but there was no telling what would happen in the coming days.

Maybe Uncle Denny had gotten wind of the lengths Stockdale had been willing to go to purchase his property. If that were the case, Uncle Denny had missed his window. Now, it was just another downtown building in need of repair that held a business beaten by the online giants.

By the end of the day, Kenzie was ready for fresh air and solitude, but she needed to check in with Uncle Denny, just to be sure everything was okay. Gram and Aunt Ginny were his main connections, and she was responsible for sending them out of town.

Judge Daniels dismissed court for the day, and the volume in the room rose to deafening.

Frank approached her desk, giving the bailiff a nod that seemed meant to tell her he was okay to be there. He leaned in close, his skin still holding the spicy soap scent. "I'm going to follow Billy and see if anything interesting happens. You will go straight up to Sophia's office and go home together."

"I'm staying at Gram's, remember?"

He dipped his chin. "Don't you think you'd be more comfortable at Sophia's now that we know who this guy is?"

She shook her head. "We have all that surveillance. And, anyway, Billy isn't the big monster I'd envisioned. He's harmless."

"No one is harmless with a gun."

Kenzie rubbed at the back of her neck. "I'll go see Sophia, but I'm sleeping at Gram's."

"Fine." He turned away.

It was too easy, but she didn't even care what his plans were now.

Kenzie took the stairs to Sophia's office, but she was still in session. After a few minutes, she decided to leave a note and go see Uncle Denny.

She jogged down the stairs and out the back door, looking over her shoulder every few minutes like a teen sneaking from her home in the middle of the night. She was three blocks down the street when she realized she'd left her purse in Sophia's office.

Sweeping a hand into her skirt pocket, Kenzie's fingers grazed her keys with the pepper spray. At least she had those and, hopefully, enough gas to get to Uncle Denny's, home, and back to the courthouse in the morning.

Chapter 54

CLARA

There were days that seemed too much like our old ones, too much like we were back from a horrible dream. They fooled me into thinking my life would go forward as I'd planned it: making a home for my family, helping with the hardware store, spending time with good friends and neighbors.

And then something would shake me from my ease, like a glimpse of the official letter that still lay open on our dining room table. I hadn't been able to touch it since Bristol opened the envelope. It was as if the paper was able to burn my skin; it was dangerous.

I snagged my Betty Crocker cookbook from the counter and dropped it over the letter. Only a corner peeked out from below the red-and-white cover.

Leaning back on the counter, I tried to relax, breathing in the scent of the chocolate chip cookies Ginny and I had baked in the oven. One more tray of dough sat on the counter, waiting to be cooked.

"What do you think?" Ginny's voice came into the room before she did.

"Of what?"

"My face, silly." She blinked her eyes, showing off a wide strip of eyeliner on each lid. "Do you think Barry will like it?"

I tipped my head to the side. "Barry will like you if you show up wearing men's coveralls. The boy has had eyes for you since elementary school."

She grinned.

"I'm so happy you're finally giving him a chance. He's such a nice guy."

Ginny shrugged. She picked up a warm cookie from the cooling rack and took a bite. "I think these get better every week. Kind of like Barry. He was a real square in school, but maturity looks very nice on him." Her face actually blushed.

"Oh my goodness. You really like him."

She took another bite.

"Promise me that you and Barry will buy a house in this neighborhood, and we'll raise our families side by side."

"Of course. Barbeques on Saturday afternoons and card games in the evenings."

That was what I would focus on—the future—when Bristol returned home and our lives could truly begin.

The telephone rang, startling me from my thoughts.

"Hello. Danes' residence." Nine months after our wedding, it still gave me a thrill to answer the phone with my married name.

"Mrs. Danes, this is Sherry Stanton from Dr. Swift's office. He asked me to call you with your test results."

"Yes. Thank you. I'm actually feeling better." The words rushed out as if saying them would fight off any illness Dr. Swift may have found.

"Mrs. Danes, you're expecting."

My mouth fell open. "What?"

"You are expecting a baby. Congratulations."

"But," I lowered my voice, "I'm taking the pill."

"I understand. Dr. Swift wants you to stop. He believes everything will be okay with the baby, but you should not continue to take the medication."

"Okay. Thank you." I twisted the phone's coiled cord in my fingers.

"I'll call you back when we get you scheduled for another appointment. Have a good day." She hung up, leaving a dial tone ringing in my ear.

"What was that?" Ginny eyed another cookie.

I knew I shouldn't share this news before I told Bristol. "I'm pregnant." The words jumped out before I could stop them.

Ginny's head snapped my way. "You're pregnant. Like, expecting a baby?"

I nodded.

"Oh my goodness." She hopped up and down. "I can't believe this. I'm going to be an aunt." Ginny threw her arms around me. "You'll be a mother."

Excitement spread from Ginny to me until I found myself with happy tears streaming down my cheeks.

"What in the world is going on here?" Bristol rubbed a hand over his head, and his mouth curled in a sweet smile.

Ginny stepped back. "Oh, dear. I really need to be going. I have a date tonight, you know." She leaned over and gave me a kiss on the cheek.

"You two kids be good now." She hugged Bristol on her way by, and like a thunderclap, Ginny was gone before I could grab her.

Bristol wrapped me in his arms. "How was your day?"

I shrugged. "You're home early." Business had slowly returned to the hardware store, keeping Bristol busy when he was there alone.

"I don't want to miss a minute with my beautiful wife."

Looking up at him, I saw the way his smile didn't reach his eyes. There was a sadness there. The sadness that comes from a man knowing his life is outside of his own control.

"What were you and Ginny so excited about?"

I'd always imagined telling Bristol about our first baby would be a special moment, planned out and memorable, but time felt so fragile and fleeting. "The doctor's office called. I'm expecting."

Bristol stepped back, leaving me cold without his embrace. He turned and paced to the end of the kitchen, then returned to me, his face solemn.

"Are you happy?"

His eyes met mine. "Of course I'm happy. I just didn't expect this ... now."

"I know." I touched his upper arm. "The timing isn't what I'd planned either, but maybe they'll release you from service, let you stay home because you're a family man now."

He ran a finger over my ear. "A pregnant wife doesn't change the draft. If it did, we'd be in the middle of another baby boom."

The timer rang, and I turned away, pulling the last sheet of cookies from the oven.

"This baby is exactly what we need. He or she will give me the extra motivation to get my job in Vietnam done and get home. You'll send pictures every week. It won't be what we planned, but it will be wonderful." He grabbed a hot cookie, juggling it from hand to hand. "I'll be back before the baby even knows I'm missing."

Chapter 55

KENZIE

When she arrived at the furniture store, Uncle Denny was finishing with a customer, a sight that made Kenzie sigh with relief. She wasn't worried about Uncle Denny's ability to support himself. Aunt Ginny, Gram, and Uncle Denny would always look out for each other, but the last time she'd been there, she could see the beating his pride was taking as business evaporated.

Uncle Denny shook the woman's hand, and she turned to leave, a receipt dangling from her fingers.

"I was just about to close up for the night." Uncle Denny opened a drawer in his desk and shuffled stacks of papers. "What brings you by?"

Kenzie's heart pounded, sending a pulsing throb into her throat. "I want to know about Brooklyn Stockdale."

He didn't look up as he took a seat in a chair far too worn for use in a furniture store. "What would a guy like me have to do with someone like her?"

"I know she wanted to buy this place."

"Yeah, so what?" His voice became gruff like the light within him had turned off.

"So, I think it's strange that you didn't take her offer." She rubbed up and down her arms. It was chilly here, the warmth of the day's sun not making it into the deep building's center.

"You need to start minding your own business. Every time I turn around, you're asking more questions that have nothing to do with you." He stared at her, but his gaze seemed to go through her.

Kenzie recoiled from the venom in his words. "I'm not a child anymore. There's no reason to speak to me that way."

"Yet, you're not acting like much of an adult either. Look." He held up his arms. "You sent your grandmother halfway across the country without so much as a plan for her care. She needs to be looked after." He slammed a fist onto the desk.

Her eyebrows shot up. "Is it me you feel justified in talking down to, or is it all women? Gram is an adult. She is capable of caring for herself without you."

"You don't know what you're talking about." He came around the desk with keys dangling from his fingers. At the doors, he locked up and turned the sign to closed.

"Why don't you tell me what's really going on?"

"Fine." He headed for the stairwell. "Come with me."

For the first time in her life, Kenzie felt uneasy with Denny, but he was her uncle, her family. She trailed him down the steps into the basement, where overstock and broken pieces collected dust.

The lighting was dim down here, having never been updated like the top three stories had. Instead, flickering bulbs illuminated only enough area to move around without stubbing a toe on the clutter.

"Do you need help with something?"

Denny grunted as he scooped papers and envelopes from the top of a dresser. Once it was cleared, he scooted it to the side. "I've got something for you to see." He leaned down and plugged a work light into an outlet.

Kenzie blinked at the sudden flood of brightness. Behind her eyelids, she could still see the outline of the room, burned into her vision. She rubbed the heels of her hands against her eyes, conscious of the heat emanating from the lamp.

When she looked again, she thought the image in front of her must have been imagined, but as she stepped forward, it clarified. Where the dresser had stood for as long as she could remember, a door was now visible.

"Where does that go?"

"This is what I wanted you to see. It's why I didn't take the offer from Mrs. Stockdale. What's back here is far more valuable." He pulled an envelope from his pocket—a brown coffee stain on the corner—and opened the flap, pouring out a key. After fitting it into the slot and turning, he used both hands to pull a lever, which slid the pin from a large lock. With his weight leaning back, Denny yanked on the handle. The door cried and groaned on bound hinges.

Once open, Denny moved the work light into the space. "Right back here." He motioned for Kenzie to enter first.

Swiping at cobwebs, she took three tentative steps, then stalled. "What is this place?" She looked back at her uncle as he stuffed the envelope into his pocket. She'd seen that stain before, but her mind was swimming with confusion.

Something skittered in the corner, drawing her attention.

Before she could turn back, a hard object collided with her head, knocking her to her knees.

Kenzie slapped her hand over the back of her head. Warm blood seeped between her fingers. She reached out with the other hand, finding the dirt wall. "What happened?" Her weakened voice echoed through the space.

Everything went black.

For the slightest moment, she thought she might have passed out, but then the door behind her rumbled into place.

Kenzie crawled to her feet, lunging for the exit, only to hear the thick pins clink into place again. "Uncle Denny? What's happening?" In the darkness, all she could see was the memory of the envelope.

She pressed her ear to the cold wood, hearing nothing but the hum of air flowing through the cracks.

"Denny!"

Kenzie smacked her hands against the solid surface until her bones began to ache. She turned in the darkness. Goose bumps prickled her arms as fear stole her strength. On top of that, her head throbbed.

Shaking out her hands, she grasped for ideas.

Blood dripped along the back of her neck.

Kenzie pulled the keys from her pocket. With shaking hands, she unwound a keychain that had an elastic band with rubbery beads. She placed the keys and the pepper spray back into her pocket before scooping her hair into a ponytail. It came together at the sight of her cut. After two attempts, she was able to wrap the band around her hair and pull it tight, at least relieving the natural pull of the skin on the wound. If that didn't stop the bleeding soon, she might be able to hold one of her socks there with the makeshift hairband.

With that in place, she swung her arm in front of her. What had she seen before she'd gone down?

The walls were unusual. They'd felt odd under her hand.

Rather than take the risk of falling and injuring herself further, Kenzie got to her hands and knees and crawled to her left until she came in contact with the wall. She scratched at it with her fingernails. It came away like cold, hard clay. She was underground. Not just in a basement but buried in the earth.

Leaning against the wall, she huddled into herself, pulling her knees to her chest.

Her thigh pinched.

Kenzie adjusted her cell phone in her pocket.

She must have been hit harder than she'd thought.

With renewed hope, she pulled the phone out and opened the lock screen. A photo of Hector stared back at her. "I'm coming home, buddy. Don't worry."

She punched in 9-1-1, then brought the phone to her ear. Nothing.

Looking at the screen, her heart broke. No service. Of course it wouldn't connect in this grave.

She engaged the flashlight app. The room came into focus. It wasn't the small space she'd imagined. The opening traveled away from her like a tunnel burrowing deeper into the earth. Cobwebs draped from the top to the floor, and she was sure she felt spiders in her hair.

Kenzie shivered. Her mind worked against her, providing images of snakes and spiders. She returned to the door, searching every inch of the wooden structure for a handle, but there was nothing on this side, not even a dummy knob.

Why would anyone create this kind of prison?

"Think!" She couldn't get out of here by muscle, but there had to be another way. She shone the light toward the gaping darkness again. Tunnels led to other places. Maybe this one would set her free if she found the end?

Or maybe it would dump her into a bat cave or snake pit.

"When I get out of here, I'm giving up all films with caves."

The open space didn't answer the spoken thoughts. Instead, it seemed to push fears on her with the draft in the air.

Gram would remind her that fear is not from God. That thought, at this moment, only served to create a more vivid concern over who would meet her in the darkness.

No, she didn't need to go. Denny would come back. He was her uncle. He might be a grumpy old man, but he wasn't cruel. There had to be a mistake. She'd never had a reason to be scared of her uncle. Was there something wrong with him now? Had they all missed symptoms of an illness that should have been treated?

Kenzie returned to the door, sliding her back down the rough surface.

Someone would come for her. Court reporters with hamsters did not die in old forgotten tunnels. They were not murdered by their elderly uncles. They were the kind of people who went on to lead long lonely lives, eventually dying of old age surrounded by crocheted blankets and, hopefully, a caring neighbor.

Chapter 56

CLARA

No one talks about the preparations before a man leaves for war. There are details that must be managed, tasks to tick off a long list. Bristol hired Barry to manage the store on a daily basis, a decision I wasn't sure about.

What if he and Ginny broke up? Most of Ginny's old boyfriends were not friendly with her once she'd given them the boot.

I would continue to manage the books, and Ginny would keep the place tidy and take care of inventory.

Though we could hardly afford it, Bristol hired a boy down the street to take the garbage to the curb each week and maintain the yard.

Something pounded against the front door, making me jump from my thoughts.

It swung open, and Bristol pushed a large box through the opening.

"What on earth is that?" My hand covered my still-flat stomach, a move I'd taken to without thought.

He grinned. "That baby will need somewhere to sleep, and it's a father's job to put up the crib."

"She won't be here for months." I regretted the words as I spoke them.

"And I won't be here then." He pushed the box into the hall. "Let me do this. It's important to me to know you two are taken care of. Also, don't call my son 'she.'"

I tipped my head back. "Don't call my daughter 'he.'" How did people manage nine months not knowing?

Bristol spent the afternoon removing items that had accumulated in our second bedroom, while I decided what should stay and what should go. He assembled the crib with the ease of a man who'd grown up in a hardware store, making me more than grateful for his forethought.

Soon it would be just me and the baby in this house. How could anyone prepare for something like that?

"Knock, knock." My brother's voice floated down the hall.

Bristol hopped up, and we closed the door behind us, not ready to share our news with anyone aside from Ginny.

We found Bobby and Star standing in the entryway, the door still open behind them.

"Come on in," Bristol said. "What brings the two of you by?"

Bobby scratched at his beard. "We were hoping to have a few words."

Bristol motioned toward the living room and then closed the front door.

Bobby sat on the sofa with Star cross-legged at his feet on the rust-colored carpet.

A long leather strap encircled Bobby's neck, a metal peace medallion hanging at his chest. He fingered the ornament as if summoning his words. "Look, man, you don't have to do what Uncle Sam is telling you."

Bristol lowered himself onto the recliner. "How's that?"

"We know people who can get you set up in Canada. Guys are doing it all the time."

"And if I get caught, I'm not only humiliated but I'll also be put in jail."

Bobby leaned forward. "There's no humiliation in refusing to kill babies."

Bristol rolled his head back. "I think you know me better than that. When I come home, are you going to be on the front line spitting at me?" He rubbed his fingertips on his forehead, making tiny waves of skin flow back and forth. "You're my brother, man. I love you, but I'm not running out on my duty as an American."

Bobby's frame softened, and for a moment, he was my big brother again, the boy who'd let me tag along on his adventures, who'd put Band-Aids on my scrapes and kept my secrets. "I love you too. That's why I want to do anything to keep you from that place. You won't come back as the same man."

I watched as their gazes connected, a conversation seeming to happen silently in the air between them. What if Bobby was right? What if the man who returned to me was someone new wearing my husband's body? I bit my lip, wishing the tears to stay down, to allow me this moment of strength for my husband, but they wouldn't obey and fell furiously down my cheeks.

Chapter 57

MATTY

The girls—we named them Michelle and Jennifer—were vocal. Each time I visited the nursery, I could identify my two by the red faces and loud cries. Though I longed to have my family home again, I was grateful for the recovery time Gretchen was given in the hospital with so much help on hand.

My mother-in-law was due to arrive the day after the twins and Gretchen were released. This would also be a good thing for my wife. I wasn't sure it would do me any good. Mrs. Darden thought of me as an inconvenience more than a member of her family.

I arrived at the office to find a box of cigars on my desk. All around the room, men stood and came by to offer their congratulations, a slap on the back, and an open hand.

I passed out the cigars until only two remained.

Morgan sidled up to my desk and leaned on the edge.

I handed him a cigar.

He bit off the end and spit it into a nearby ashtray. "Two girls, huh? That will keep a man busy."

"You got girls?"

Morgan flicked his lighter open. "Seven of them."

I lowered my cigar. "Seven?"

"That's right. Mary Ellen, Catherine, Hannah Marie, Rebecca, Caroline, Deborah, and little Maggie." For the first time in our partnership, I saw an ounce of care in Morgan's eyes. "They're the best of me, and a whole lot of their saintly mother."

"I may need some advice one of these days."

"Here's all you need to know. Make as much money as you can. Girls are expensive. And do what your wife says." He puffed on his cigar and then offered me a light.

I wasn't much of a smoker, but I followed Morgan's example and inhaled the sweet smoke. It came back out in a puff of coughs.

Morgan slapped me on the back—hard. "Take it easy with that. It's a slow inhale. No rushing."

I scratched my chin, thinking again of the man who'd delivered my daughters after just losing his own.

Connie stepped toward my desk, waving a hand in front of her nose. "They picked up Betty Campbell's brother at the school. He knocked a girl down at lunch and broke her arm."

Morgan sighed. "We let the vandalism to the principal's car go because the boy lost his sister. Doc Campbell paid to have the window fixed and all. But this is going too far. Where is he?"

"In the back of a squad car on the way here."

"We'll meet them downstairs." Morgan snuffed out his cigar. He tapped the guy at the desk next to mine. "I'll be back for that."

So much for celebration.

Downstairs, we found a very angry Ben Campbell being helped from the back of a squad car, his hands in cuffs behind his back.

I looked to Morgan. "Do you think those are necessary?"

"If the boy is going to keep going this direction, he might as well get used to the restraints."

I shrugged, but there had to be a better way to get this kid to stop acting out. "You can uncuff him. Morgan and I will take over from here."

"Good luck to you both." The officer clicked the key into the lock and released Ben's hands. "He's a real piece of work."

Ben scowled toward the officer who was already heading back to his car. "I'm out of here."

Morgan grabbed his shoulder. "And where do you think you're going?"

"Home."

"Not this time." Morgan turned the boy toward the station. "I hear you hurt a girl pretty bad today. Your daddy can't pay to fix that one."

"He won't care. She had it coming." He ducked his shoulder, and Morgan's grip tightened.

I opened the door, and Morgan pushed the boy through and into the small conference room on the right.

The room was sparse—only six chairs and a rectangular table.

Morgan pushed the boy into the seat at the end of the room. "You think it's okay to shove a girl, huh?"

The boy's face transformed with a glare. "She had it coming to her. You weren't there."

"I don't care what she did. Real men do not hurt women. That goes for tykes like you too."

Ben moved to stand, but Morgan gave him another shove downward.

"I ain't no kid."

I took the seat on the other side, resting one elbow on the cold surface of the table. "How old are you, Ben?" Without consulting my notes, I couldn't remember his exact age.

"Almost fifteen." He was short for his age, but his arms showed muscle growth, having sloughed off the spindliness of youth.

"So, that means you're coming close to adulthood, and that comes with very severe consequences for actions you've only received a slap on the hand for so far."

"Where's my dad? I don't got nothing to say to you." His arms crossed tight over his chest, and his scowl accosted the table.

I looked at Morgan. Knowing now he was the father of seven made me think he'd have answers. Instead, I found him clenching and unclenching his fists in a way that made me wonder how close he was to clocking the boy.

A low growl hummed from Morgan's chest. "So help me, boy, if you ever come within thirty feet of my girls, I'll end you, and Daddy won't be able to bring you back."

For the first time, I saw a glimmer of fear on the kid's face.

"What's that you were saying, Detective Morgan?" Dr. Campbell stood in the doorway. He ran a thumbnail under the edge of a nail on the opposite hand, so casual, you'd think he was observing a play put on in his honor.

"Doc, your boy has gone too far. We're getting reports all over town that Benjamin is harassing people, vandalizing, and making himself into a general nuisance."

"Nonsense. He's a good boy who's been through a lot. I think you could grant him some grace in this circumstance." Dr. Campbell didn't move from his spot, but his intimidation seemed to take over the room.

I stood, needing the height to regain my authority. "The judge will determine how much grace Ben receives. That's not up to us."

Morgan gave me a look I couldn't decipher, and he shook his head.

"Judge Bailey and I go way back. We were just talking, and he thinks this shouldn't go any further, seeing as my son is in the midst of grieving his sister's death." He looked from me to Morgan. "And the detectives on her case seem to be useless."

Connie came up behind Dr. Campbell. "Excuse me." Her words were polite, but the tone didn't match.

Campbell moved to the side, allowing her entrance.

She handed a slip of paper to Morgan.

I might not have read the words myself, but the tension in Morgan's features said it all. We'd been stripped of our power to bring any discipline to this boy.

"This isn't over." Morgan grabbed Ben by the upper arm and lifted him to his feet. "Keep your nose clean. Your daddy won't be able to save you forever."

Campbell cleared his throat. "Detective Morgan, I'll have you keep your hands off my son." He looked to the kid. "Come on, Ben. I'll get you home before I return to work."

Ben hesitated at the door, turned his head back to us, and slowly smiled. It gave me the heebie-jeebies.

When they'd both left, I looked to Morgan. "Do you think Ben is capable of murder?"

The look he returned to me was one of deep contemplation.

Connie waved another slip of paper in the air. "It won't matter if he is. You two have been taken off the Betty Campbell case by order of the mayor. Perry is taking over."

Morgan raised his hands in the air. "That's ridiculous, and I'd say a conflict of interest. Perry is a second cousin or some such thing to Dr. Campbell. He can't look at this case with an objective eye."

"You and I both know that most people in this town can't throw a stone around without hitting a relative. Second cousin isn't going to mean a thing to the chief." She shrugged. "And he's the only detective left after you two."

I rubbed at the tension mounting in my neck.

"The chief wants you all in his office ... now." She turned to go. "And he said to bring all your notes on the case."

Chapter 58

KENZIE

Kenzie's cell buzzed in her hand, startling her. She fumbled it, dropping the phone on the ground, then retrieved it, hoping one of her desperate texts had made it out.

Instead, it was a notification. She'd reached the last 15 percent of the battery.

Kenzie stared into the darkness, shining the light as far as it would reach, before turning the flashlight app off to save the remaining power.

In the darkness, her senses seemed heightened. Somewhere beyond her spot, a rodent scurried. And there was a new scent fighting for dominance over the smell of earth.

What was that, and where was it coming from?

She rose to her feet, sniffing the air. It grew fainter.

Turning to the door, she smelled around the edges. Captivity had already turned her into a dog.

Near the base, the scent was its strongest and most recognizable. Smoke.

Not the kind that swirled off cigarettes or puffed from a cigar smoker. This was the smell of burning wood.

She pressed her palms against the surface of the door as she'd been taught in elementary school. It was cool, meaning she could open the door—if it hadn't been already locked—and not face fire on the other side.

Forming fists, Kenzie again pounded on the barrier between her and safety.

"Denny! Get me out of here! Gram will know you did this." The threat was ridiculous, but in a situation like this, any option was worth trying.

Any option but moving deeper into the tunnel.

"You were right, Frank. I should have listened to all your advice." She thought back to the day before when she'd caught sight of him dropping the tracker back into her purse. Why couldn't he just track her phone like a normal overly protective friend?

How many times had Sophia suggested she get an iPhone? Couldn't those be tracked? Her Android was barely beyond the capability of a flip phone.

She took in a deep breath, telling herself that smoke didn't mean a building was on fire. Denny could just as well be destroying evidence. Of what, she had no idea.

Leaning against the door, she closed her eyes and offered one of her rare prayers to God. Would He listen to someone who barely acknowledged His existence?

By touching the side of her fitness tracker, she made the display came to life, which shone the smallest bit of light into the surrounding space. She'd already been down here for an hour. Frank would have tried to check in by now—or would he have? His plan was to follow Billy and get more information about what he was up to.

None of them thought Denny was a threat. She wasn't even sure if Frank knew about her uncle.

Kenzie coughed, the smoke growing within the room. She weighed the options and decided to turn the flashlight on for a quick look. With the low battery, the phone refused to allow the flashlight app to function. She used her fingerprint to open the phone and used the light from the screen.

Below the door, smoke swirled. It was dense and dark, clawing through the air that swept it up and pushed it toward the top.

Kenzie's heartbeat hit new highs.

She tore off her skirt, leaving her chilled in leggings, and stuffed the fabric below the door.

Touching the surface again, she couldn't tell if it had grown warmer, but the hope that this fire was contained had dissipated.

Kenzie shone the dim light toward the far end of the room again. Three percent remained on her battery. She considered all Gram had been through in 1970 and since. There had to be an ounce of that courage somewhere in Kenzie's DNA.

"It's better to die trying to survive than to sit here and give up."

A crackling sound answered her from the other side of the door.

The fire was near. She didn't have time to talk her feet into moving.

Kenzie held the light in front of her with an outstretched arm. She kept the other hand up, shielding her face.

The room narrowed to a tunnel that required her to duck, the movement bringing a new wave of pain to the back of her head.

"No one would build a tunnel that led to nowhere." Smoke scratched at the inside of her lungs, and she pressed on.

The path took a sharp left.

Kenzie's foot caught, and she fell to the ground, the phone skidding in front of her.

Fear caught in her chest as pain clamped around her knee. Her breaths were short and punctuated with anxious cries.

She crawled toward the light, reached her hand out to grab it, and froze.

The cell leaned against denim. A pant leg.

Smoke pushed her forward, but fear shoved her back. Kenzie needed to get that phone. With all the strength she had, she snatched it from its resting place and shone the dim light toward the owner of the dusty denim.

A skeleton lay slumped against the earthen wall.

Her scream bounced off the walls, deafening in the confined space.

Then the light disappeared, the phone's power sapped, and Kenzie was left in the dark with only a corpse for company.

Her eyes began to burn.

Kenzie stuffed the phone into her pocket and removed her watch. It wasn't a lot, but the light would chase away creatures and give a tiny warning before she stumbled into another body.

Deciding it was safer to go forward than back, she crawled past the dearly departed and worked her way farther along the pathway.

A barrier stopped her forward movement almost immediately.

Pressing her weight against the object, she heard the squeak of old nails moving within wood.

Smoke stole the oxygen. She pressed her face to a grate in the barricade, inhaling the sweet air outside of her confinement.

"Give up now, and you die," she whispered to herself.

Kenzie rolled to her back, her feet on the wood. She scooted back to get momentum, her head sliding into what remained of the skeleton's leg.

It toppled forward, landing on her.

Kenzie screamed, pulled her legs back, and slammed them into the barricade.

It cracked.

She repeated the process three more times.

On the last kick, her right leg broke through. Pain tore from her calf where a nail had sliced her flesh.

She scurried out from her trap beneath the bones and forced her body through the opening.

On the other side, the tunnel was more like an earthen tube. She no longer had a choice but to crawl.

After what felt like hours, but was more likely minutes, she came to a place where the tunnel went off to the left and also continued forward.

It seemed endless, and the air that had once seemed to come from nowhere felt stagnant here.

Either from the hit on the head or lack of oxygen, Kenzie grew dizzy and tired.

"Which way?"

Her question echoed back to her.

Chapter 59

CLARA

The morning Bristol was to check in with the draft office, our alarm sounded at six o'clock. I hadn't slept but for fits and starts since we'd laid down the night before. My mind was a whirlwind of fears and hopes, all connected to Bristol's appointment. Was it wrong to pray that my husband would be somehow found inferior for service?

Though I searched for a defect, all I found in the man who pretended to sleep next to me was a lean, tall man with the strength of a giant. In the years since high school he'd filled out, maturing into the kind of man women noticed. I longed for him to return to his awkward days as a teen.

I read an article in the doctor's office about a man who broke his own knee to get out of service, and in the middle of the night, I'd come up with a plan to ask Bobby to injure my husband. Now, with the light filtering through the bedroom curtains, the insanity of my thinking clarified.

Rolling over, I rested my hand on Bristol's chest. He was awake but still, his body rising and falling with each breath. I clung to this moment, committing each inhale and exhale to my memory. Tomorrow was not guaranteed. Right then I promised God that if He let me keep Bristol home with me, I'd never take another day for granted.

"We can't lie here forever." The hum of his words filtered through my palm.

"Just another minute or two."

He rubbed his rough hand over my hair and kissed the top of my head. "I love you, Clara, with all my heart."

My throat tightened. "I love you too." The words were weak, not holding the power of the feeling that engulfed me. "No matter what happens, I will always love you." I regretted the words as soon as they were out, the declaration sounding too much like permission for my husband to die on a battlefield.

Bristol pushed up, rolling me to my side. "The morning is waiting. I'm meeting Harold and Tony at the IGA parking lot at seven. I can't leave them waiting."

Knowing he had others he knew going through this same process brought a level of peace, but I still wished I could have been the one to go with him to Salem.

Bristol slid his legs into trousers and buttoned up a short-sleeved shirt.

"Do me a favor and try to look a bit less healthy when they do your physical."

He turned back to me, the first smile of the day on his face. "Like this?" He curved his back and ambled around the room with a pronounced limp.

I burst into laughter. "That should do it."

"I'll do my best. And I'll give them the list of things your mother is always telling me need improvement. That should help." He waggled his eyebrows. "It's a long list."

I slapped a hand against my forehead. My mother could find fault in perfection.

Rising, I stretched, wrapped my robe around me, and went out to the kitchen to prepare a quick breakfast. "Are you sure you don't want me to drive you to the IGA?" I called over my shoulder.

"Nope. I could use the walk. Who knows, maybe I will trip over a crack in the sidewalk and break my leg."

"We can only hope." Bristol was the silly to my serious. He balanced me in a way I hadn't realized I'd needed until he was here.

The morning went by too quickly, and long before I was ready, we were standing at the front door, Bristol with a bag over his shoulder.

"I will be back by dinnertime, but if I'm not, don't wait on me." He pulled me in and kissed me hard on the lips, the scent of his aftershave swirling around my head. "I love you." He patted my tummy. "And I love you too."

"And we both adore you." I held his face in my hands, memorizing every line. He'd be off to Vietnam in mere days. How could I go on living without him?

Bristol took my palms in his, kissing each of my fingers. "I'll see you tonight."

I blinked back tears and nodded.

A part of my heart broke as I watched the love of my life walk down the sidewalk. "I love you, Bristol Danes!" My words were loud enough to alert the neighbors, but I didn't care. Nothing mattered outside of our family.

Chapter 60

KENZIE

There were voices in her dream. They were coming for her. Maybe this dark place was the entrance to Heaven. When she could get her eyes to open, she'd see the bright white of the robes and gold of the streets, but her lids were heavy—too heavy to lift.

"She's here."

They're welcoming me. How nice.

A hand touched her face, shook her shoulder.

That was a bit rough for Heaven.

"Kenzie. Can you hear me?"

"Frank?" Her voice was a growl, rough with the pain of talking.

His head dropped to her shoulder. "Oh, thank God."

"What happened? Where am I?" Her eyes fluttered in the bright light. It smelled sweet, like candy. Shelves lined stone walls.

A woman with a hairnet over her dark hair and a white apron smeared with brown stood over them. "Should I get the paramedics?"

Frank nodded.

"I'm fine." She tried to sit, but a wave of deep chest coughs sapped her energy.

The woman dashed up the stairs at the end of the room.

"What is this place?"

"It's where the magic happens." His face was bright with mischief.

"Not the time, Frank." She let her eyes dip again.

"I thought that would be the perfect clue. We're in the basement of the chocolate shop. This is where they make the chocolates."

She could just make out the chocolate scent beyond the stench of smoke that clung to her like a wet blanket. "How did I get in here? And where did you come from?"

"I may have put another tracker *on* your car." He held up a hand. "Remember, you were the one who mentioned that first."

She shrugged, no longer concerned by the petty issue of privacy.

"When I got here, the building was already burning, but the fire department had made good progress in containing the fire. I told them that you could be in there." He turned his head away. "They wouldn't go in until they had clearance. I was stomping around, trying to figure out the next step, when I heard two ladies talking. They were worried about the fire getting into their shop through the tunnel system."

"I was in the tunnel." She tried to sit again, but the movement restored the pain in her scalp. "I'd taken one of two paths, praying I'd picked the right way. There was another barricade, a smooth one, but I didn't have enough room to break through. The smoke was chasing me."

"I nearly fell into you when I got through. You were just outside the entrance to the chocolate shop. When I convinced the ladies to let me down here, they showed me a door in the wall. It hadn't been opened in many years. Neither of them had any idea where the key was. They're going to want me to make a few repairs. I busted that thing apart."

She chuckled, the action like flames in her throat. "I'm glad you did."

"Me too."

Kenzie let him pull her into his lap. "Tell me more." She closed her eyes, letting his voice bring her peace.

"Well, I'm guessing the tunnel system had something to do with prohibition. The look of the lock and the hinges reminded me of that time period. There were old bottles of beer in the tunnel. I'd guess they were from the sixties or seventies. I'd guess the underground system was used for a bit of partying back in the day."

"Uncle Denny."

"Was he with you?"

"He ... he locked me in." She blinked back tears at the memory.

Frank's face went pale.

"Where is he?"

"I don't know."

The stairs pounded as a man and woman in paramedic attire scrambled down.

Before Kenzie could say another word, her face was covered with a plastic mask and precious oxygen filled her lungs.

Frank's voice grew distant as she let the medics tend to her wounds. She could work it all out later, when her brain was able to think again. But for right now, she'd let whatever was in that needle the woman plunged into her arm take her away to a happier place.

Chapter 61

CLARA

I made mashed potatoes and pot roast for dinner. It was one of Bristol's favorite meals. We'd be feasting from now until the day he shipped out.

I slid the potatoes into the oven to stay warm with meat while I waited for Bristol to arrive home from his check-in with the Army.

Again, I walked to the living room window that looked out on our street. The sun had dipped halfway behind the mountains, casting long shadows from the trees. In the orange and yellow hues that bathed our neighborhood, I could feel the sense that something wasn't right. The world had shifted, and we'd be off balance for a very long time.

The phone rang, and I jumped, dashing toward the kitchen. "Hello? Bristol?"

"It's Ginny. I was calling to see if he'd gotten home yet. Mom is driving me crazy with questions."

I couldn't respond, my body was shaking.

"I'm coming over. I need to drop Mom at Louisa's for their bridge game and then I'll be there."

"Thank you." I dropped the phone on the cradle, ringing the bell inside.

I paced our small kitchen, shaking the tension from my arms. Bristol had said he might be late. It was an hour's drive from Salem. Yet, the clock on the oven ticked toward seven.

Grabbing the phone again, I flipped through the phone book until I found the number for Harold's house. I underlined it with a pen, then set the phone down again, not wanting to take any time away from his family. He and Sheila had been married only the week before, wanting to tie the knot before Harold left for Vietnam. What a way to spend your very first days as husband and wife, knowing separation would arrive quickly.

The mixed vegetables had gone from bright colored squares and circles to mush. I'd need to throw them out and start a new pot when Bristol arrived.

At seven thirty, I was over my concern for others and dialed Harold's number.

A man answered. "Hello."

"This is Clara Danes."

"Oh, Clara, I'm glad you called. Is everything alright with Bristol? We waited as long as we could, but Tony was a mess with worry about being late."

"What do you mean? Is Bristol still in Salem?"

There was a long hesitation. "No. He didn't show up this morning."

"At the IGA parking lot?" As if there was another location.

"Yes. We waited until the very last minute, then we had to go. I'm sorry."

"You didn't see him at all?"

"No."

I hung up the phone and slid to the floor, covering my face with my hands. What was happening?

"Clara?" Ginny's voice, all sing-song and hopeful floated in. "Oh my goodness." She knelt beside me. "What happened? Are you okay? Is it the baby?"

I shook my head.

Ginny took my hands in hers. "Clara, tell me what's happening."

I took in a shaky breath. "I called Harold Sims. Bristol had plans to ride with him and Tony Watts this morning."

"Yes. You'd mentioned that before."

"Bristol never arrived."

"I don't understand." Her eyes were round, a crease forming between them. "Where did he go?"

All I could do was shrug. Bristol hadn't gone to his check-in, but he also hadn't come home. Where was he?

"My brother came by a couple nights ago." My face burned with betrayal. Bristol had never given me a reason to doubt him, yet my mind kept hearing Bobby's words about running away to Canada. "Never mind."

"He tried to get him to dodge the draft?"

I nodded.

"What did Bristol say?"

"Of course, he said he could never do a thing like that." I ran my fingers deep into my hair, scratching along my scalp. My grandmother once told me that our convictions are not really known until they are tested. Could Bristol have folded under the pressure of Vietnam, a baby, and his dad's declining health?

"Whatever ridiculous thoughts are running around in your head, just put them to rest. Maybe he needed to get away for a few hours. There's been a lot on his shoulders. But you and I both know that my brother is not the kind of man to abandon his family."

"Yet Uncle Sam is forcing him to go. What does that do to a person?" I suddenly became aware of a burning scent coming from the oven. Pulling on mitts, I swung the door down and was met by a wall of smoke.

Coughing, I stepped back, opening the back door just as the smoke detector let out a vibrating wail.

Ginny removed the pot roast and set the pan on the back step while I knocked at the alarm with the broom handle, finally cracking it free from the ceiling where it fell to the floor and broke into pieces.

My ears continued to ring even after the alarm had stopped blaring.

"You really know how to throw a party." Ginny peeled off the oven mitts and tossed them on the counter. "Bristol will have heard the dinner bell. I'm sure he'll arrive any minute." She tested me out with a half-smile.

"Cute."

A pounding at the front door broke the silence.

I hurried to answer it, knowing Bristol wouldn't knock, but still holding out hope that my husband would be on the other side of the door.

Instead, I found two uniformed men. "Is it my husband? Is he okay?" Then I took in the insignias. These were military police officers. Nothing good could come of this visit.

"Ma'am, are you Clara Danes, the wife of Bristol Danes?"

"I am." Ginny came to my side, wrapping her arm around my waist from the side. "How can I help you?"

"Are you aware that your husband was commanded to appear at the draft office today at oh eight hundred?"

"If that means eight in the morning, yes I was."

"And are you aware that your husband did not report as ordered?"

I held up a hand. "Listen, Bristol wouldn't do what you're thinking. He's not the kind of man who runs from his duty. Something must have happened on the way."

The taller man nodded his head. "We hear that all the time. We're going to need to look around your place."

I stepped back, allowing them entrance. "Go ahead. Be my guest."

The two men went room to room, as if Bristol were hiding under a bed or in a closet. It felt way too much like the night the police searched for clues to Betty's murder. Another crime my husband was assumed to have committed but never could have done.

Bristol Danes was not a killer or a draft dodger or the kind of man who would run out on his family.

I was nearly sure of it.

Chapter 62

MATTY

Morgan and I shared few words as he collected everything we had on the case. Well, the official reports, anyway. I kept my personal notes because there could come a day when they would be needed. I just had a gut feeling about that.

Perry was already in the chief's office. Through the open door, I could see him leaning back in a chair and laughing it up over some joke.

"This is ridiculous." I slapped a stapled stack of papers onto the file. "No one should be able to control the police department."

Morgan scratched his head. The fury of earlier had been replaced with complacency. "The doc and the mayor went to high school together. Once a month, they drive down to the valley and play golf at one of those fancy clubs. The chief has been known to join them on occasion."

"And Judge Bailey?"

He nodded. "You're getting it. Campbell knows how to collect power."

The chief's voice shot out from his office. "You two quit lollygagging and get in here. My wife is making her meatloaf for dinner, and I have no intention of missing it while it's hot."

I blew out a breath, lifting the pages on my desk.

"Let's get this over with." Morgan's jaw worked back and forth.

For the first time, I was starting to understand the man I'd been assigned to work with. Too bad that hadn't come before we were thrown off the case.

"Have a seat." The chief motioned to the one remaining chair.

Neither of us moved to take it.

I dropped the file onto the desk in front of Detective Perry. "This is what we've got."

He thumbed through it. "I imagine I'll need to start over from the beginning."

A low moan rumbled from Morgan's chest.

"You understand." Perry picked a piece of lint from his trousers. "If my name is on this case, I'll need to be sure the evidence is clear and accurate."

"Is there anything you need from us?" I kept my gaze on the chief.

"Perry? Any questions for these two?"

"If you all don't mind, I'd like to take some time with the notes. I'll find you if I need clarification." Perry stood and tucked the file under his arm. "Starting from scratch," he muttered as he walked out.

My shoulders slumped. Frustration and humiliation were at battle within me. There was something to Morgan's question about Benjamin Campbell.

"Yawl. Callahan is off sick today. You'll fill in for him at the crosswalk on Main when school gets out."

My eyebrows lifted. "You want me to be the crossing guard?"

"Is the task of keeping elementary school children alive too small for you, detective?"

"No sir." I had two baby girls who needed me to hold my temper. I just needed to remember that. "Is that all?"

"You're dismissed." He held a hand up to my partner. "Morgan, close the door."

Traffic guard would be a humiliating punishment, but I'd rather block traffic for little kids than be Morgan at this moment.

I couldn't make out the words, but the tone that warped through the chief's office wall was as sharp as any knife.

I caught movement behind me and turned. Connie stood with a bright yellow crossing-guard jacket hanging from one hand while the other held a stop sign mounted on a long pole. Lucky me.

"If it makes you feel any better, the chief found himself on school duty for a month when he was new."

"There's no way you're old enough to know that."

She handed me the pole. "The woman who had this job before me just happened to be my Aunt Connie."

I laid the stop sign on my now empty desktop and took the coat, threading my arms through the sleeves. "Can I assume you were named after this aunt?"

"You can, and you'd be right." She patted her hair, which was so stiff with spray it hardly moved. "Be sure to wear a hat." She returned to her desk.

The door burst open, and Morgan pounded out. His face shone with a color that could only be compared to a very ripe tomato.

"What happened?" I regretted the question as it was flowing from my mouth.

Morgan turned a glare on me. His head tipped to the side. "I'll tell you the worst of it." His head bobbed in short motions. "Campbell is sending that kid out of town."

"To military school, I hope."

"No such luck. He'll be living with family somewhere on the East Coast." He rubbed his fingers together to indicate great amounts of money.

"At least he's out of our hair."

Morgan crossed his arms. "True, but I was really starting to think that boy might have something to do with Betty Campbell's death."

"You think he killed his own sister?"

"Why not?"

"Do you think he had the strength to strangle her?" I returned to my desk chair, leaning as far back as I could without tipping.

"According to Dr. Swift's report, Betty was very intoxicated. I think he could have done it." He scratched his head. "I get stuck on how he moved the body to the creek though."

"Does this mean Bristol Danes is off the list?"

"You talk as if you and I have any say over this case." He pointed toward the chief's office. "I've been warned in no uncertain terms to stay away. No input. No theories. Nothing. The chief says I've harassed the family."

While I would never call Morgan a soft touch, he had done no such thing. If I had been in charge, we would have gone much deeper with our investigation of those closest to the victim. There seemed to be an unwritten list in this town of who was innocent based on public standing. It made me question my choice of town to raise my family in.

I glanced toward the door.

Clara Danes stood trembling, a friend beside her.

"What's that about?" I looked to Morgan.

"I'm not touching it. Get that ridiculous coat off and find out."

I glanced at my watch. I had time to take a quick statement before heading to the school. I removed the coat and slung it over my chair, then went to Connie's desk where the women stood. "How can I help you?" If she was here to report her husband as a murderer, Morgan would never let me hear the end of it.

"It's Bristol. He's gone." She blinked back tears and pulled a soft blue button-up sweater tight across her chest.

"Come with me." I led them to my desk and pulled an extra chair from the desk behind me. "Have a seat."

Clara took the metal beast of a seat that always sat near the end of my work area, and her friend took the one with wheels that I'd pulled over.

"What do you mean, he's disappeared?"

Clara leaned forward, putting her face into her hands.

The other woman took over. "Bristol was to report to the draft office yesterday morning. At around seven, two military police officers arrived at the house looking for him."

"And you are?" The woman was familiar, but I couldn't place her.

"I'm Ginny—Virginia Danes—Bristol's sister."

I wrote this down in my notebook. "Were you there when the MPs arrived?"

She tipped her head to the side.

"The military police."

"Yes. Clara needed my support. She was all busted up over my brother leaving for Vietnam."

Clara raised her head. Her eyes were rimmed with red, and bright patches shone through her makeup. "Bristol is a good man."

I nodded my head. It was my job to always be suspicious, but I thought she could be right about her husband. "Where do you think he's gone?"

"I'm sure something has happened to him." She leaned closer to me. "Bristol wouldn't have left us if he didn't have to."

Morgan walked by, clearing his throat. As he came close to me, he whispered, "Draft dodger."

"He is not." Clara burst from her seat, but Morgan was already around the corner. "My husband would never walk away from his duty. He isn't that kind of man."

"Okay." I motioned for her to return to the seat. "What do you think happened to your husband?"

"Someone must have hurt him or kidnapped him." Her voice was so high, I resisted covering my ears.

"Ma'am, men are rarely kidnapped. Your husband has been under a great deal of stress lately." I crossed my arms. This was not how I'd hoped things would work out for the Danes family, but I couldn't blame the man for running. Given the choice now—with what I knew about what I'd seen in Vietnam—I'd have packed my family up and taken off for the northern border. But Bristol hadn't taken Clara with him. That I couldn't abide. "Look, I'll see what I can do, and I'll ask around. Your brother is Bobby Hansen, is that correct?" I knew it was.

"Bobby doesn't have a thing to do with this. Bristol is gone, but not because he wants to be. He would never leave us like that."

The word *us* stuck in my mind, and I took notice of the way she held a hand over her stomach. Clara Danes was pregnant. Now, she really did have me wondering. I got to my feet. "Listen, I've got somewhere I need to be, but directly after, I'll do some poking around and see what I can find out. I'll be in touch tomorrow regardless, and you let me know if your husband makes contact with you, understand?"

She nodded, but there was a hardness in her eyes I'd never seen there before.

I glanced at my watch. I really did need to get going. I snagged the bright coat that surely removed any confidence the women had in me, and I ushered them toward the door. On the way out, I nodded to Connie and held the door for the women. "Ginny, will you be able to stay with your sister-in-law? I think it would be good for her to have someone at the house with her."

Ginny nodded, put her arm around Clara, and they walked off toward the visitor parking lot.

Chapter 63

KENZIE

Kenzie woke in a hospital room, not remembering how she'd arrived. She blinked a couple of times, then sat up, memories from her time in the tunnel coming back in waves.

Frank and Sophia jumped up, coming to each side of her bed.

Sophia took her hand. "You're okay now."

"There was a body. I mean a skeleton." Had she dreamed that nightmare?

Sophia looked to Frank, her features twisted in concern.

"I'm not delusional. I did see it." Her mind spun with everything that had happened. "Uncle Denny." She flung her legs over the side of the bed. "Where is he? I need to talk with him." Her brain could not comprehend a reason he would have purposely placed her in the tunnels. Unless he knew she could survive there. Did he know the store was on fire? There were too many blanks in her memory, too many spaces where she couldn't remember the details of how she'd arrived in an earthen coffin under a store she'd played in since her toddler days.

Then she remembered the envelope. Kenzie lay back on the pillow. "Denny wrote the notes. It was the coffee stain. I saw it on an envelope he had."

The door swished open. Gram hurried to her side, pushing Frank out of her way.

Aunt Ginny followed close behind.

Gram touched her weathered hand to Kenzie's cheek. "I am never leaving town again. I don't care how cute some baby is, I'm staying with you until the day I die."

Kenzie couldn't help but smile. "I'm so sorry, Gram. I'm okay."

"I'll be the one who determines when you're okay. You'll be in my room for the time being. Ginny's going to scoot herself over and let me stay in her room until you're properly back on your feet."

"No, Gram, that's asking way too much. The couch is fine."

"Nonsense."

Aunt Ginny wriggled between Sophia and the bed. "I can already hear your grandmother's freight train of a snore through the thin walls. Having her in my room for a bit won't make that much difference." She tapped at her ears. "I just pull these babies out, and she can't bother me."

Gram tipped her head. "I do not snore."

"And that guy doesn't lift weights." She pointed to Frank who actually blushed at the attention.

"For the love." Gram gave Frank a quick once-over. "Who are you?"

Sophia covered her mouth with a hand.

"I'm Frank, ma'am. I'm a friend of your granddaughter."

Gram crossed her arms and appraised him. "A friend, you say. What kind of friend?"

"Gram." Kenzie couldn't have been more embarrassed even if her grandmother had pulled out baby pictures of her in the bathtub. "We're friends. He's been helping me find out ... what happened to Grandpa."

Gram looked back at Kenzie.

"How did you get here so fast? Weren't the two of you supposed to be in Chicago for a couple more days? Have I slept that long?"

"We came home as soon as I got the call from Denny."

"Denny?" She pulled the blanket up to her chin, suddenly cold. "So, Uncle Denny is all right then?"

Aunt Ginny shook her head. "I'm not sure that man's been all right since he lost Floyd in Vietnam. And no, he died in the fire, honey."

"But what call?" Even through her anger at Denny, her heart broke at the thought of him perishing in the store that had been his family legacy.

"It was brief. Denny said he was sorry. That there would be a note in the mail, and that we could find you and Bristol in the tunnels." Gram shook her head. "We got the note when we arrived back. He didn't kill Bristol, but he knew who did, and he kept the secret all this time out of loyalty. He wanted us to know where you were. He believed you were safe and would find your way through the tunnels."

"I found him." Tears blurred her vision. "I'm so sorry, Gram." She'd been that close to her grandfather's bones. For some reason, she felt like she should have recognized that it was him.

"I know. It's okay. Now we can put him to rest properly."

"He didn't run away."

"I never doubted him. Bristol was the kind of man worth waiting for." Gram gave Frank another look.

"But what happened?"

Gram's smile was sad. "His Uncle Albert. Bristol came by to confront Albert about Betty. The child everyone thought was Betty's youngest brother was actually her son."

Kenzie nodded. "Yes. Frank and I figured that out. Theodore Campbell."

"Well, the father of that child was Denny's twin, Floyd. When Denny and Floyd shipped out, Floyd told Denny that he'd come to his senses. He and Betty had decided to get married when he returned and raise their child. He didn't know that Betty had already died at home." Gram shrugged. "I just wish we knew what happened to Betty. It would put all the pieces in place finally."

Kenzie scratched near the tape that held an IV tube in her hand.

"There's more we need to tell you." The lines in Gram's face deepened. "Denny confessed to killing Brooklyn Stockdale. She wanted the store and kept pressing him to make a deal. He owed a great deal of money, and she tried to negotiate with him, knowing this. Denny was in debt to the roof of that building. She must have known something was up when he kept refusing her offers. She couldn't have known the real reason. He didn't want anyone to find Bristol. He said he went there to tell her to back off, but the next thing he knew, he'd hit her over the head with a vase."

"I'll need a copy of this note." Sophia looked solemn. "Judge Daniels will hear this right away."

"Looks like Stockdale was innocent." Frank shrugged. "That one, I didn't see coming."

Sophia wagged a finger in the air. "He may be innocent of murder, but I still think the guy is a creep. The judicial system will eventually get him on something."

"I'm thinking about Teddy, alone in that trailer." Kenzie took a drink of water from the cup near the bed. "All this was for him, yet look how his life turned out. It would have been better to be honest in the first place."

"Ginny and I plan to visit Teddy. He is family, after all."

"I'd be glad to take you two ladies out there," Frank offered.

"What do you think?" Ginny looked to Gram. "Should we let Kenzie's *friend* take us on a ride?"

Kenzie covered her face.

"Do you think Kenzie will trust us alone with him?" Gram asked.

"Gram!" Kenzie's face was on fire.

The room burst into laughter, and Frank caught her gaze, his smile saying more than amusement. Maybe she could give him a chance. Not all men were bad. Her grandfather hadn't been.

Chapter 64

CLARA

Every day after Bristol disappeared was agony, but none more than the day our little girl took her first breath, coming into the world without a father to welcome her.

In the early days of my pregnancy, I'd been forced to accept that Bristol would be absent on this day, but I was able to hold on to the hope that he would return to us after his tour. How could I keep that hope alive when I didn't know where he'd gone or if he was coming back?

Ginny stepped into my room, a bouquet in her hands. "I stopped at the nursery. She's beautiful."

"She looks a lot like your dad did." Bristol and Ginny's father had passed away a month earlier, a relief in many ways. In Heaven, he was whole again. I couldn't help but wonder if he'd found Bristol there.

Ginny sat on the edge of my bed. "I can see that. She does look like the old man version of her father." Ginny's eyes shone.

It was easy for me to get caught up in my misery, but my best friend had lost her father just months after her brother's disappearance. I wondered how she managed while caring for me and her mother so well.

"Barry took a week of vacation. He'll tend to the hardware store while you're in the hospital. Mom is helping there too, so everything is in good shape. Nothing for you to worry about." She patted my leg covered in blankets.

Nothing could convince me that there were no worries. I had a newborn daughter who still didn't even have a name. My ability to feed her and keep a roof over her head depended on me keeping the store open and profitable. Barry had proposed to Ginny a few weeks earlier. They planned for a spring wedding, then my dear friend would have to give more of her time to her own family, and I refused to be the third wheel in her marriage.

A nurse wheeled in a bassinet. "I thought you would like some time with your daughter." She lifted a swaddled bundle from the bed and placed her in my arms. "Do we have a name for this little angel yet?"

I stared at my daughter—her pink lips rounded into a pucker and a blond wisp of hair showing from below her tiny cap. "I think I'll call her Hope. Hope Virginia Danes." My vision clouded. This child was exactly what I needed, a bit of her father to keep me going until he returned. She represented hope, and my heart was full of love even as it overflowed with grief.

Chapter 65

MATTY

I set off to check with anyone and everyone who knew Bristol Danes. My first stop was at the home of Clara's parents. Though she'd adamantly denied that Bristol may have skipped town to avoid the draft, Clara had admitted her brother had offered help if Bristol decided he was open to that kind of escape.

Though Bobby was supposedly a college student, word around town was he rarely attended classes, spending his time instead organizing and participating in Vietnam protests.

I knew firsthand what it was like over there. I knew the horrors; they woke me up in the dead of night, leaving me sweaty and breathless with fear that resided in the marrow of my bones. Vietnam was not a war I wanted to fight, but it was part of me now, and the hippies who spit and yelled names at returning soldiers, I couldn't abide that behavior.

Where was that peace they spoke of when they attacked the already broken of spirit?

I approached the door alone, having shed my need for supervision on a case that no one in the station took too seriously.

On the blue door hung a brass lion's head with the knocker held in his jaws. I pulled it back and let it clink onto the surface two or three times.

A neatly dressed woman answered, her hair pulled back in a tight bun and a checkered apron covering the front of her dress. She made me think of the woman on the cover of Gretchen's cookbook.

"Mrs. Hansen?"

"Yes. This really isn't a good time if you're trying to sell something." She wrung her hands.

"No, ma'am. I'm Detective Yawl with the Oscar's Creek Police Department. Would you mind if I came in and asked you a few questions about your son-in-law, Bristol Danes?"

Her hands went to her hips. "If this is about Betty Campbell, you are not welcome here. Bristol is not the kind of man who could perpetrate a crime like what happened to that poor girl."

"No, ma'am, this is about his current whereabouts. Your daughter has reported Bristol missing."

She returned to wringing her hands. "Of course. I'm sorry. Please come in." The door opened wider, and Mrs. Hansen stood to the side. "I hope you don't mind, I'm busy preparing some food to take over to Clara. Could we talk in the kitchen?"

"Of course." The Hansen residence was a sprawling ranch house with sparse decor. If I dared to run a finger over the top of a door, I doubted I'd find even a speck of dust.

In the kitchen, Mrs. Hansen had Tupperware set out in a neat row. Some might describe them as soldiers, but I only knew the kind of military that hacked through jungles and prayed for helicopter evacuations.

I shook my head, forcing my mind into the present. "Do you have any idea where your son-in-law might be?"

"Not a one. He's a good man. The type of man you want for your daughter. Do you have children, Detective?" She stirred mayonnaise into a bowl of pasta.

"I do. Twin daughters." Saying this was still fresh on my tongue, a phrase that would become commonplace in the years to follow. "They're a week old today."

She stopped stirring. "Oh my. Does your wife have everything she needs? I could bring over a casserole."

I held up a hand. "She's set for now. Thank you. Her mother and sister are with her, and they are filling the freezer with extra meals for after they return home."

"Oh dear, it will be hard for her to be away from family with two little ones. Please, be sure to give her my number. I'll do whatever I can to help out."

It felt nearly rude not to take her offer, but I was there for a reason. "Ma'am, is your son at home?"

"Bobby? He was supposed to go back to school last night, but the poor boy came down with a sore throat. He and Star stayed on for another night." Her eyes went wide. "Not in the same room. We aren't that kind of family, I assure you."

"I understand. Could I talk with Bobby for a few minutes?"

"I don't see why, but I'll get him." She brushed her hands on her apron and walked out of the kitchen. "Bobby, what on earth are you doing?"

I approached the corner to find a young man with long hair held tight to his head with a strip of leather halfway out the door. "Bobby Hansen? I'm Detective Yawl, and I'd like to have a word." I readied myself for a chase, but he leaned back on his heels, resigned.

Bobby waved at someone beyond my view, and a moment later a woman in a flowered dress that brushed the ground when she walked joined him.

"I don't talk to the fuzz," Bobby said.

"Robert James Hansen, don't you ever let me hear you speak that way to a man of the law. Sit yourself down in the living room and answer whatever questions this man has for you. He's trying to find your sister's husband."

The look that flashed across Bobby's face was answer enough. He had no idea Bristol was leaving.

"I understand you went to see Bristol and Clara a couple of days ago, is that correct?" We took seats in the living room, the young woman on the floor.

"I did. I told him to get out of here. Bristol's a good guy, maybe a bit square, but I like him. You can't blame me for not wanting Uncle Sam to turn him into another baby killer."

Every time I heard someone utter that phrase, the nerves in my neck twitched. "Did you offer Bristol any advice to help him skip out on the draft?"

Bobby crossed his arms, his eyes blank.

"Bobby, I'm not looking to get you in trouble. Clara is very upset. Did you tell Bristol where to go or who to talk to?"

He sat still as if he'd entered a trance.

Mrs. Hansen stepped behind the couch, took hold of Bobby's right ear, and yanked it upward. "Answer this nice man's questions. I raised you better than this."

My mouth fell open before I remembered my position and snapped it shut.

"I didn't do anything." Bobby's face squeezed in pain. "Bristol didn't even want to know where he could go. He wouldn't let me give him any information. I'm telling the truth."

His mother released his ear. "Thank you." She looked to me. "Does that answer your question, Detective?"

"Yes." I stood. We needed a mother like that on the force. "I'll get going. There are a few other stops I need to make."

"Thank you. I truly believe you'll find Bristol." Mrs. Hansen led me to the door.

Outside, I took a deep breath, only then realizing how stifling it had been inside.

I drove until I was near the Danes' home, then started walking the route Clara had described to me, the one Bristol generally followed when he took one of his regular walks.

As I approached downtown, I thought about how Clara mentioned he would pray for the small businesses along his way. A man like that didn't seem the sort to turn his back on his duty to his country.

Traffic was busy for Oscar's Creek, which didn't mean much in most towns around the country. I walked into the five-and-dime, finding the owner busy behind the counter ringing up an order. When he'd finished and the lady moved on, I stepped up.

"Good morning. I'm Detective Yawl."

"I know who you are, son. This place isn't big enough for anonymity. I've seen you and that lovely wife of yours in church too. Looks like you'll be a daddy soon."

A grin took over my face. So much for the determined and neutral expression of an investigator. "She had them last week."

His eyebrows shot up. "Them?"

"Yes, sir. Two healthy girls, the spitting image of each other and, thankfully, their mother."

He tipped his head back and laughed. "It's a good thing you're with the force. You're going to have your hands full." The man looked nearly as happy as I was with my little ones. I imagined he must be a grandfather by the gray scattered generously through his dark hair and the laugh lines that crinkled around his eyes and bracketed his mouth. "What can I do you for?"

"Well, I was wondering if you happened to see Bristol Danes yesterday morning." I started to pull the photo out of my notebook, but he stopped me with a raised hand.

"I know Bristol. I've known that boy since he was knee-high to a grasshopper. Cutest little towhead you ever did see. He was his daddy's shadow. Good kid."

"Did you happen to see him yesterday morning?"

The man rubbed his hand along his jawline. "He comes walking by just about every day. Let's see, yesterday morning." He shot a finger up. "Yes. That's right. He was later than usual. I was out sweeping the sidewalk when I saw him talking with his uncle Albert as he unlocked for the morning. I remember it, because they were so serious, and I'd heard about Bristol's draft notice."

There was a shift in his tone. "I served in the Second World War. It was voluntary when I enlisted, and we were there for a solid purpose. We did a job and came back heroes. There's no excuse for the way these boys today are treated." He blinked back tears. "No excuse at all. They're out there giving what they didn't offer freely, and they return to hatred and ridicule. It makes me sick."

"You have my agreement on that." The memories of protesters lining the streets at our homecoming would haunt me for the rest of my life.

"Did you serve, son?"

I nodded. "Vietnam, '66 to '68."

He raised his hand and gave me a salute that nearly broke my police image to pieces. It was my honor to salute him in return.

***

An orange sign in the furniture store window read, "Father's Day Special." Inside, the shop was humming with housewives looking at recliners. One lady flopped her head back and pretended to snore, with one hand curved into a C as if she were holding a can or glass of something. Her friends burst into laughter.

A salesman approached, his expression ready for the pitch. "Good morning. We've got some great sales happening now."

"Nope." I held up my hand. "I'm actually looking for Albert. Can you point me in that direction?"

"Mr. Flanigan is a very busy man. Is there something I can help you with?"

I whipped out my badge and gave him a good look at my credentials.

The color drained from his face. "Right this way."

I followed him to the back of the store where an office was set up on the other side of a temporary wall.

"Boss, you have someone to see you."

"Not now, Jones." I still couldn't see the other man, but his voice was as rough as sandpaper.

The salesman looked back at me, then to his employer. "It's a detective from OCPD."

A long sigh. "Send him back."

The salesman waved me over and took his leave without even a good-bye.

"Albert Flanigan?"

"Yes. What can I do for you?" He didn't bother to stand; instead he leaned back in his chair and dropped his feet onto a cluttered table.

"I'm here about Bristol Danes, your nephew."

"I heard Bristol took off for the North." He shook his head. "I didn't take that boy for a coward, but I guess when your mettle is tested, you find out how strong you really are."

"I understand you spoke with Bristol yesterday morning."

He dropped his feet to the floor with a thud, then leaned forward, his elbow on the desk. "Yesterday morning?"

"Yes. The day he was to report to the induction center." I stepped closer, daring him to lie. It was amazing how often people offered untruths that weren't even necessary.

"Oh, that's right. I saw him for a minute or two. As far as I knew, he was going to do his duty." He crinkled his eyebrows. "Come to think of it, he seemed jumpy. I should have seen this coming."

"How long was your visit with Bristol?"

"I wouldn't even call it that. He said he wanted to say another good-bye, which was odd because we'd stopped in the day before. My wife, Marnie, she's a mess about our boys being over there."

A woman came rushing around the corner. "Sir, your neighbor called. The Army is at your house."

Color flooded away from Albert's face. He grabbed his jacket and ran for the door, leaving his hat behind.

Chapter 66

KENZIE

Kenzie sipped hot peppermint tea in the living room while Aunt Ginny went on about the baby in Chicago, showing off the newly printed photographs again.

The doorbell rang and Hector let out a whistle.

Gram got there before Aunt Ginny or Kenzie could get up from the couch.

"Frank. I'm so glad to see you." She opened the door wide, as if he needed extra room to enter.

"It's nice to see you too, Mrs. Danes."

Gram crossed her arms. "You've got news."

"I do."

"Well, come on in here and let us have it." Gram pointed him toward the recliner.

"I'll get the tea." Aunt Ginny scurried off to the kitchen.

Frank took a seat. "Should I wait for her to come back?"

"I can hear you." Aunt Ginny shouted from the kitchen.

Kenzie set her mug on a coaster. She shifted on the couch, bringing her feet to the carpet. "What happened?" A thread of worry still wove itself through her, as if any little thing could pull down the pieces of her life.

"Detective Yawl was contacted by Benjamin Campbell's attorney. He's coming in to make a statement about the death of his sister."

Gram blinked back tears. "I'm so glad to hear that. Maybe Teddy can have some peace now."

"Yawl pulled some strings. If you'd like, we can observe."

Kenzie looked at her grandmother.

Gram pushed wisps of white hair away from her eyes. "I know it wasn't my Bristol. I know it in here." She tapped her heart. "I'm just so worried that my heart might be wrong."

He shook his head. "I think you can trust your heart." The remains of the man in the tunnel, the one who'd used his last days to scratch out love notes to his wife and unborn child, that man was not a killer. "If Benjamin is seriously ready to tell the story, this is the moment we've been waiting for."

"Some of us longer than others." Aunt Ginny tipped her gaze to the ceiling, tears welling over her lower lashes. "I want to be there when the truth comes out. I want to be there when the name of whoever killed Betty forever replaces my brother's name in the mouths of those who accuse."

There was a strength in the room, emanating from two women the world would see as elderly and weak. They were the ones who'd carried the burden of the unknown through decades of change in this shifting world. It filled Kenzie with the steel of pride, the hope that she could carry on in the steps of the women who'd come before her.

Gram's hand took hold of Kenzie's. "There is a time to wait, and a time to know all. It's time for the truth."

***

"Clara Danes, you don't look a day older than the first time I met you." Detective Yawl was waiting in the lobby when they arrived.

"And your lying isn't any better now than it was back then." Gram and Yawl embraced in a quick hug, the kind of gesture only people who've seen sorrow side by side can share.

When they parted, their hands remained linked. "I'm so glad you got your man back, though I'm awfully sorry for the circumstances."

"You were good to try to find him. No one else would hear a word of my story. I'll forever be grateful to you for that." She let her hands drop. "How are those sweet twins?"

"Old. They're both grandmothers. Can you believe it?" Yawl pushed the button for the elevator.

Kenzie watched as Aunt Ginny, Gram, and the detective looked around the lobby as if remembering a time long past, filled with memories that were as fresh as the moment.

The swishing of the elevator doors focused the group on the present.

They stepped out onto the third floor.

A man sat behind a reception desk.

"Hey, Connie, the chief is expecting us." Yawl took the lead.

Gram gave him a questioning look.

"When Connie retired, I kept messing up and calling him by her name. He finally said not to bother with his real one." He winked. "It's Colin."

"Right this way." The man led them down a hall into a room with a large flat-screen television at the far end. Waters were set around the table as if they were expected for a reception rather than the telling of a long-awaited story. Colin picked up a remote from the center of the table and powered on the television.

Benjamin Campbell came into focus.

"Did I make it in time?" They turned to find Teddy standing in the doorway alongside an officer.

Gram pushed to her feet. "I'm so glad you decided to join us." She touched his arm. "This will be difficult, but you have a lot of people here who care about you."

Teddy stepped to the side, and another man came through the door. Billy.

"I wouldn't have made it if it weren't for my boy here." Pride radiated from his toothy smile.

Warmth flooded Kenzie's chest.

Billy's gaze darted to Kenzie, then away.

Frank's hand took hold of Kenzie's, wrapping her fingers in warmth.

The decision to keep quiet about suspecting Billy was the right choice.

Two detectives walked onto the screen, taking seats across from Benjamin, and a man who introduced himself for the record as Benjamin's attorney sat beside him.

Billy pulled out a chair and Teddy sat, his skin still sallow with disease, but light had returned to his eyes.

"Mr. Campbell, you asked to give a statement about what happened the night of January 17, 1970. Is that correct?"

"Yeah." He nodded, and though he was restrained, Kenzie was grateful they could watch this interview from another room. He looked to his attorney who gave a slight nod. "That night, January 17, 1970, my father, Dr. Charles Campbell, was at the hospital for a delivery. It was not unusual for him to stay over in an empty room while he waited to be needed."

He shifted in his chair. "My room was above the front porch. I had one of those windows that pops out from the roof. It was late, well past when I was supposed to be sleeping. I'd been up reading a *MAD Magazine* with a flashlight." He huffed a short laugh. "My mother forbade me from looking at them, so I waited until everyone was asleep." He shrugged. "That seemed like the big sin at the time. How fast the world changes."

"What happened next?" one of the detectives asked.

"There was a noise outside. I don't remember what it was, but it caught my attention. Betty had gone to the movies with friends—at least, that's what she'd told our mother. They were strict with her. Always pushing her to be someone they could be proud of—you know, to act like the town doctor's daughter should." He looked up toward the ceiling, and there seemed to be emotion pushing up from what Kenzie had assumed was complete darkness.

"Betty wasn't so bad. I mean, I loved my sister. She was good to me. It's just that she wanted freedom. Kids back then were desperate for it, and parents were desperate to hold on to it. They were afraid of it, that freedom would ruin us.

"Our uncle, my mother's brother, died in Vietnam. After the funeral, someone tried to comfort my mother by telling her he'd died fighting for freedom. Mom spat on the ground. 'To Hell with your freedom. I want my brother back.' I'd never heard her swear before then. Maybe that's why I remember it so well."

The detective cleared his throat.

"So, I looked out the window, and I spotted Bristol Danes nearly carrying Betty toward our front walkway."

"Could you see them clearly?" the detective asked.

"There was a full moon, and our road had streetlights. I could see who it was. He kind of leaned her on the fence. I think he was hoping she'd take herself the rest of the way. The porch light came on and flooded our yard. That's when Bristol stepped back into the shadows. I didn't know what he'd done to my sister, but I was furious. I grabbed my robe and started down the steps. My mother and Betty were already in the living room, so I waited for them to move on so I could leave without being seen, but they stopped there. From where I sat on the stairs, I could just see the back of Betty's head.

"'What is wrong with you?' Mom said. 'You smell like the bottom of a beer bottle. You just wait until your father gets home from the hospital. Then you'll have something to cry about.' I couldn't see her, but I heard the floorboards as she paced.

"'Dad can't do a thing.' Betty flung her hand above her head. 'I'm an engaged woman.'

"Mom's gasp said it all.

"'Floyd and I are getting married. We're doing it first thing when he gets back from Vietnam. We're taking Teddy and getting our own place. We're going to be a family.'

"'You don't know what you're talking about. You're a foolish child.'

"'He's my son.'

"'You wouldn't. After everything we've done to protect your reputation.'

"Betty got to her feet, the argument seeming to sober her a bit. 'My reputation? No, you did it to protect your reputation. Well, guess what? I don't care. I'm taking my son.' She stomped back to her bedroom. It was on the first floor, just down the hall.

"Mom went after her, and the sounds ..." He ran his fingers over his ears as if hearing it all over again. "I should have gone in. I should have stopped her, but when I came to the door, it was like I couldn't move.

"There was a gurgling sound. I'll never forget it. I wake up in the middle of the night hearing it all over again. I stopped thinking about not getting caught, and I stepped into the doorway. Mom had her hands wrapped around Betty's neck like one of these cuffs." He lifted his hands. "But they kept cinching tighter and tighter."

Ben buried his face in his hands.

Kenzie turned to Gram, seeing tears coursing down her wrinkled cheeks.

"I snuck out the back door and darted down the street, looking for Bristol Danes. I knew who he was because he ran the hardware store, and he had a very pretty wife who caught my attention from time to time. I think I knew Betty was gone, but I needed someone besides my own mom to blame.

"I couldn't go full speed in my slippers, but I made good time and caught up to him a few blocks down the hill. 'What did you do to my sister?' I grabbed his arm, and he spun around.

"The guy just shook his head. 'Nothing, man. I helped her home after she took a fall on a curb.'

"I didn't want to believe him. Guys like that made me crazy with anger, so squeaky clean, but he was easily a foot taller than me." Benjamin held his cuffed hands up. "You can imagine by my height now, I've never been real tall.

"I don't remember all the details of what was said, but I finally headed back home. I do remember that I was freezing. That could have been the biggest motivation.

"As I came to our house, I saw a car pull into the driveway. It was my dad. I really didn't want to be caught by him. He'd be seeing red already. I didn't understand what Betty was saying about taking our brother with her when she left, but I knew it had really upset our mother.

"Dad marched in through the front door. He was wearing his hat and trench coat. I went around the back of the house, stepping onto the back porch. Muffled voices came through the wall. We weren't the kind of family who spoke openly. I knew that if I wanted to get what Betty meant about taking Teddy, I would have to get my information in a less-than-honorable way. I think I may have been a bit bent out of shape that she was planning to take Teddy and not me. I didn't understand that Teddy really was her son. Dad and I had remained in Oscar's Creek when Mom and Betty went to stay with Mom's aunt. I guess I didn't pay too much attention to my mother's and sister's bodies, so I didn't pick up on anything before they went. I stayed with a friend when Dad went to visit them. When he got home, he told me Mom had delivered a healthy baby boy, my brother. There was no reason to question him.

"I edged down the hall, standing just outside my sister's room."

Teddy's chin trembled, and Gram reached over and touched his arm.

"Mr. Campbell, what happened next?"

For the first time, Benjamin Campbell showed weakness. Kenzie could see the young boy in him, the child who witnessed something few adults could handle. This story, Betty and Benjamin's, was the making of a monster told in the details of the night when it all came to a point of eruption.

"Her face was all wrong, blue. And her eyes, I will never forget the way they stared at me.

"Dad tugged her body to the floor and tried to bring her back. My father was a good doctor, but even I knew Betty would never take another breath.

"My dad wept then. I'd never seen him cry before. He leaned over her body and shook with sobs. It was more than I could take. I turned and ran upstairs. I buried myself under all my blankets and stayed there. I didn't want to hear anything else, but where my room was meant I could hear everything. The garage door opened and closed, then opened and closed again before he drove away."

The detective tapped a pen on his notebook. "Do you have any information about how her body came to be at the creek?"

Benjamin shook his head. "I stayed under those covers until the next morning when Mom got me out of bed to get ready for Boy Scouts."

"Did she say anything about the night before?"

"No. I remember the relief when she peeled back my blankets and brushed her fingers through my hair to wake me. I thought, 'Oh wow, that was a horrible dream.' Mom made breakfast as usual, and I even asked if Betty was up. She told me Betty had been out late, so we'd let her sleep a little longer.

"Dad came in while I was eating. Mom asked him about the birth. They acted as if everything was normal, but my mother couldn't hide her bloodshot eyes. Dad told her he'd take me to Scouts, and she thanked him. It was pouring down rain, and she didn't like me out in the weather. That's what she always said, 'out in the weather.' " Benjamin's sigh spoke volumes about the respect he held for his mom even fifty years later.

"We weren't a block from the house when my dad spoke the words that still haunt me. He kept his hands on the steering wheel, ten and two, his eyes facing the street in front of us. Rain pelted the windshield, the wipers beating back and forth. Then he said, 'You are never to say a word about what you saw last night. If you do, I'll kill your mother and your brother and make you bury the bodies.' I think he wanted me to believe he had done it, and I let him."

Kenzie's body chilled. This man had carried that threat within him for all these years, even after his father died. It was amazing the lies people were bought into, let burrow into their beings, and believed as truth.

Gram had always lived as if Grandpa Danes was out there. She was a wife waiting for the return of her love. But she must have known, somewhere deep in her soul, that he was gone.

And Kenzie believed she'd never have a solid and lasting relationship with a man. She'd believed the lie that the Danes women were not cut out for that kind of connection. But in reality, her father was the only man who'd walked away willingly.

Maybe Sophia was right, she needed to at least meet the man who gave her half the DNA in her body. Fathers held a lot of power in a person's life, even the absent ones.

Chapter 67

CLARA

*2*⁰²⁴

The sun was already warm as the morning light shone over our group huddled around the newly dug grave that housed the body my dear Bristol once resided within.

My dear Kenzie held one of my hands while Ginny had the other. It was a long time coming, this moment of closure, and my heart felt lighter while a new kind of grief sat in the shadows waiting for me to take it on.

In all the nightmares I'd woken from over the fifty-plus years I'd waited for my husband to return to me, his murder by one of his own family members had never entered my mind. I remembered Albert as a man who would do anything to protect his family, and on some level, that must have been what he thought he was doing.

He and Marnie mourned the loss of Floyd with earnest pain, and all the while, my husband's body sat in a tunnel under the store.

It was the discovery of a letter in Bristol's pocket that answered my question of why.

Floyd had written to his cousin, telling Bristol all about Teddy Campbell being his child with Betty. He spoke of his sorrow over letting the Campbells take his son without putting up a fight and his intention to do the right thing by Betty and their boy upon his return to America. He asked Bristol to talk with his father, to help smooth things over.

Yet the thing Floyd hadn't known when he wrote that missive to Bristol was that Betty was gone. He was too late.

And Albert chose the secret. He silenced the echoes of his son's indiscretions.

But as Albert was stealing the life from my husband, Floyd was bleeding out from an explosion in a jungle on the other side of the world.

I released the hands that held mine and stepped toward Bristol's newly installed headstone. Kissing my hand, I transferred that kiss to the cold stone, then looked up at Heaven. We will be together again, but there was still life for me on Earth.

Beside me, Frank put an arm around Kenzie's shoulder, and to my sweet relief, she didn't pull away.

No secrets, no shame, just family and hope.